680

A SUMMER of SUNDAYS

A SUMMER of SUNDAYS

Lindsay Eland

EGMONT
USA
NEW YORK

EGMONT

We bring stories to life

First published by Egmont USA, 2013
443 Park Avenue South, Suite 806
New York, NY 10016
Copyright © Lindsay Eland, 2013
All rights reserved
1 3 5 7 9 8 6 4 2
www.egmontusa.com
www.lindsayeland.com

Library of Congress Cataloging-in-Publication Data

Eland, Lindsay.
A summer of Sundays / Lindsay Eland.
pages   cm
Summary: Always lost in the shuffle of her large family, an eleven-year-old girl decides that this summer she'll make sure she stands out, and a discovery in the library basement may help.
ISBN 978-1-60684-030-6 (hardcover) — ISBN 978-1-60684-413-7 (ebook) [1. Family life—Fiction. 2. Self-acceptance—Fiction.] I. Title.
PZ7.E355Su 2013
[Fic]—dc23
2012045141

Printed in the United States of America

To Mom and Dad, Suzanne and Alisa. You four have been there from the very beginning, all the times in the middle, and I will love you until the very end.

To my Grandma and Grandpa, MomMom and PopPop, Muzzy and PapaGil, and Betsy and Rubble. Not only do your names and your stories grace these pages, but you have also graced my life and filled it to overflowing.

And finally: to anyone who has ever felt left behind, forgotten, or stuck in the middle—this is for you.

～～～

I LIKE the middle of brownies, and the center of a chocolate chip cookie. The gooey middle of a just-out-of-the-oven cinnamon roll is as close to heaven as you can get.

But being the middle child is no gooey-cinnamon-roll center, that's for sure. And if someone tells you anything different, well, he's either a grown-up who wants to make cooked broccoli sound oh-so-delicious or he's a grown-up *and* he was an only child. And an only child has no idea what it's like to be third in line for the bathroom.

But I do.

Being the third kid of six, stuffed in the middle, well, you get awful lost, especially when you're a cookie-cutter cutout of all your siblings. Same muddy-water hair. Same brown eyes. Same little notch in my left ear. Just like all my brothers and sisters.

I've been called the "third of six," the "third Fowler child," and the "third girl." I've also been called "May" (the oldest), "Emma" (the second oldest), and even "Butters" (our dog). Then there's the common, "You're CJ's sister," or "Are you related to Bo?" or "Oh, you look just like your brother Henry." I've been called all those names way more than Sunday Annika Fowler, which is the name my parents gave me almost twelve years ago.

But really, I answer to whatever. It's much easier than waiting around until they figure out which one I am.

Yep, being the middle child is definitely not gooey delicious like cookies or brownies or cinnamon rolls. Being the middle is half in and half out, too young and too old.

Being the middle is being forgotten.

But this summer, all that was going to end.

ALL nine of us—six kids, two adults, and one droopy-eared dog—stood by our big blue van, waiting for Dad to close up the packed trailer and start the car so we could begin the four-hour journey to the barely-there town of Alma.

Dad had been working there all summer long remodeling the library. Work had been pretty scarce for him, so he had to take whatever he could get, even if that meant moving away from us for a few months. He called every night and sent us pictures of the library as he put in new floors, windows, and trim. We sent him pictures of us right back. But seeing his face on a screen wasn't the same. His empty seat at the dinner table and the lonely spot in the driveway where his truck was always parked felt like a big gray cloud hanging over us.

After a month and a half, he called Mom and told her that he couldn't stand being away from us for one more second. Personally I found that hard to believe. But he didn't have to sleep in the same room with Emma or hear CJ talking about poop all day or listen to May whine about driving or watch over Henry, so maybe it was true.

"We'll spend the end of summer together," he'd said over the speakerphone. "And you can all help me get ready for the reopening of the library."

May and Emma had whined and cried and pleaded to stay behind, then whined and cried and pleaded some more.

It hadn't worked.

Me? I couldn't wait to go to Alma and work on the library.

There wasn't a place I could think of that was more magical than a building bursting with books and stories and words. A place where the quiet was so thick and warm it felt like a blanket. And who knew, maybe in a small town like Alma I'd stick out a little more.

CJ, Bo, and Henry were just as excited as me, except for a different reason: building a new fort. On the day we were leaving, I watched CJ stow away in his backpack: his walkie-talkies, a length of rope, a small shovel, duct tape, and the beginners carpenter set he'd bought at a garage sale the first week of summer. He'd built a too-small dog-house and an unfinished fence with it, changed the locks on the house, nailed a few windows shut, and now all the closet doorknobs fall off. I had watched as he put his backpack—lumpy and obviously heavy—inside the trailer. From the looks of the laundry on his bedroom floor, he wasn't planning on changing his underwear or socks very often. . . .

May trudged down to the car and gave one last try. "It's summer vacation, and Mom is supposed to help me learn to drive. I'll die if I don't get my license this summer. It's so not fair."

"Well, as far as I can remember, May," Dad said, tossing a pillow into the backseat, "they do have roads in Alma. And I don't think I've ever heard of 'death by lack of license' before. I think you'll survive."

"If you're going to force me to go against my will, then I refuse to leave without this," Emma said, setting her precious sewing machine and a box of supplies by the growing stack of suitcases. "But it looks like there's hardly any room left.

Dad smiled and picked it up, slipping it in between the seats and giving the white plastic cover a quick pat. "Looks like it fits. Now tell your mom we'll be ready to leave in an hour."

Anxious to get on the road, I dragged one of the suitcases to the trailer, and Bo picked up a smaller one, lugging it after me. "Here you go, Dad," I said.

He turned and smiled, taking the suitcases. "Wow, Bo, you sure are strong. Thanks for the help."

"I helped, too," I said, seeing as the suitcase I carried was twice as big and three times as heavy.

He tugged my ponytail. "I know, Sunday. But Bo's a lot younger than you and he's—" Dad glanced over at CJ, who was trying to secret something away in the car. "Oh no you don't, CJ. You are not bringing that saw. Besides, I have all my tools there. I can cut a board for you."

Mom walked up then, catching the end of the conversation. "Cut what? What saw? Do I even want to know?"

CJ sulked back to the house with the saw, and Dad waved off the incident. I wondered if he had gotten his fill of us already and was rethinking the whole plan.

But after stuffing suitcases, pillows, our dinner triangle, one dog, six kids, Mom, and anything else my siblings and I managed to cram into the trailer, Dad started up the van and we were off, chugging along down the highway.

Dad pulled off the interstate two hours later and stopped in front of a gas station. "All right, everyone, I need to check the trailer and fill up on gas. Be back to the car in five minutes. I'd like to get to Alma by mid afternoon."

As my brothers and sisters filed into the convenience store to grab candy bars or gum or chips or drinks, I went to the single dirty bathroom outside of the gas station and waited in line. As I finally clicked the lock to the restroom door, I heard my brothers and sisters talking, laughing, and arguing on their way back to the car, and I hoped that someone remembered that I liked Reese's Pieces the best.

Then I heard the van doors slide shut and the engine rev up.

My heart raced.

Surely they knew I was here, still in the bathroom. CJ would know he had more elbow room than normal. Someone would notice that I wasn't there to help Henry if he got carsick again. And Bo, well, he'd never forget me. I washed my hands real quick and didn't even bother to dry them before I opened the creaky door and burst outside. I stared at the spot where the car had been. But looking down the highway, all I saw was the hot, wavy sun bubbling off the surface of the pavement.

Gulping on gas-fume air, I glanced around the now-empty station trying to convince myself that they'd parked in a different spot.

No.

I'd dealt with a lot as the middle child. Cold showers, my name forgotten or mixed up, and last Christmas I'd gone to the bathroom and missed our family picture (I was added in later), but at least I'd never been left behind.

Until now.

The realization sank like a rock to the bottom of my stomach.

I looked back at the highway. Maybe Mom's cell phone had service now. I fished in my pockets for two quarters, my hands trembling. But all I pulled out was an old, worn tissue and a single penny.

My heart *thunk, thunk, thunked* inside my chest. This couldn't really be happening. It was a dream, just like when I woke up on the first day of fifth grade and thought I'd grown a mustache.

I'd wake up any minute and find myself asleep in the van. *Wake up, Sunday. Wake up. Wake up!*

I pinched my arm and winced.

The hot sun beating down on the blacktop was real, so was the smell of gasoline.

This wasn't a dream.

A lump formed in my throat, and tears stung my eyes. *Think, Sunday. Think.*

Glancing through the window at the cashier, I thought about asking if I could use the phone. Surely the old lady squinting down at her magazine would let me.

But I couldn't. She would ask why I needed to make a call, and then I'd have to tell her, and then maybe she'd call the police or something. Besides, any minute my family would realize what happened and they'd come back. Any minute. Any minute.

But a few minutes turned into fifteen.

They'll come. They'll come. They'll come.

I sat down on a small orange bench outside the gas station, between a wad of slick pink gum and the initials RM + CL = Love. At first I clenched my fists, my finger-nails biting into my skin. I imagined what would happen when my family came back full of guilt. My mom would cry and wrap me in a big hug. Maybe my parents would buy me a new book so I didn't have to borrow one from my sisters. Or maybe they'd let me have two ice cream sandwiches after dinner instead of one, or let me sleep in my own room for a night.

But as the seconds ticktocked past, the anger dissolved into fear. What if they never came back? Why didn't they realize I was gone? And what if they were glad I was gone? CJ always complained about not having enough room. Emma would have a spot to prop up her feet now that my head wasn't in the way.

My eyes never left the horizon.

One after another, cars sped down the highway. I held my breath as each one emerged out of the wavy sun, hoping that maybe the next one would be my family. But as each car or truck or van flew past, I struggled to keep tears from sliding down my cheeks.

A whole two hours later our blue van pulled back into the gas station. I tried to hold back my sob of relief. *See, Sunday. They came back. And now they feel awful.*

The door opened and May got out, rushing past me

without a glance. I watched her back until it disappeared behind the scuffed bathroom door. I turned and walked to the van, bracing myself for the apologies and tears.

"I can't believe we just drove an hour in the wrong direction, Adam," Mom said. "We'll barely be able to unpack before it starts getting dark."

I stared, shocked. Not a single "We are so sorry, Sunday!" Not even a "We rushed back here as fast as we could."

My dad ran his hands through his hair. It wasn't the first time that he'd driven in the wrong direction. It was hard to pay attention to road signs when he and Mom were breaking up fights between my brothers or negotiating with my sisters. "I guess we got turned around. Don't worry, it'll be fine."

Mom sighed and leaned her head back.

My heart dropped in my chest. I tried to think of a way to bring up how they'd left me behind and completely forgotten me. Nothing came.

I climbed into the van and took my seat on the worn fabric. CJ knocked me with his elbow. "Move over, Sunday. You're taking up all the room."

I pushed him back and scowled. Bo blinked his eyes open, yawned, then lay his head on my shoulder, sinking back into sleep. I looked out the window, the sharp reflection of the sun off the parked cars stinging my eyes. Even Bo had forgotten me?

"Is May still in the bathroom?" Mom asked, her gaze flickering to me in the mirror.

I stared back. "Yeah."

May dashed back, the smell of watermelon lip gloss following her. Then the door slid shut, my dad shifted the van into first, and we were off.

No one had noticed that I wasn't there.

For two hours I was completely forgotten. It was as if I didn't exist. As if I'd become one of the extras in the background of a movie . . . a nobody.

I didn't say anything to my parents. I knew they'd feel bad. My mom would probably cry and maybe they *would* buy me a book or something like that. But I didn't want a book or an ice cream sandwich or anything else to make it all better. I just wanted to be sure that I'd never be forgotten again. Ever.

No more mixed-up name. No more being left behind. No more "one-of-the-six." I needed to do something so that my family would never forget me.

I looked out the window, blurry green fields rushing past.

Maybe moving to Alma for the summer would be my chance to do something to stand out.

Yes.

After this summer, people would say, "Oh, that's Sunday Fowler. She's the one who—" And then they'd say the spectacular thing that I was going to do. Of course, I didn't exactly know what that was yet, since there wasn't anything I was spectacular at, but I'd figure it out.

Maybe I'd deliver newspapers while riding around balanced on top of a unicycle: SUNDAY FOWLER: UNICYCLE NEWSPAPER GIRL.

There was supposed to be a lake near the town. I could swim across it all by myself: ALMOST-TWELVE-YEAR-OLD FIRST TO SWIM ACROSS GIANT LAKE.

But whatever I did, the town of Alma would never forget Sunday Fowler.

And neither would my family.

3

"**WAKE** up, everyone," Mom called.

Dad rolled down his window and stuck his arm outside as a warm breeze filtered through the van. "We're almost there." In the rearview mirror, I watched his eyes squint into a smile.

Bo, who had been leaning on my shoulder for the last hour, woke up and rubbed his eyes. Though my arm had fallen asleep a while ago, I didn't have the heart to nudge him awake. He looked up at me and smiled, his eyes still sleepy and a red line creased across his face where he had pressed his cheek against my shirt.

"We're here," I told him softly.

Bo was six years younger than me, and ever since he could walk he'd been like my miniature shadow.

"Sunday," he'd say, climbing up the ladder to my bed every single night. "Will you read me a book?"

I never minded.

I followed his gaze as Dad made a turn onto Main Street. He drove real slow, and for once we were all quiet as we took in our home for the rest of the summer.

"The library is near a park, and our house is right next to it," Dad said.

The street was lined with small stores, most reminding me of my grandparents—wrinkled and droopy with age but still beautiful in their own ways. The biggest dog I'd ever seen bounded down the sidewalk right in front of a thrift store. His massive feet flipped over a big silver bowl and flung water all over the small old lady who clung to his leash as if her life depended on it. Actually it looked like her life *did* depend on it. He galloped by a few clothing shops, a five-and-dime, a real estate office, and a small restaurant called the Crepe Café. A pretty lady with flowers in her hair flipped over the CLOSED sign on the café and started out onto the sidewalk. She passed by a couple walking hand in hand and a group of kids gobbling down ice cream cones.

It was the most perfect town I'd ever seen.

Not like something from *Little Women* or *Anne of Green Gables*, but it was just small enough for a middle-of-the-middle child to be noticed.

Now I just had to figure out how.

Dad made another turn and drove down a street lined with houses on the left and a wide green park on the right.

A man sat on top of a lawn mower, driving through the tall grass like he was on a highway. I didn't know a lawn mower could move that fast. His stripes zigged and zagged all over the place. He slowed down long enough to tip his hat at our car before he was off again.

CJ put his head out the window to watch. "Cool."

"You're sure it will fit all of us?" Mom asked, obviously wondering how in the world we were all going to stuff ourselves into a house that was only as big as the ones we'd passed. They were nice and all, but I could picture the house straining at each joint to keep us crammed inside.

"Yes, Lara, don't worry. I made sure I saw the inside of the house. It's perfect for us."

She sighed.

We turned down a street that bordered the park. A tall, skinny stone building sat at the back with thick chiseled letters above the doors that read ALMA TOWN LIBRARY. It didn't look like it needed too much work, at least not on the outside. There weren't any flowers in the big flower-pots, the few steps leading up to the doors were dirty, caked with dried, dead leaves, and the windows could use some scrubbing, but all that could be done in a day. I got an ache in my stomach. How long would it take for me to be noticed and recognized? I figured I needed the whole rest of the summer.

"That's the library?" May asked, cracking her gum close to my ear. "Looks awful small."

Emma smoothed down the strands of hair that flew around her face from the breeze fluttering in through Dad's open window. "Doesn't look like there's much to do," she said. "I bet we'll finish ahead of schedule."

"And then we can leave, right?" May asked. "Because I need to practice driving."

CJ leaned over to me and mumbled, "All the practice in the world wouldn't be able to help her."

It was true. May was a terrible driver.

"And I can't get my license if you guys are going to be too busy to drive with me," she complained. "Besides, what if they don't even have a place to take a test or-or-or they won't give me my license 'cause I'm not from here?"

"We'll make time," Mom reassured her. "And don't worry, you'll be able to get your license."

But from the way May chewed her bottom lip, I could tell she was still worried. All I knew was that I didn't want to be within five miles of any car May was driving.

"Most of the work now is just cleaning up, organizing, and helping out the new librarian," Dad said as he tried to get a good look at the library and drive at the same time. "Your mom and I will be plenty busy, but there'll be time to practice your driving."

"I bet there's a lot to organize," Mom said. She could

organize just about anything. From pictures we drew when we could first hold a marker to the knotted-up fishing line Dad had out in the garage, once Mom got ahold of something it was separated, categorized, slipped neatly into the space she'd arranged for it, and then slapped with a label.

I gazed up at the library and could almost smell the scent of old books and hear the crack of their spines. "I'd like to help, too."

"Of course *you* would, little Miss Goody Two-shoes," Emma whispered behind me.

I glared at her, then turned back around.

"So where are we gonna live?" Bo asked, swiping his hand across his nose.

Mom pointed to a large house beside the library. "Is it that one?"

Dad nodded and smiled. "That's it." We all craned to see as the van pulled into the driveway. Everyone clambered out as soon as the car rolled to a stop.

CJ, Bo, and Henry barely stopped to look before they had raced up the walkway, up the stairs, and were pulling at the front door. May stretched and yawned while Emma walked to the very middle of the front yard and stared up. Mom smiled at Dad and he reached down and kissed her hand.

Me, I just stood off to the side drinking in the sight of it.

The house was tall and wide and white with a long front porch, a round window right at the top that was probably the attic, and an old red watering can sitting by the front door. The yard was big and the grass had the same zigzag stripes as the park.

"Come on, Dad!" CJ whined, tugging on the doorknob. "Open the door. We want to see the inside."

Dad turned to me and tossed a small ring with two keys on it. "Can you open it up for them, Em–May–Sunday?"

The boys stepped aside as I twisted the key in the lock, then barreled forward, almost knocking me off my feet when they heard the click of the bolt.

They scrambled through the house, running from room to room, racing up the stairs and then flying back down again. They swarmed around me.

"I bet I could jump out of the window in the big bedroom and land in the tree outside."

"No way!"

"There are bathrooms everywhere."

"And-and-and one of them has a huge bathtub!"

"It looks like someone pooped in the toilet upstairs!"

"Really? I wanna see!"

"Gross, CJ," I said. The three of them giggled and raced back upstairs to look at the toilet again.

I set the keys on a small table by the front door and looked around. The house was fully furnished with things that looked like they were for a much fancier family. One with six less kids and no pets. The sound of smashing porcelain came from upstairs. I cringed, hoping that Super Glue worked on whatever it had been.

My parents walked right by me, followed by my sisters, who were already dragging their suitcases inside.

"We get first dibs on rooms, right, Mom?"

"And you told me that if there's enough, then I get my own room, since I'm the oldest."

"Yeah, right. That isn't fair. I need a place to put my sewing machine, so I should have my own room."

Mom sighed. "All right, just a minute. Let's look in the all the rooms first, and then we'll decide who goes where."

Dad started walking through the house like he did when he had just finished building a new one back home. He let me go with him a few times to look before the owners moved in. I always stood beside him as he examined the crown moldings and trim, running his hand along the seams of all the joints.

"How does it look, Dad?" I asked, walking up next to him. He was staring up at a ceiling fan.

He turned to me and smiled, letting his hand rest on my head. "It's nice. I think we'll—" he started, but was cut off by CJ, Bo, and Henry thundering into the room, knocking him back onto the couch and then piling on top of him, screaming about the bathrooms again and the poop in the toilet.

My stomach twisted.

I used to add myself to the pile, my laughter mixing in with my brothers' and my dad's. But one evening last fall, my aunt stopped me just after I launched off the floor. She was visiting from California and didn't have any kids. She spent most of her time at our house rubbing her temples and hiding in my dad's office, where she slept. We were in the living room, and I lay down on top of my brothers, who were sprawled on top of my dad. "Will you get up, Sunday?" she said. I felt heat fill my cheeks.

"Aren't you a little old to be doing that kind of thing? I mean, really, it's . . . it's . . . well, you're just too old."

And maybe I was. I didn't feel too old.

But I did feel stuck.

Stuck in the middle of being too old, but still too young. The middle of the middle of the middle.

I turned from the giggly screeches and went to find my sisters and Mom. I knew I wasn't going to get my own room, so I was curious to see who I'd be bunking with.

I knew I wouldn't be rooming with Henry, who would sleep in Mom and Dad's room since he sometimes still wet the bed or woke up with nightmares.

And May would get her own room just because she seemed to be able to get just about anything she wanted.

So I figured I would either be with CJ and Bo or Emma.

I couldn't decide which would be better. CJ snored, and Bo slept as light as a feather. But I shared with Emma at home, and she chattered away in her sleep.

I found my sisters in a bright, cheery room with pale yellow walls, a single bed, a bunk bed, and windows that faced the park. A bathroom was attached to one side.

"But there aren't enough rooms, May, and I am not sleeping with CJ and Bo just so you can have your own."

"Fine. I'll share this one with you."

"Fine."

"Fine."

Silence hung between them.

Mom came in. "Have you two come to an agreement?"

Emma rolled her suitcase to the bed next to the bathroom. "Yeah. Me and May are in here."

Mom wiped her hands on her jeans. "Well, it looks like that's settled. You two get unpacked." She turned and jumped at the sight of me. "Oh, Sunday, I didn't realize you were there. Do you know where Butters is? I don't want her wandering over to the library or pooping in other people's yards."

"Pooping? Who's pooping?" CJ called from below.

"Poop, poop, poop," Bo and Henry crowed.

"Don't keep yelling 'poop,'" Mom called down.

I stifled a giggle as CJ whispered "poop," then grinned up at Mom mischievously. "Well, you said not to yell it."

She rolled her eyes, but I could tell she was trying not to smile. "So, have you seen Butters, Sunday?"

I sighed. The only time someone remembered my name was when they needed help. "Not since we got here. Should I go find her?"

"Please." Mom sighed, swiping her forehead. "Thanks."

Butters was outside snuffling the bushes that bordered the porch. She was a basset hound, long like a sausage with floppy ears that felt like velvet, and sad brown eyes. Though she was technically everyone's dog, I taught her all her tricks, and she always found her way to the foot of my bed at night. Hopefully she'd find me tonight.

"Come on in, Butters," I called to her. I grabbed my own suitcase from the back of the packed van and lugged it behind me. Butters snuffled and padded after me, her long ears dragging on the ground and her little claws tapping on the wood. I left her sniffing around the house, her nose glued to the floor and her tail wagging as I went up the stairs to find out where I was going to be sleeping.

The hallway was empty and quiet except for the muffled voices coming from behind each of the closed doors.

Remembering the bunk bed, I knocked at May and Emma's door. I didn't like painting my nails and didn't really care what my hair looked like as long as it was out of the way, but the thought of talking about boys or friends made my insides flutter. Maybe I could tell them about Robo, the boy I liked. I knocked again.

"Who is it?" Emma's voice was right up against the wood, but she didn't open it.

"Me, Sunday," I yelled.

The door opened a crack. "What do you want?"

I tried to push my way inside, but she held the door firmly. "I thought I could take the top or bottom bunk."

May stepped to the door and opened it a little wider. "Sorry, Sunday," she said, in a tone that she only used when she didn't really mean it. "Can you find a different place to sleep? Three's too many in a small room like this one."

"But me and Emma share a room back home. And there's an extra bed."

May smiled at me like I was a little girl. "I know, but I just don't think it'll work. Besides, Emma and I are closer in age, and well, you understand. Right?"

I felt my cheeks burn. "Yeah. Of course."

"Thanks," May said. "I knew you would. Now, come on, Emma, I'll paint your nails and then you can do mine."

The door closed.

Eleven-almost-twelve obviously did not let me into my older sisters' circle of friendship. I'd be staying with Bo and CJ. It wouldn't be too bad. I'd just change in the bathroom and put cotton in my ears to keep out CJ's snoring.

The worst part would be trying to hide my flashlight when I read at night. Bo'd always be asking me to read to him or bothering me about turning the light off.

I heard giggling and scuffling coming from behind another door and rapped hard.

Bo flung it open and smiled. "Hi, Sunday," he said. "Look! Me and CJ get to sleep in this bed and watch." He dashed to the queen-sized bed, where CJ already sat. They nodded at each other and each drew a dark blue curtain together until it met in the middle and I couldn't see either of them. "Insta-fort!" came his muffled reply.

"Cool, guys."

I could tell they were in heaven.

Smiling, I glanced around the room. No other bed.

Bo poked his head out from behind the curtain. "Hey, where are you going to sleep, Sunday?"

I shrugged. "I don't know."

"You could sleep in here if you want," he offered, wiping his nose on the fabric.

"Thanks, but—"

"No she can't," CJ said from behind the curtain. "She's too old and there isn't enough room. Besides, she'll probably tell on us if we jump on the bed, or she'll talk on the phone to some boy all night."

My smile disappeared. I'd never once told on them for jumping on the bed, and I'd never had a phone conversation longer than fifteen minutes with anyone, let alone a boy. I grabbed a small pillow off a chair and threw it where I thought he sat behind the curtain.

"Ouch, Sunday," he squealed. "I'm gonna tell Mom."

"Really? Who's the tattletale now? And that didn't hurt. Besides, I wasn't going to sleep in here anyway. You snore louder than a rhinoceros. I just wanted to see your room."

CJ was silent. I started for the door.

"You're not too old, Sunday," Bo called after me. "You're just . . . just Sunday."

Part of me thought it was a sweet thing for him to say. That I still belonged . . . at least with him. But another part of me cringed.

Just Sunday.

That's exactly what I didn't want to be. Just Sunday was the one left behind at the gas station.

Just Sunday blended into the background.

I pasted on a small smile and forced myself to whisper a halfhearted "Thanks, Bo" before I shut the door. The giggling started back up immediately. Standing in the empty hallway, I looked at the closed doors.

I didn't belong in any of them.

Still, I needed to find somewhere to sleep. That's when I remembered the little round window I'd seen when we first pulled up. The one where an attic should be.

The door at the top of the stairs looked like all the

others in the house except for the large brass knob. I twisted it and found a dark stairway leading up. The air was mustier than in the hallway, but the smell made the dark space above me seem more enticing—maybe even magical. The thought of finding an old wardrobe like the one Lucy went through into Narnia filled me with excitement. The stairs creaked with each step. At the top, I found a light switch and flipped it on. There was a bed, neatly made, a fan that whirred when I plugged it in, and fine dust covering an old beat-up trunk where clothes peeked out from the lid.

A small bookshelf against one wall held two rows of worn books. After glancing at the spines, I pulled out a paperback copy of *The Secret Garden*, fanning out the yellowed pages before turning back to face the room.

The room was perfect and I had it all to myself.

Setting my suitcase down and placing the book on the nightstand, I bounced on the bed a few times and then went to the little window, pushing the pane open to let the air blow in. My eyes were level with the tops of the trees. Our van was below, and Dad was emptying the small trailer onto the driveway. A squirrel looked on and chattered as birds swooped from one tree to the next. Beyond, I could see the library, the crazily mowed lawn, and the tops of the buildings in town.

And then I looked across the field and saw a house.

It was off to the right, old looking, maybe even con-
demned. The door opened and a man walked out, placed
his hands on his hips, and stared in our direction. He had
thick white hair and seemed too big for the small porch.

He stood just like that for a few seconds, then turned
and walked back inside. Curtains fell across two windows,
and I could almost hear his door lock.

Our next-door neighbor. I guessed that was what he
was even though there was a pretty big field separating us.
Well, he didn't have to worry about me snooping around.
Maybe CJ, but not me. I had plans for this summer.

It was going to be a summer of Sunday's.

4

LATER that evening, after all that remained were the bits of pizza crust that lay scattered on our plates, Dad asked if anyone wanted to walk over to the library with him. "We won't do anything tonight, but I'd like to see how many of the new light fixtures still need bulbs."

CJ, Bo, and I volunteered.

The sky had darkened to a deep and eerie blue, giving the trees, our house, and the library thick black shadows.

"I bet the library is haunted," CJ whispered low.

Bo squeezed my hand tighter. "Really? Should we go back?"

"It's not haunted. CJ's just trying to scare you." But I stepped closer to Dad, just in case.

The stone steps were shrouded in darkness. "Just wait at the bottom of the stairs for a minute while I turn on the outside light," Dad said. "We don't need anyone tripping and falling."

He walked up, unlocked the door, and slipped into the blackness of the building.

My heart sped up as the door closed. I glanced back at the house, keeping my eyes glued on the light pouring out through the windows. Mom stood at the sink in the kitchen. May chattered on her cell phone up in her room. My small round window was black.

A twig snapped and I whirled around.

"What was that?" Bo whispered. He leaned against me.

"I don't know."

Leaves rustled, and my eyes found the house across the field. The blinds were drawn, but a single window was lit dimly. It clicked off.

I shivered.

"I bet it's a bear or . . . or . . ." CJ's voice shook. "Or the ghost of someone that died in the library."

I clenched my teeth and pushed him a little. "Stop it, CJ. I mean it."

He pushed me back.

The library stairs lit up with an orange haze, and the door clicked open. "All right, come on in. It's pretty dark, but you'll be able to see well enough."

The three of us rushed up the steps and inside.

Dad was right. Only two bulbs were working. They lit the round circulation desk and a set of stairs that went down to a door with an EMPLOYEES ONLY sign.

Bo rushed to Dad's side, and though I knew CJ got scared sometimes—he's still never seen the entire movie of *The Wizard of Oz*—he immediately began to explore the darkness.

I stood under the single light at the circulation desk and ran my hand along the scratched surface. Bending down I looked in the RETURN slot and found three books.

Harry Potter and the Sorcerer's Stone and two others I hadn't heard of.

Harry Potter was one of my favorites. I still remembered the first time I opened the copy I'd received for Christmas. It had rained that day, and the hot chocolate that sat steaming on the nightstand gradually cooled as I sank into Harry's world.

I set the books down on the desk and looked at the picture that hung on the wall behind. It was of a woman who looked older than Mom and Dad but not quite as old as Grandma and Grandpa. I squinted at the small golden plaque on the base of the frame.

ALMA, PENNSYLVANIA, I read, and then walked behind the desk so that I could see the words better. HOMETOWN OF THE NATIONAL BOOK PRIZE—WINNING AUTHOR LEE WREN. *THE LIFE AND DEATH OF BIRDS*, NATIONAL BOOK PRIZE 1969. Then it gave the dates of her birth and death.

Wow. The librarian back in Pittsburgh told me the

National Book Prize was one of the biggest awards you could get as a writer.

A famous author had lived here?

Maybe when I left Alma at the end of the summer, people would say, "Sunday Fowler lived here."

"CJ . . . I mean, Sunday?" Dad asked. He climbed on top of a stool, reaching for one of the burned-out bulbs.

I walked out from behind the desk. "Yeah?"

"Could you do me a favor?"

"Uh, sure."

He handed me the flashlight tucked in his pocket. "Go down into the basement and see how many bulbs I need down there. I brought a few with me but I don't think I have enough."

I glanced down the dark steps, the EMPLOYEES ONLY sign lit up by the new bulb Dad had just replaced.

"Thanks," he said, not waiting for my answer.

I took the flashlight, walked down the stairs that were thankfully illuminated, and then pushed the doors open. My single light bobbed in the blackness, and I scanned the walls until I found a switch. None of the lights were working. I stepped farther inside, first counting the lights above and then scanning the rest of the room. Four bulbs.

There were two desks sitting in the middle of the room, and a big contraption against the far wall that looked like some sort of heater or air conditioner with silver pipes snaking up the walls and across the ceiling. Spiderwebs hung in the empty corners while wisps of an abandoned web caught the beam of my flashlight. A metal bookcase was against the other wall, filled from top to bottom with boxes. I stepped over to inspect them. More books, gritty with dust.

Shining my flashlight over each shelf, I found that all the boxes looked the same. But when the beam reached the top shelf, something glinted. Shifting the light back over, I saw it again.

There was an old step stool sitting beside the bookcase. I dragged it over and climbed up. Standing on my tiptoes to reach, I pushed aside the nearest box to see better. It was some sort of a heavy file cabinet or safe. It had a latch with a tiny silver lock like on a suitcase.

Maybe it wasn't locked.

I stretched up even more, but my fingertips were only able to brush against the smooth surface.

"Come on," I whispered, reaching, stretching.

Then there was a flash of light behind me and a roaring "BOO!"

I screeched and toppled off the back of the stool, landing directly on CJ.

He pushed me off. "Ouch." He hobbled to stand, then dissolved into giggles. "You should have seen your face, Sunday! It was hilarious."

"You could have killed me, CJ!" A sharp pain bit at my ankle as I groped for the flashlight and got to my feet.

"Well, I didn't, did I?" he shot back.

Dad's voice boomed from the top of the stairs. "What's going on down there? Everything okay?"

"CJ scared the daylights out of me!"

"I was just trying to be funny."

"Well, you have to be careful, especially in the dark," Dad said. "Are you ready to go, Sunday? How many lights?"

"Four."

"Great, thanks."

I started up the stairs but stopped and shined the flashlight once more at the top shelf. From where I stood, I could see the box perfectly, the little silver lock glinting.

"You coming, Sunday?" Dad called down to me.

What was in there?

"Yeah, I'm coming." I let the doors close and then ran up the steps.

Tomorrow I'd get the box down and open it.

"'Night, Sunday," Mom said from the door to my room.

I yawned and laid down *The Secret Garden* on my chest. "Good night."

"How do you like the book so far?"

"I love it, but I've already read it before. Remember? Last year?"

Mom shook her head, running her hand through her hair. "No. I think I remember May reading it a while ago." She yawned. "But anyway, try not to stay up too late."

My heart sank. Of course she didn't remember. "Okay."

The door closed, and I read until my eyelids drooped. Before sleep completely took over, I tore a small strip of paper from my notebook and slipped it in between the pages. Then I clicked off my reading light and tucked myself under the covers.

Maybe I could be like Mary Lennox and find a boy locked away in a hidden bedroom. Or maybe I could find a lonely hermit and bring him out of his house.

Of course, that meant I had to find myself a hermit or a hidden boy.

Maybe I could crack an unsolved crime.

JEWEL THIEF CAUGHT THANKS TO SUNDAY FOWLER.

Whatever it was, I needed to come up with something soon if I ever wanted to become more than just "one-of-the-six."

5

UNFORTUNATELY I didn't think of any other ideas to help me make my mark as I slept. Nothing came to me over our breakfast except maybe trying to break a world record again. But trying to eat the most Reese's Pieces hadn't worked last spring. Instead CJ broke a city record for eating the most donut holes in one minute. Let's just say my fame disappeared when his name was printed in the *Pittsburgh Post*.

After breakfast, Dad made us all walk over to the library together, weighed down with cleaning supplies, a vacuum, brooms, buckets, and Mom's organizing bins.

"Who donated all the money to do this work?" Emma asked, huffing, even though she'd managed to grab the two empty buckets.

Mom grunted. "It was an anonymous donation by someone," she said. "And a pretty big one."

An anonymous donation? I never could understand why anyone would want to be anonymous when they were doing something good like donating money. And now, trying to think of a way to be recognized, it seemed even sillier. Who in the world would want to do something that people would notice and then not tell a single soul? Not a middle child, I knew that much.

"Here we go," Dad said, unlocking the door and pushing it open. "Put the supplies over there. Just try not to block the bathrooms."

We trudged in, one after the other, and dropped the supplies, then looked around.

The main room looked different as the morning sun filled the dusty windows. It wasn't nearly as eerie, and I felt silly for being scared. Now the library reminded me of the fairy tale "Sleeping Beauty": the castle, and everyone inside it, asleep because of a spell cast on it by the wicked witch.

And we were going to awaken it.

I took in the room, dusty corners to cobwebbed ceiling. A staircase I hadn't seen last night ran up the side where more shelves were piled with books. There was a railing around the second floor that allowed you to look down on the circulation desk. I spotted the staircase that led down to the basement. If I got a chance to sneak away without anyone noticing, I could pull down the silver box and see what was inside. Maybe there was something else sitting on one of these shelves, like an antique book

worth millions or old pictures of the library. Or maybe
the famous author Lee Wren had carved her name into
one of the desks.

I let my hand glide across the top of the circulation
desk and winced as a splinter dove into my skin. As I
tried to pull it out, I thought of Lee Wren walking into
the library and placing her books right here. Maybe she
drank out of the water fountain or stood right where I
stood now. I'd try to read her book this summer.

The room behind the desk was filled with shelves and
shelves of books that had been thrown together in the
midst of the remodel. Some were stacked one on top of
the other until they met the wooden shelf above, and
others leaned against one another barely able to stand.
The shelves were old, and most of them looked like they
were going to fall apart at any moment. There were a
few desks covered with carvings. They didn't match the
smooth wood floors Dad had put in, but he was going
to refinish the furniture while we cleaned and organized.

I walked around some more, letting my mind wander.
An image of a big Reopening Day Party complete with
balloons and streamers, food and games, took shape
inside my head. Maybe I could organize something like
that to stand out? A newspaper article with the headline TWELVE-YEAR-OLD ORGANIZES PARTY OF THE CENTURY
scrolled through my head.

But it would have to be big and have something really—

Dad clapped his hands, jolting me out of my thoughts. "All right, everyone!" he said. "Let's get started."

May piped in immediately. "You and Mom promised that one of you will take me driving every day, remember?"

"Yes, I know—"

"I'll go with Mom and May when they leave," Emma interrupted. "I thought I saw something about a theater production and they might need my experience making costumes." Ever since she helped out with costumes for the high school's production of *Grease*, Emma thought she was ready to stitch for Broadway.

"Yeah, yeah," Dad said. I could tell he was getting annoyed. He looked over at CJ, Bo, Henry, and me. "What engagements do you have that I should know about?"

CJ shrugged. "Well, I want to make a fort in the trees over there sometime."

Henry chimed in with a "Me, too!"

"I'm going with Sunday," Bo said, slipping his hand in mine.

I grinned. Good old faithful Bo. "Well, I don't have anything," I said. "I guess I'll just stay here and help."

Emma huffed, and when I turned she stuck up her nose and sneered--her sign for "Miss Goody Two-shoes."

Bo let go of my hand and moved next to CJ and Henry. "Then I want to go with them."

The warmth from his small hand vanished from my skin. "Bo—" I started. "I won't be cleaning the whole time."

"But I want to make a fort. I hate cleaning and putting things away."

CJ let his arm drape across Bo's shoulder. "Yeah, he wants to make a fort with us."

"Yeah, a fort," Henry echoed, his finger in his nose.

I hoped I sounded convincing when I said, "Fine. I don't care." There I was again, standing on the outside.

"Okay, then," Dad said. "Every day you each need to help out here, even if it's just taking out the trash or getting everyone breakfast or lunch. Your mom and I and the new librarian will be doing most of the work, but we still expect help. Understood?"

We all nodded.

"Good." He turned to Mom. "What do you think we should do first, Lara?"

Mom sighed, then walked around a bit. I could practically see her organizing things in her head. She turned and looked at us ready to delegate jobs. I always thought that if she wasn't a mom she'd be pretty good at working in the army. "First, let's move the books to this side of the room so that we can clean the other half. Then start separating them. Decide which ones are beyond repair and which are good enough to save, and try to place them in order by their call numbers. The new librarian is coming in a few days and will help, but I'd like to get a head start. Once the books are moved over, we can look at the furniture and see what needs to be fixed and what needs to go into storage. Are we ready?"

We all answered, "Ready."

"Then let's go."

We moved like a well-oiled machine, having organized and cleaned up our own house in the same way. I was happy to eventually sit and flip through the books, smelling the musty yellowed pages and listening to the crinkle of the plastic library covers when I opened them. Most of the due dates stamped on the inside slip were from years ago and most had publication dates from the sixties, seventies, eighties, and nineties. Seeing *Bridge to Terabithia*, and *The Mixed-up Files of Mrs. Basil E. Frankweiler*, and *Homecoming*—books I had read last year—was like meeting old friends. I wondered if the librarian would let me keep the ones that couldn't be put on the shelves anymore and set them off to the side.

Though I thought of trying to sneak away to the basement to see what was in the silver box, the stacks of books were endless.

May and Emma had slipped off together to make lunch, and it wasn't too long before we heard the familiar clang of our dinner triangle. Mom had insisted on bringing it with us. "It'll feel more like home with it hanging off the porch, and besides, that's the only way that we can call everyone in for dinner."

The boys dropped the books where they stood, and we all walked back over to the house and sat down on the porch to eat the egg salad sandwiches, apples, and chips.

Seizing the opportunity to slip away, I wrapped my lunch in a paper towel and started back for the library. "Mom, I'll go see what the basement's like."

"All right, Emma . . . I mean, May. Ugh. I mean, Sunday."

CJ laughed. "Don't get scared."

I walked into the library, then down the stairs through the EMPLOYEES ONLY doors, setting my half-eaten lunch on one of the desks. The basement was still dim since there was only one small window, but Dad had replaced the bulbs, so the black shadows that had been eerie last night were only dusty corners now. The two desks I had seen by flashlight were older and more run-down than the desks and chairs in the main library. I stood on my tiptoes to get a glimpse of the silver locked box.

I should have looked for the key before I came down. Then again, who knew how long I would have by myself before one of my brothers or sisters came poking around? I needed to get the box down and find out what was inside before one of them found me.

After setting aside a stool with wobbly, unstable legs, I pulled up one of the old chairs, tested to see if it would hold me. I grabbed a small cardboard box and set it aside, then reached for the silver one.

It was heavy, so I put it down on the desk, then ran my hand over the dusty top. It was mostly smooth with a few scratches. I took a deep breath and pulled on the lock, hoping that maybe, just maybe, it was broken.

It held fast.

There were a million and one places the key could be in the library, if it was even *in* the library.

I considered returning the box to its place on the top shelf.

But maybe it held something special inside like a treasure map to a fortune. Or maybe there was treasure inside the box itself?

I had to find out.

After glancing around the small room, I checked both of the old desks. The drawers were empty except for a lone queen of hearts and a few pencils sharpened down to nubs.

Maybe the key was upstairs.

Just in case one of my siblings came down while I went to look, I lifted the box off the desk and placed it against the wall, where it blended in with the rest of the messy room. Taking another quick bite of my sandwich, I ran up the stairs, then glanced out the window toward the house.

Whew. Everyone was still eating.

I turned and looked for where a key might be kept.

The circulation desk was the most likely place. I walked behind it, opening every single drawer.

The first had little animal stamps and an I LOVE READING stamp. I remembered how much I loved to get a stamp on my hand at the library when I was younger and pressed a small penguin against my skin. Nothing showed up and I moved on. Another drawer had pencils, pens, paper clips, tape, and a stapler. I rummaged through the clutter and finally noticed something silver.

A small key!

I grinned and placed it on the desk. That wasn't so hard. Still, I should check the other drawers, too.

Once I'd gone through every drawer I had collected seven keys. Actually I'd found eight, but one was too big, so I put it back.

A voice yelled from just outside the library window, "Just meet us back here at five, okay?"

Dad! There was shouting from my brothers, and my mom asked, "Do you *have* to talk about poop all day long?"

I swiped the keys into my hand and rushed back down the stairs just as a stampede of footsteps entered the library.

Leaving the box right where it was, I began to try the different keys. *Nope. No.*

"Where's Sunday?" It was Bo. Usually I liked that he searched me out. But not now. I just needed a few more minutes. I held my breath and tried another key.

Not that one.

His footsteps tromped down the stairs just as the fourth key slipped easily into the lock. I turned it, then pulled down. The box opened!

The basement door swung wide, banging into the wall. I sat on the box, trying to act like I hadn't been doing anything at all. "Hi, Bo," I said, trying to catch my breath.

"Hi, Sunday. What are you doing?"

"Oh, just taking a little break. I was looking through some of these boxes." I got up, slipped the key into my pocket, and went to a cardboard box, lifting up some old books and two cassette tapes that looked like the ones Mom and Dad had showed us once. "You know, just seeing what's down here."

"Bo?" It was Henry now.

"We're in the basement!"

Henry blasted into the room and looked around. "What's down here?"

"You know, more old dusty boxes," I said, walking to the doors and hoping they'd follow me. "Nothing much. Now, why don't you guys go upstairs and see what Mom and Dad need help with?"

Bo sat down on one of the chairs, then Henry did, too. "No, I want to stay down here with you."

"Yeah, me too. CJ might like this for a fort," Henry said, glancing around.

"NO!" I said quickly. "You should make one outside. Besides, we have to organize down here."

"Oh."

I sighed.

"Sunday?" Now it was Mom.

"Yeah?"

"Can you come up here and help finish sorting this stack? And boys, I still need you to help move more books."

I followed Bo and Henry out of the basement and turned to get one last look at the box.

I had to find out what was in there.

THE NEXT three days were filled from sunrise till sunset with so much stacking, separating, wiping, sweeping, vacuuming, and dusting that I never got a chance to sneak away to the basement. I saw the silver box glinting now and then in the bit of sun that slipped through the small basement window, but with Bo on my heels and CJ getting into mischief every time I turned around, there was never anything I could do about it. On the third day, after the triangle clanged announcing dinner, I realized I was just going to have to go to the library by myself. I'd creep out while my brothers were taking their baths and my sisters were holed up in their room.

Dad locked up the library, and we all met in the dining room. Spaghetti and bread sat steaming on the table.

"The director said that I could help with costumes for the play," Emma said. Her eyes sparkled, and she talked in quick bursts of excitement. "They're doing *A Midsummer Night's Dream*. I'm thinking simple but elegant."

"That's wonderful," Mom said, though I could tell she was calculating the number of hours she was going to spend behind Emma's sewing machine.

"Mom let me drive home," May said, twirling a glob of spaghetti around her fork.

Mom nodded and gave Dad a shaky smile.

I'd witnessed both of my parents in the car with May and decided that even though Mom's face and neck broke into hives, and she and May always ended up crying at the end, Mom was a little better under pressure than Dad. He always got frustrated with May's lack of driving skills and wound up throwing his hands in the air, yelling, and then taking the wheel and driving back to the house.

"And how did it go?" Dad asked.

May let the spaghetti drop off her fork and shrugged. "It went pretty good."

"Pretty good?" Emma cried. "She almost killed us! First she barely missed a mailbox when she looked out the window at a dog, then she ran a stoplight and got honked at, and then she knocked over the trash cans in the driveway because she—"

"I just misjudged the distance!" May shouted.

"They were right in front of you!"

"That's enough," Dad said. "I think you have the driving

part down. It's just the paying-attention part that needs some work."

Emma laughed and mumbled something under her breath but was silenced by a glare from Dad.

After dinner was finally over, I waited up in my room until I heard the water running downstairs and my sisters' door close. Then I found Dad. He was sitting at the kitchen table waiting for the timer to ding, signaling that the last dozen of his Fowler Family Chocolate Chip Cookies were ready to come out of the oven. On the counter, earlier batches of cookies were cooling on wire racks next to four loaves of Mom's pumpkin bread.

"Dad, I think I left something over at the library. Can I run and get it?"

Lucky for me, the timer dinged at that moment. Dad sprang out of his seat, rustled in his pocket, and handed me a set of keys before rushing to the oven and pulling out a tray of lightly browned cookies. He smiled with almost evil delight. My dad loved chocolate chip cookies almost more than life itself. If Mom didn't hide some of them, we'd be lucky if we got to eat two each before they were gone.

He lifted them one by one off the tray and onto a cooling rack. "The key to the library is the gold one," he said, not taking his eyes off his task. "Make sure you turn out the lights and lock up after you're done."

"Okay, thanks."

I slipped out the front door, dashed for the library, and was inside before anyone saw me.

I ran down to the basement, pushed through the door, and went to where the silver box sat. My fingertips tingled with anticipation. Whatever was inside, it had to be really important or it wouldn't have been locked up and set high on a shelf.

Maybe it was a confession.

SUNDAY FOWLER UNLOCKS CRIME OF THE PAST.

Hefting the box onto the desk, I took a deep breath and gently opened the small door.

A bundle of envelopes, yellow with age, sat on top with the word *Librarian* written in blue ink—just old, musty documents. I plopped them into the cardboard box, my excitement dwindling.

The only other thing was a stack of typed papers held together by a large red rubber band. I picked up the bundle and read:

CHAPTER ONE

The town of Price was as old and tired as the wrinkled ladies who sat outside fanning themselves on porches in the afternoon sun. Everyone and everything seemed to melt together. The girl, Lilly, rubbed her stomach, hungry. Like always. But the creek below her on the other side of the Johnstons' house was calling her name, and she had a frog that needed something to eat. Since she was the one who captured him, she thought it best that she feed him before herself. It was only fair.

Lilly, wearing the overalls she was only allowed to wear on Saturdays—every other day she had to wear tight-necked dresses—picked her way down the path, poison ivy thick and drippy on the one side and jaggers reaching out for her skin on the other. Not paying too much mind to anything else besides catching a few crickets and then getting back home, she almost missed the boy in the weeds.

If it wasn't for his greased-back dark hair shining in all that green, and his glasses catching a glimmer of sunlight, she probably would have, and inwardly chastised herself for not paying better attention.

"Hey," she said. The boy sat among the ivy, the ugly leaves caressing his skin. "You know you're sitting right smack-dab in the middle of poison ivy?"

He nodded but didn't say anything.

"Well, aren't you gonna get out?"

He shook his head no. "I'm not allergic. I'm not allergic to anything."

"Are you stupid or something?"

"Nope. I get all A's."

Lilly laughed. She either liked him already or hated his guts. "Well, maybe they didn't teach you anything in your school 'cause everyone's allergic to poison ivy." Of course, she didn't know if that was completely true. Still, she'd listened to enough of her daddy's yelling to realize that if you say something as if it were true, why then, everyone believes it is.

"I'm not."

Lilly's smile disappeared.

Nope. She definitely did not like him.

Her hand itched to reach out and take a swipe at him. But she didn't want to get poison ivy herself— something her daddy would be awful unforgiving about. Lilly shrugged and continued on her way. "Suit yourself."

When she came back up the path, her jar full of plump black crickets and one grasshopper, the boy was gone. Lilly smiled to herself. He must've come to his senses and realized she was right. She was right about most things and wouldn't admit it if she wasn't. That's why the boy stirred her up. He seemed pretty certain, and the only thing she hated more than being wrong was being made to look silly.

The next day, Lilly was sitting on the front porch while her daddy was in his bedroom sleeping on and on, when who should walk up but that dark-haired boy with his ridiculous-looking glasses.

He stopped at the little run-down fence and wiggled a loose white post. "You're Lilly, aren't you?"

"Maybe."

"The man at the corner store told me you were. I'm Mark."

"Maybe you are smart," she said in her best sarcastic voice. "Well, Mark, how bad do you itch?"

He smiled wide, which irked Lilly something awful, then held out his arm, the skin smooth as buttermilk without so much as a single bump or mark. "Told you. I'm not allergic."

That was when she officially went from not liking the dark-haired, ridiculous-looking boy to hating that dark-haired, ridiculous-looking boy.

I smiled at the pages in my hand.

"Hello? Is someone down there?" Mom's voice called from the top of the stairs.

I jumped, my heart pounding. "It's only me. I'll be up in a minute. I just thought I left something down here."

"Is that you, CJ?"

I sighed. "No, it's Sunday."

Her footsteps started down the stairs, and I rushed to close the box and put it back against the wall. "Do you know where he and Henry and Bo are? They dried off after their baths and then disappeared."

I tucked the papers under my top, thankful that I was wearing my loosest T-shirt—the one I'd gotten for reading the most books during the summer last year (I was hoping to win this year's T-shirt, too). "No, but I haven't been here long."

The footsteps stopped. "Are you coming up?"

"Yeah, in a minute."

"Well, make sure you lock the doors."

"I will."

I patted the pages under my shirt. Why had they been locked away in the basement of the library? Maybe it really was a long, drawn-out confession of a crime. Or maybe it was a story written by someone in town? Like someone's diary.

My heart skipped a beat.

Or it might be nothing at all.

I started up the basement stairs, careful to keep the papers pressed against my stomach. Either way, nobody in my family could know about this.

I FLICKED off the main light in the library, then turned the key in the lock. The hazy twilight melted with the ground, and the evening air was crisp. Fireflies blinked on and off, and the hidden crickets were just beginning to sing. I started back to the house, excited about the rubber-banded pages.

"What are you hiding?"

My heart stopped for a second and I jolted to a halt, clutching the papers tighter against my skin. I searched the dusk. The voice came from behind a large tree. "CJ, is that you? I swear I'm going to kill you."

I waited for my brother's laughter. Getting scared by him again; he'd never let me live it down. A twig snapped, and the leaves shivered above me. I swallowed down the urge to scream. "CJ, you better come out. I mean it." I tried to make my voice strong, but it came out more like a timid squeak.

I watched the darkness. There was a small rustling of

grass and branches. A figure stepped out from behind a tree. Whirling around, I bolted toward the house.

"No, wait!" the voice called out behind me.

I stopped and turned slowly.

The fingernail moon revealed the figure of a boy. The large figure. A big, round boy in white shorts and a white shirt. Even though it was almost dark I could tell that the shirt he wore was as clean as the day it was bought. I don't think there was a piece of clothing in our entire house that was that clean.

"I'm Jude Zachariah Caleb Trist the Third," he said. "What are you hiding inside your shirt?"

I ignored his question and kicked myself for not being nearly as sneaky as I thought I'd been. "That's a lot of names." Then again, he was a lot of boy. He stepped closer and I stepped back. "What do you want?"

Now he ignored me. "I'm eleven years old," he said.

"Oh, really? I'm almost twelve." I stood up straighter. The manuscript slipped and I grabbed it quickly to keep it inside my shirt.

"Really? You look pretty small. I thought you were maybe seven."

This boy was getting on my nerves even more than CJ. "I might be small, but I'm still almost twelve. You can ask my mom."

"All right." His voice seemed almost cheery like I'd

really invited him. He walked up and stood beside me.

"What do you mean, 'all right'?"

"All right. I'll go and ask your mom."

"Y-y-you can't."

"Why not? I know you have one. I've been watching you and your family all day long. Are all those kids really your brothers and sisters?" He stopped and sniffed the air. "What's that smell?"

I knew without even taking a breath that it was a combination of Dad's cookies and Mom's pumpkin bread.

"It's nothing," I said, and started back to the house. "Must be coming from that house across the field."

He laughed. "No way. He's a lunatic."

I have to admit, the word *lunatic* made me stop in my tracks. But only for a second. This boy was the lunatic.

"You still haven't told me what you're hiding." He caught up to me. "If you stole something from the library, I'll tell."

I turned on him. "I didn't steal anything. I'm just looking at it. And you're not going to tell anyone."

He lifted his chin. "How are you going to stop me?"

I clenched my left fist real tight, my fingernails biting into my palms. "Because . . . because. I'll . . ."

The door opened and Mom stepped onto the porch, knocking over the red watering can. It clanged as it hit the wood. "Emm—I mean, Sunday. Are you still out there?"

"Yeah, I'm coming." I turned back to Judah Zachariah Whatever-His-Name-Was. "Just go home," I said.

"No. And I will tell."

"No you won't."

"Yes I will."

"Sunday, who's out there with you?" I heard my mom's footsteps on the stairs. "CJ, if you snuck out the back door again, I swear I will ground you for life."

The boy and I locked eyes in the dark and I sighed. "Fine." I turned back to Mom. "There's a boy here. He says he wants to ask you how old I am."

Mom came the rest of the way down the stairs. "What? A boy?"

Jude I-Have-Six-Names brushed past me and met my mom with an outstretched hand. "I'm Jude Zachariah Caleb Trist the Third. My mom works at the bank. Is she really twelve years old?" he asked, pointing at me.

"Almost twelve," I corrected. I didn't need to look like a fool (though I was sure I already did) arguing in the dark with a boy I didn't even know with hidden papers stuffed underneath my T-shirt.

Mom smiled. "It's nice to meet you. And yes, Sunday is almost twelve."

He nodded but didn't move.

"There. See? Now you can go home."

"Sunday!" Mom scolded. She shot me a look, her eyes

flashing as they caught a bit of moonlight.

"Well—" I whined.

Mom turned back to Jude-the-Intruder. "If you don't think your mother will mind, you're welcome to join us for dessert. We were just about to have some pumpkin bread with butter."

Jude didn't even hesitate. He followed my mom up the stairs and into the house, where I heard Henry crying because he didn't get the first piece.

Mom turned around. "Let me just bring in an extra chair. You coming, Sunday?"

"Yeah." I followed them into the house, then dashed up the stairs to my bedroom, where I stashed the papers underneath my bed. Then I rejoined everyone in the dining room, ignoring the boy who was just standing there staring with his mouth hanging open like a goldfish. The plate that held the pumpkin bread was nothing but crumbs, well, besides the heels, which were everyone's least favorite parts. I picked one up, slathered it with butter that melted instantly into the still-warm bread, and ate it.

CJ, Bo, and Henry had pumpkin bread masks over their faces. They'd poked out holes for their eyes, noses, and mouths.

Mom lugged a chair through the door and set it next to me at the table. "There you go."

CJ looked at me and then at Jude. He let his bread fall off his face into his hands, then took an obscenely big bite. "Who are you?"

"Jude Zachariah Caleb Trist the Third."

I could tell Henry was impressed.

"How old are you?" CJ asked.

Jude made himself look taller, even though he was already big—in more ways than one. "Eleven."

CJ lifted one eyebrow and looked at him skeptically. "You got hair on your chest?"

Jude's cheeks blushed pink, and he glanced around the table at my sisters and parents, but they weren't paying any attention. "No."

CJ seemed satisfied and handed Jude the last slice of bread.

I watched the intruder lick his lips. "Thanks."

"Sit by me, sit by me!" Henry said, patting his chair. "I can squish myself real small. Watch."

"That's really good," Jude said. He squeezed himself onto the sliver of chair next to Henry.

I rolled my eyes and listened in on Mom and Dad.

"I need to take a mop to the floor again now that the books are mostly sorted." Mom let her pen glide across the notepad already halfway filled.

Emma was taking turns nibbling the smallest bites imaginable from her slice of pumpkin bread and pressing the buttons on her phone. Since she'd gotten the phone a few months ago, Dad joked that he should've just had it surgically implanted in her ear.

I glanced back at Jude With-a-Zillion-Names. He looked even bigger sitting next to Henry. I couldn't help but feel sorry for Jude Trist-Caleb-Whatever. He'd been pressed and stuffed into that bright white shirt and the buttons looked as if they were struggling to stay in the buttonholes. He was like a marshmallow on the end of a stick sitting over hot, gray coals. But he looked content, with a thick slice of pumpkin bread in his hands and butter dripping down his right wrist. His eyes were large and wide as he looked from one of my siblings to the next. I noticed his gaze fell on Emma more than once. Emma was the beauty. Always had been, probably always would be. She had the same features as the rest of us, but for some reason she wore them better. I felt myself bristle. It wasn't as if I liked this boy or even wanted him to like me. He'd been completely annoying and had threatened to tell on me. But still. It was hard to sit by and watch Emma get admired while I didn't get so much as a second glance. Or even a first glance.

Eventually everyone got up from the table, and it was clear that Mom had forgotten that she'd invited a strange boy with too many names into our house for dessert. But Jude was wrapped up in watching the chaos and I could tell he didn't know which way was up.

I grabbed his arm and walked him to the door. "Thanks for coming," I said, opening it.

He craned his neck to take a look at CJ, who had tied a basket from the top of the stairs and was trying to coax Henry into getting inside so he could hoist him up to the second floor. I closed the door on Jude a little more and he snapped out of his trance. "Wow, that was . . . was so much fun. Is it always like this at your house?"

"Complete craziness and so noisy you can hardly hear yourself think? Yes."

"What's the name of your sister, the one playing with her phone?"

I lifted my chin. "Emma. She's practically engaged, though." It wasn't a complete lie. Tommy Anderson had proposed to her on the bus in sixth grade and she'd said yes. Emma was a freshman in high school now and Tommy Anderson had moved away, but still.

Jude's smile deflated. "Oh."

"Your mom is probably wondering where you are, don't you think?"

He looked down at his watch, the huge white face glinting a little from the light escaping through the door. He almost bolted down the stairs. "Yeah, I should go," he called back. "I'll see you tomorrow."

I called back, "All right," though it was only when I

closed the door that I realized I'd be seeing him again. And he knew I had hidden something underneath my shirt from the library.

Just my luck.

I tromped up the stairs, Butters at my heels.

Once inside my room with the door closed, I kicked the thought of the boy out of my head along with my shoes, which landed by the trunk of old clothes. After slipping into my pajamas and flicking on the fan, I grabbed *The Secret Garden* and flopped onto my bed. I'd been reading it every night since we arrived and only had three chapters left.

After I read the last words, I closed the cover with a satisfied sigh. The book had been just as brilliant the second time as it had been the first.

The whirring fan rustled the pages I had snuck from the library. Rolling over onto my stomach, I reached under the bed where I had hidden them and pulled the stack onto my lap.

After flipping through the musty pages, I smoothed my hand across the top and pressed my nose to them. I'd always loved reading a new book. Opening up one to the first page was like starting a new life. And the story I held in my hands now was even more exciting. Whose was it? Was I the very first person to read it?

I found where I had stopped and continued:

But the universe thrust Lilly and Mark together at almost every turn, it seemed. Lilly thought that perhaps it was punishment for the time she had pretended to read her Bible when really she had been reading <u>Moby-Dick</u>. Or maybe Fate had some unknown plan for her that she had no interest in being a part of. But because she couldn't seem to get rid of Mark, she took to beating him up. Even that, however, didn't keep him away. It seemed only to make him like her more. Lilly couldn't take that one bit.

She had plans for her life. Plans for getting out of Price, where nothing ever happened. Plans for making something of herself. Plans to prove to her good-for-nothing daddy that he was wrong about her. And one thing Lilly knew for a fact was that none of those plans included a boy with too-thick glasses who wasn't allergic to poison ivy.

My eyes started to droop. Yawning, I got up and slipped the pages underneath the mattress—safe from my nosy brothers and prying sisters.

For now, the story was just mine.

8

I HAD just poured the milk into Bo's cereal bowl the next morning when there was a knock at the front door. Jude. I don't know how I knew it before the door even opened, but I did.

Mom, who'd probably been up and dressed since five o'clock as usual, walked to the door and opened it wide. "Good morning. Jude, right?"

He nodded. "Good morning."

Mom could get his name right, but not mine? I plopped into a chair, grabbed my spoon, and stabbed at the mound of flakes swimming in my bowl.

"It's good to see you again. Have you had breakfast?"

"Hi, Jude!" Bo said, jumping up and spilling half of his cereal onto the table. He rushed over like he was going to wrap the boy in a hug, then hung back behind Mom.

"Hi." Jude walked in, looking more comfortable and normal in his loose blue T-shirt and shorts than he had yesterday in that white getup he'd been packed into. Still,

I marveled at how clean he was. He looked like something out of a commercial for laundry detergent.

"Sunday," Mom said, leading Jude to the dining room. "It's your friend Jude."

Jude smiled at me and took a seat as if that's what he did every other morning of his life. "Hi, Sunday," he said.

I swallowed a bite of cereal, wiped the dribble of milk from my chin, and mustered up a halfhearted *hi.*

"What can I get you? I'm sure you could still eat a little something?" Mom asked. "Toast maybe?"

He smiled. "Yeah, sure. And thank you again for the pumpkin bread. It was the best thing I've ever had. My mom makes it sometimes, but not as good as yours."

I rolled my eyes. He must've taken a class on how to win over moms. She smiled, pleased, and then disappeared into the kitchen.

"Where's everybody else?'

"Me and Sunday always eat breakfast together." Bo smiled at me. "CJ and Henry are washing off the wall in the bedroom, 'cause they played tic-tac-toe on it last night. Mom said she'd skin them alive if they ever did something like that again. May and Emma are getting ready, trying on clothes and putting gunk in their hair, shaving their legs and plucking their eyebrows out. Stuff like that."

I stifled a laugh, thinking what my sisters would do if

they knew Bo was telling a random boy about everything they do in the bathroom.

Mom came in and set a plate of buttery toast in front of Jude along with a glass of orange juice and a jar of strawberry jam. "Now, don't hesitate to ask for more," she said.

"Thank you."

"You have any brothers or sisters?" I asked.

Jude shook his head no through a mouthful of toast.

"Really? It's just you and your parents?"

"Yeah, well, just me and my mom. And then there's Wally, my mom's boyfriend."

"Oh. Your parents are divorced then?"

He looked down at his plate and nodded.

"Sunday!" Mom said, giving me another look.

I shrugged. "I was just asking. He knows that Emma and May pluck their eyebrows out. I think we should at least know a little about him."

"What does 'divorced' mean?" Bo asked. His chin was covered in a white crust of dried milk.

Mom smiled and took Bo's near-empty bowl. "Come on, Bo, let's get you washed up."

They disappeared into the kitchen.

I waited until they were gone, then whispered. "So, you aren't gonna tell, right?"

"Tell?" Jude acted like he didn't know what I was talking about. "Tell about what?"

I sighed, exasperated. "About . . . well, forget it." If he didn't remember, I wasn't going to remind him.

"Oh, about the thing you were hiding last night?"

I nodded.

"No. I won't tell."

"Thanks."

"Can you tell me what it was, though?" He took a swig of orange juice and wiped his mouth with of his hand.

"No."

"Why not?"

"'Cause . . . 'cause I hardly know you, and because I don't know if it's anything yet. I took it so I could read it and see."

"So it's a book, then?" He popped the last piece of toast in his mouth. "Oh, come on, tell me."

"Why should I? You were going to tell on me and, like I said, I hardly know you."

"Sure you do. My name is Jude Zachariah Caleb Trist the Third. I'm an only child. My parents are divorced, and my mom's boyfriend is a dork." He paused. "And I wasn't going to tell."

"Yeah, right."

"I wasn't." He took his plate and stood up. We walked to the kitchen and put our dishes in the dishwasher. "I just saw your family over the past few days and, well, I wanted to say hi. My mom says you should always be friendly to newcomers."

"You only wanted to meet Emma. Admit it."

His cheeks filled with red. "No, I didn't even see her up close until last night. It's like I said, I just wanted to meet you and your family."

"I don't see why."

I walked outside and sat down on the porch stairs, picking at a scab on my knee. Jude plopped down next to me. Butters trotted out through the open door and disappeared into the bushes, her nose to the ground. "So tell me again why you wanted to meet my family."

Jude gave a halfhearted shrug. "I don't have any brothers and sisters. I don't know what it's like."

"Well, it stinks," I said, thinking of sitting at the gas station alone. But Jude wouldn't understand that. I bet he never felt invisible. He would never get left behind.

"It's okay being an only child. But sometimes it gets lonely, and my mom can be overprotective." He turned to me. "You don't like being in a big family?"

"It's not that I don't like my family. They're all right. It's just that it's easy to get forgotten." I looked at him. "But how about you? You said your stepdad's a dork."

He glared at me. "He's not my stepdad."

"Oh, yeah. Sorry. Your mom's *boyfriend* then. Why don't you like him?"

Jude shrugged. "He's just always trying to do stuff with me. Teach me things and be my best friend. Like, right now he's trying to get me to play with him in the father-son baseball game at the fair that's coming up."

"And what's wrong with that?"

"I had a dad and he was lousy, and I don't want another one. All my mom's other boyfriends were lousy, too. They were only being nice to me so they could get close to my mom. That's what Wally's doing. Besides, my mom and I are fine when it's just the two of us. We don't need anyone else."

"But you come over to my house to see what it's like to have brothers and sisters? That doesn't make any sense."

He untied and retied his shoelace. "Just forget it. You wouldn't understand."

I raised my eyebrows. "Well, excuse me."

We sat for a few moments before Jude broke the silence. "So why are you trying to hide the book or whatever it is you found?"

I looked hard at him and lowered my voice. "Because I need to make my mark this summer."

"Make your mark?"

"Yeah, you know, do something that sets me apart from everyone else. Do something big. Something that will get me noticed by everyone. Something important."

"What's so secret about that?"

"Because if one of my sisters or brothers finds out, then all the attention will go to them."

"How?"

Standing up, I walked the rest of the way down the stairs. "That's how it always goes with my brothers and sisters. Now, stop asking so many questions."

"But if I don't know what you're trying to do, how am I supposed to help?"

I whirled around. "Help?"

"Yeah. Help you make your mark, or whatever."

Stepping closer, I looked him up and down. "You really want to help?"

He nodded. "Sure. I don't have anything else to do. My best friend, Griffin, spends the summer with his grandparents, and most of my other friends live in the next town over and are probably at camp. Besides, it'll give me a good excuse to say no to Wally if he asks me to go somewhere."

"And you won't tell a single soul—especially anyone in my family—about anything that I come up with to try?"

He crossed his heart and then spat on the ground. "That's how my grandpa taught me to make a promise. He said if you ever break a promise like that, then your spit rises up from the ground like fog and turns into a ghost that haunts you the rest of your life."

"You believe that?"

Jude shrugged.

I turned up my chin. "Well, I do. So don't you break

it, Jude Zachariah—" I couldn't remember the rest of his name.

"Caleb Trist the Third," he finished. "I won't."

I nodded and found myself smiling at him. "I'll tell you everything later, okay?"

"All right."

Dad hailed us from the library stairs, his tool belt hanging around his waist. "Sunday! You coming to help?"

"Yeah. I'll be there in a sec." I turned to Jude and asked if he wanted to come along.

"Sure. But I have to call my mom. She freaked out last night when I came home late."

Jude went to use the phone, and I ran over to the library. Dad had brought one of the desks outside and was staring. "What are you doing?"

"Oh, I'm going to start refinishing the desks and some of the shelves. I have to sand them down and then stain or paint them. What do you think? Stain or repaint?"

I shrugged. "I don't know."

"The librarian is coming today so she'll decide. Your friend coming over, too?"

"Yeah. Is that okay?"

He smiled and ruffled my hair. "Sure."

I stepped into the library and started in on another stack of books. From the looks of it, Mom and the librarian were going to have to order a whole lot more copies.

I flipped through book after book, sorting them into separate "bad condition" and "good condition" piles. Finally, when I thought that Jude must've gotten lost on the thirty-second walk over, I heard his voice.

"You're making the costumes?" he asked.

I stood up and stepped out the open door. "Where in the world were—" But I stopped. There he was, his eyes big and round just like Butters's when she wants a treat, gazing up at Emma. "I bet your costumes are the best," he said all swoony-like.

Emma smiled at him, which I could tell just about sent him over the edge. "Thanks."

I should've known. One of my siblings was already stealing a friend I'd had for not even a full two hours.

I rolled my eyes, tromped down the stairs, and grabbed Jude's hand, tugging him up into the library.

"Come on, loverboy. I thought you were going to help me." The door closed behind us, and the trance my sister had put over him broke. At least for the moment.

I sat him down next to stack of books. "Start sorting."

"Is Emma gonna—" he started.

Glaring at him with an I-will-kill-you-if-you-say-anything-more-about-my-sister look, I shoved a book in his hand. He turned it over, confused.

"Snap out of it, Jude. Look at the book and see if we should keep it."

He looked at me, his eyes still hazy. "What?"

"See. If. We. Should. Keep. It."

He shook his head, the last of her trance disappearing, and smiled. "Oh, yeah."

Instead of ringing the triangle for lunch, Mom and May carried over a plate of sandwiches, celery sticks slathered with globs of peanut butter, two pitchers of pink lemonade, and some of Dad's Famous Fowler Family Chocolate Chip Cookies.

I grabbed a slice of celery and licked out the peanut butter in one swipe, then sat down on one of the steps. Jude eyed the cookies and the sandwiches dripping with jelly and cream cheese (Bo's and my favorite).

"You can have some. Mom always makes enough."

Jude reached for a sandwich just as a clean white car pulled up. A woman stepped out and glanced around at the pile of us spread all over the library stairs and grass. She held a brown paper bag in one hand, the name JUDE written in neat bold letters across the front, and a tall water bottle in the other.

"Is that your mom?" I asked. She looked young and nervous but pretty. Her brown hair was pulled in a neat ponytail, and she was dressed really nice in a skirt, high heels, and a silky blouse like Mom wore on Christmas Eve.

Jude nodded, his cheeks red as an apple, and got up.

A man got out of the passenger side. He was tall and thin and wore a mechanic's outfit streaked with black grease and oil, the complete opposite of Jude's mom. He had a rough yet kind look about him as he reached out to shake hands with my dad. "Is that—?" I started.

"Yes."

Mom had already made her way down the stairs and was greeting Ms. Trist with a warm hug. Dad looked like he was explaining what he'd done with the library. Wally nodded and smiled.

But everywhere else, chaos was breaking out, and I watched Ms. Trist's reaction change from "this woman is nice" to "these kids are out of control."

CJ was chasing after Bo with a booger on the end of his finger yelling, "If I catch you, then you have to eat it."

May was crying because Dad was going to make her apologize to the people down the street for hitting their garbage can earlier that morning trying to parallel park. Emma was complaining about a stain on her tank top, and Henry had his pants down around his ankles and was peeing on one of the trees.

"May . . . I mean, Sunday," Mom called. "Why don't you come over and meet Jude's mom?"

I walked over and shook her hand, trying to block her from as much of the scene as I could. "Hi, I'm Sunday."

Ms. Trist's mouth twitched as if she was trying to keep her smile right where it was. "It's nice to meet you," she said. "It seems like you all are . . . " I saw her glance at CJ, who was lying on top of Bo, the booger inches away from his face. " . . . busy?" She laid her hand protectively on Jude's shoulder. "Jude is a delicate boy."

"Mom! I am not."

Wally strolled over and put his arm around Jude's mom. "He's not delicate, Rachel."

Jude rolled his eyes and shrugged away the hand that Wally tried to place on his shoulder.

Ms. Trist smiled. "Well, he might be a little shy—"

"Mom!"

Jude's mom kissed one of his pudgy cheeks. "It's true. He's not used to a lot of . . . rough play."

I think that was code for "please don't let that unruly boy shove a disgusting booger in my son's face." I understood exactly where she was coming from.

Ms. Trist handed Mom the brown paper bag. "I packed Jude a lunch. He only eats organic foods. There's an extra arrowroot cookie for you, Sunday." She turned to Jude. "And for a snack I've packed your third serving of fruit. You'll need to get two more servings of veggies tonight. Okay?"

Jude nodded, his face a deep crimson. "I'll be fine."

Mom raised her voice. She had to be louder than

Emma, who was yelling something at May. "We'll take good care of him!"

Emma stomped off to the house, and CJ, Bo, and Henry (who had his pants pulled back up) ran over to Ms. Trist and smiled, revealing lemon rinds stuck to their teeth.

"We better go, Rachel," Wally said, heading back to the car. "I have to be at the shop in five minutes."

"I'm coming." Ms. Trist glanced around nervously once more, then handed Mom a business card with every single number and email address she had in case we needed to get ahold of her. "For any reason at all," she said.

Mom took the card and tucked it into her back pocket. Ms. Trist smothered Jude in a hug, had him promise to be home at five, and then slid into the passenger seat.

"Your mom seems nice," I said, biting into a sandwich.

"Yeah." He pulled out containers and plastic bags, each labeled with his name and a description of what was inside: tofu and brown rice, vitamins, mini tomatoes, and two lumps that could've been cookies. Last he drew out a bag of sliced mango and a bottle of water with a sticker that said ORGANICALLY COLLECTED IN THE UNDERGROUND SPRINGS OF THE ALPS.

Jude stared down at his lunch, which didn't look all that bad. That is, if you took away the tofu, vitamins, brown rice, tomatoes, and probably the cookies. "She's trying to get me healthy."

"Yeah. I sort of guessed that." I crunched down on another stalk of celery. He eyed it. I grabbed the container of tofu and stuffed it back into the brown bag. Then I handed him a celery stick with enough peanut butter to seal his tongue to the roof of his mouth for a day.

"Don't worry, this'll count as one of your servings of vegetables and one serving of protein."

9

AFTER lunch a woman on a bike rode up to the library, pushed the kickstand down, smoothed down her dark windblown hair, and walked toward the library.

"That must be her," Mom whispered, wiping her hands on her jeans and standing. "The new librarian." She smiled and met the woman halfway down the stairs and shook her hand. "You must be Miss Dunghop?"

Dunghop?

CJ was going to lose it when he met her, and then Bo and Henry would lose it, and then Mom would lose it . . . except not in the same way.

Mom walked her up the stairs, where Jude and I were arranging books into boxes, and May and Emma were labeling them. "These are my three girls, Emma, May, and Sunday, and their friend Jude. This is Miss Dunghop."

We all smiled. She was the youngest librarian I had ever seen. She had perfect white teeth, big brown eyes, and ears that stuck out slightly from her dark brown hair.

Freckles dotted her nose and cheeks like a dusting of cinnamon and she was exactly how I pictured Miss Honey
from *Matilda*. I liked her instantly.

"Nice to meet you," I said.

There was the sudden screeching of voices coming
from the house, and we saw the boys tripping out the
front door and then traipsing over to the library.

"Oh dear. I mean, Oh good," Mom said, forcing a smile.
"You can meet my boys." She shot CJ a nervous look, but
I could tell he didn't notice.

"Boys, I'd like you to meet Miss Dunghop–"

That's when CJ burst out laughing. I elbowed him hard,
and he brought his giggles to a quiet snicker behind my
back. He whispered to Bo and Henry, who also started to
laugh.

Mom continued louder, probably hoping to drown
them out. "These are my boys, CJ, Bo, and Henry."

Miss Dunghop smiled. "Nice to meet you."

"Nice to meet you, Miss *Dung*hop," CJ said, giggling.

Bo and Henry started laughing, and Mom's face turned
the color of a raspberry. I thought fast and, grabbing both
Henry's and Bo's hands, started down the library steps.
"Come on, CJ. Didn't you want to make a fort?"

Miss Dunghop waved her hand. "Don't worry about it.
With a last name like Dunghop I've heard it all. That's
why I go by Miss Jenny."

CJ stared at her for a few moments as if he wasn't quite sure what to think, then shrugged. "All right. But I like Dunghop better." He tugged Henry and Bo the rest of the way down the stairs. "Come on. Let's go build our fort."

Mom let out a long sigh as they disappeared behind the library. I watched her cheeks slowly return to their normal color. "Now, Miss Jenny," Mom said, "would you like to come in and look around at the remodel? Then the kids and I can show you the books we've gone through."

Miss Jenny nodded and smiled. "Lead the way."

Despite all the cleaning and organizing over the next few days, Jude hadn't forgotten about the manuscript or about my plans to make my mark. He bugged me like a fly around a peanut butter and jelly sandwich.

But I had my reasons for holding out.

First, even though we were becoming better friends, I still didn't know him all that well, and I needed to make sure he wasn't going to turn around and tattle on me the moment I showed him the manuscript.

Second, I needed to make sure that he wasn't going to tell my family about what we were up to because that would ruin everything, too.

And third, well, I hadn't come up with any plans to do anything spectacular yet. I'd been so busy at the library that I was hardly able to keep myself awake at night to read the Nancy Drew book *The Mystery at Lilac Inn* or the manuscript, let alone try to come up with a plan to be noticed. Each day that I didn't come up with anything made me more anxious to get started. I didn't want to leave Alma as still just one-of-the-six.

But just that morning, Mom and Miss Jenny had told Jude and me that we didn't have to stay at the library all day long anymore. It was finally time to come up with a huge plan to make my mark.

That's why, after lunch, I took Jude up to my room.

He plopped down on the floor in front of the fan and looked around. "So, where is that book you're reading? The one you took from the library."

I stared hard at him. He could be trusted. To a certain point. "Close your eyes and turn around."

"Really, Sunday, that's silly. I won't tell."

"What if one of my brothers or sisters captures you and forces you to tell them all your secrets? If you don't know where the book is, then there won't be a chance of you spilling the beans."

He sighed and shrugged. "Okay."

I waited till he was facing the opposite way and then checked to make sure his eyes were closed. Lifting the mattress, I pulled out the pages. I carried them over to the floor and took a seat in front of him. "You can open your eyes."

"This isn't a book."

"Sure it is. It's just not a published one. Maybe some-one in Alma is destined to become a famous writer."

The headline in the Alma newspaper, SUNDAY FOWLER TURNS UNKNOWN LOCAL INTO FAMOUS AUTHOR, scrolled through my mind.

"So you don't know who wrote it?"

I shook my head no and grinned. "It's a mystery."

"I guess it could be anyone's."

"Yeah, I suppose."

"How in the world are you going to find out who it belongs to? It's impossible."

The headline disappeared in a puff of smoke and I snatched the papers back. "You sure know how to kill a person's dreams."

"I'm just saying. Lots of people write books. My mom even says she wants to write one someday."

"Well, maybe she wrote it? And if we can prove it, then maybe she'll be in the newspaper or it'll get published and made into a movie or something."

I could tell Jude liked that idea. "Maybe. She has always liked going to the library."

"I found this one locked in a box in the library basement."

"A safe? You broke into a safe?" His eyebrows rose over his wide-open eyes.

I hadn't thought of it as a safe, but the idea sounded

much more intriguing that way. "Well, sort of. So the book has to be kind of valuable, right?"

Jude shrugged. "I guess so. Or what if it's something that someone wrote and didn't want anyone to read? Like a diary or something."

I stood up, set the pages beside *The Mystery at Lilac Inn*, and sat on my bed. "It's not written like a diary and, besides, if they didn't want anyone to read it, then they should've kept it at home and not in the library where anyone could find the key and open the box." I lifted my nose in the air, more determined than ever. "I'm going to figure out who wrote this and I think we should start with your mom."

He shrugged. "Sure."

"In the meantime, you can help me think of ideas for what I can do to make myself stand out. The manuscript from the library might not turn out to be anything."

We were both silent for a few moments. The only sound was the whirring of the fan and the choking sound of the car trying to start in the driveway.

"I saw on a map that there's a lake outside of town. I could swim across it all by myself," I said. "I'm sure that would get people's attention."

Jude laughed, pushing aside the bangs that had crept in front of his eyes. "Yeah, I guess you could. But your brother Henry could do that, too."

"No, he can't swim."

"You don't need to. It's so shallow and small that anyone can cross it. And it's pretty gross. My mom won't let me get within two feet of it."

I let out a groan. I had pictured a shimmering lake with boats tied up to docks, water-skiers gliding across the water, and fishermen casting rods. Not a slimy puddle.

"You could try to break a record or something."

"I've already tried that. Didn't work. You don't have a unicycle, do you?"

"That's the last thing my mom would ever let me have."

"Yeah, I guess you're right." Visions of tents, balloons, food, and contests filled my head. "I was thinking I could throw a big party for the reopening of the library."

He smiled and nodded. "That's a good idea."

A party wasn't as grand an idea as I was hoping for, but it was something I could probably pull off. Jude could help. We'd just have to make it really extravagant if it was going to make me stand out. "It's keeping my brothers and sisters from poking around that'll be the hard part. They'll definitely know something is up."

"Yeah, but everyone will still know it was your idea."

I laughed. "You don't know my family."

I took out a notebook and a blue pen I'd brought with me from home and paced the floor.

"The party has to be big. Something that people won't

be able to forget." I wrote BIG at the top of the piece of paper. "Like . . . rides and a . . . a hot-air balloon. Things like that."

"Rides and a hot-air balloon? Where are you going to get the money for that? And how are you going to keep all that from your family?"

"Well, I'll have to tell my parents eventually. But . . ." I fell silent. Jude was right. How in the world would I ever be able to pull something like that off without everyone in my family putting their hands in? "Okay, forget the balloon and rides for now. Maybe we could see if there are people in town who could do tricks or entertain or something. I can bake food and make lemonade and I can talk to my parents to see if there is a little extra money from the anonymous donation to buy decorations."

I pictured my name etched on a bronze plaque screwed into a bench. "Hey, maybe the town will name something in the library after me. You think?"

"Maybe. I have an idea. You could write to some famous authors and ask if they could come and speak at the party!"

"That's perfect!" I scribbled the idea down. That would be huge. "Who should I write to? Judy Blume? Stephen King? J. K. Rowling?"

"Sure. You might as well try as many as you can think of. Let's make a list."

We both shouted out authors, getting distracted with almost every name by talking about their books.

"I loved *The Invention of Hugo Cabret*, too!" I said, scribbling down Brian Selznick.

Kate DiCamillo. "Have you read *The Tale of Despereaux*?"

"How about *A Long Way from Chicago* by Richard Peck?"

"That's one of my favorites. Remember the part—"

I stopped when the notebook page was filled with names. "Okay, we have to stop there. If everyone on this page says no, then we'll think of more." I glanced down at the list. "What if they don't get the letters in time . . . or what if they don't get back to us?"

Jude took the pen and scribbled Rick Riordan down. "I don't know. It's a long shot either way, but we should try."

I glanced down at the manuscript. If only I could find out who wrote it.

That would be big news in town.

News big enough to announce at the party. Big enough for the *Alma Gazette*.

Big enough for my name to be printed in bold black ink and my picture to be on the front page.

"All right," Jude said, interrupting my thoughts. "Let's start writing the letters. We should send them soon."

"Right." I pulled out a clean sheet of paper. "Dear J. K. Rowling . . ."

10

JUDE and I walked along the sidewalks toward town the next morning. He said that on our way to the post office we had to stop and try a crepe at the Crepe Café.

"They're the best."

"And your mom lets you eat them?"

He shrugged. "Ms. Bodnar uses organic milk and eggs, so Mom doesn't mind."

"Hmm." A big, flat French pancake didn't sound that appealing, but we needed to send off the letters, and I was itching to walk around downtown for the first time.

But not so itchy that I was going to let May drive Jude and me the few blocks to Main Street.

"She can't be all that bad," Jude said, huffing beside me.

Just then the van came jerking down the street, heaving forward and back like a wild stallion. It passed us, then stalled. May's muffled wail erupted behind the windows and I picked up my pace. "I guess that just depends on your definition of 'bad.'"

Jude wiped the beads of sweat that had collected above his lip and we turned right onto Main Street.

I gulped down the little town. I'd been at the library for the past week, so I hadn't had a chance to walk along the streets or glance into any of the shops. The sidewalks were swept clean, handprints and initials stuck forever in some of the cement squares. Flowers hung in pots from light posts, bursting in shades of purple, blue, red, and pink, and swayed gently back and forth. The air was warm but not heavy like it was in the city. It smelled like flowers, grass, and something baking in the oven. The giant dog I had spotted from my seat in the van when we first arrived dashed down the sidewalk, an old man half running, half sprinting after him. It looked like if he dug his heels in the sidewalk and held on, the dog would pull him along and he'd be waterskiing. I could hear him breathing from across the road. "Mr. Castor!" he yelled. "Heel! Heel!"

"That's Papa Gil." Jude said. "He's married to Muzzy. Their dog is the worst dog I've ever seen."

"I think I remember him and his wife coming to the library the other day. They brought over a pie. I didn't get to meet them because Mom and Dad sent me to take down the zip line that CJ had rigged up from the upstairs bathroom before he sent Henry down. Muzzy and Papa Gil? Are those their real names?"

"No, but that's what everyone calls them. They own the thrift store over there. My mom said they never were able to have kids, so all the kids in town are sort of like their grandchildren." He leaned in closer. "And they always have candy."

I smiled toward the thrift store window, where clothes hung a little crooked on the cardboard mannequins. When my grandpa was alive, he would always come over to visit on Sunday afternoon. "It's my favorite day of the week," he'd say to me, scooping me up in his arms. "'Cause you're my Sunday." I remember how he smelled like peanut butter and had a deep, rough voice. It would be nice to have a grandpa and grandma nearby, at least for the summer.

"Here it is," Jude said.

We walked into the small café I had spied when we first drove through town. That's where all the good smells were coming from. It looked like a picture of France I had seen in a calendar once.

So did the woman behind the counter.

She wore flowers in her reddish hair and flashed Jude and me a smile as she slid a crepe into a to-go box and handed it to a bulky man whose roly-poly stomach showed just how much he enjoyed her cooking. "Have a good day, Mr. Ryans," she said, her voice slightly accented.

Mr. Ryans licked his lips and smiled before bustling back onto the sidewalk.

The woman behind the counter was a little older than my parents. There were streaks of gray mixed in with her wiry red curls, which she had pulled off her freckled face in a loose, low ponytail. She wore a red T-shirt with the phrase I LOVE FOOD written across the chest in bright white letters, and she wore five or six silver bangles that jingled around her wrist like bells.

Jude walked up to the counter. "Hi, Ms. Bodnar. This is Sunday. Her family is fixing up the old library."

Ms. Bodnar grinned. "Oh, yes, I think I met your sisters already. May and Emma, right?"

I nodded and inwardly groaned. Now it would be a miracle if she ever remembered my name.

"Nice to meet you, Sunday." She poured some batter onto a black pan, then lifted the handle and swirled the batter until it thinly covered the bottom. "I'm so glad you and your family have come. My late husband worked at the library for a few years. He would've been very sad to see what's become of it."

"Really? He worked there?" I stole a look at Jude, but he was watching Ms. Bodnar flip the lightly browned crepe. Was the story I'd found her husband's?

"Yes. When we moved here from Paris, he did not pack any of his clothes. Not even socks or underwear. 'I can replace those,' he told me, 'but not my books.'"

I liked her already. "Did your husband ever try to

write, Ms. Bodnar? You know, a story or a novel or something like that?"

She laughed, slid the crepe onto a plate, and swiped a knife covered in chocolate across it. "No, he didn't like to write. Just read, read, read." She dropped thinly sliced strawberries across the chocolate, then rolled it up like a burrito, adding a dollop of whipped cream on top. "I am the one who likes to write."

"Really?" I knocked Jude with my elbow, though he didn't seem to notice.

She smiled and waved the comment away. "Oh, it's nothing, really, I just write little stories here and there, and I'm not sure if they are even good."

Ms. Bodnar handed the plate and two forks to Jude. "Here's a crepe for you two to split. A gift to welcome you to town."

I grinned, my mouth watering at the sight of the drippy whipped cream. "Thank you."

Jude and I sat down at one of the tables and dug in. After taking just one bite, it wasn't hard to understand how the man in front of us got his tubby belly. It was like eating a piece of the clouds.

We were almost finished when Jude stopped eating and took a quick breath in.

"What?" I asked.

"Shh!" He hunkered down and glanced quickly at an

old man with a cane who walked past the café. When he was out of sight, Jude sat up, dug his fork into the last bite of crepe, and popped it into his mouth.

"What was that about?" I asked. "It wasn't Wally."

"It's hard to imagine, but that old man is even more awful than Wally." Jude leaned in closer but craned his neck to watch the man continue down the street. "That there is the meanest man in the entire world."

"Him?"

Jude nodded and stood up, swiping up the last bit of whipped cream with his finger.

I followed. "How's he so mean?"

"Just a second," Jude whispered, and set the plate on the counter. "Thanks, Ms. Bodnar."

"Yes, thank you. That was delicious."

She waved. "Anytime."

Jude and I started down the sidewalk. The old man was one block in front of us, and I could hear his feet and the cane creating a *shuffle-shuffle-tap* rhythm on the cement.

Jude whispered, even though there was no way on earth the old man could hear us, if he could even hear at all. "His name is Ben Folger. He's the lunatic that lives across the field from you. He's lived here almost all his life. You see his cane?"

I nodded.

"Well, Terrance Von, a senior at the high school, says

he's seen him pull a knife out of it and stab a stray cat before. There's also a curse around his house. Anything that goes over the bushes into his yard"—he paused and glanced around, lowering his voice—"never comes out again. Balls, shoes . . . kids. I hear he even eats raw meat."

"You don't really believe that stuff." I laughed.

Jude stopped, grabbed my arm. "Sure I do. And you should, too. That is if you want to make it back to your own town at the end of the summer. He hates kids and every kind of animal. His basement is like a dungeon, damp and dark with rats and spiders. Terrance says that's where he keeps and tortures the people who've trespassed."

"How does Terrance Von know if he can't go onto his property because of the curse?"

Jude continued walking. "How should I know? But he doesn't seem like the type of guy who would lie."

I stared down the sidewalk, watching the old man disappear around the corner.

"So, is he like a hermit?" I asked.

"Sort of, I guess. He does come out every now and then, but mostly I think he just hides away in his house plotting evil and burying the bones of the cats he's eaten in his garden."

That sounded kind of hermitish to me. "Or maybe he sits inside and writes? I've heard that sometimes writers hide themselves away in their houses while they tap away on their computers. Do you think he could have written the story that I found?"

Jude grabbed my arm and stopped. "Does the story have murder or torture in it?"

I shook my head. "Not so far."

He released my arm and started walking again. "Then no. He couldn't've written it. Besides, I doubt he has ever set foot in the library."

"Well, maybe that's what I need to do to make my mark: befriend the local hermit and bring him out of hiding." I would be like Mary Lennox in *The Secret Garden*. The idea made my heart thump with excitement and my skin crawl with fear.

Jude stopped again, pulling my arm harder this time. "No way, Sunday Fowler," he whispered, as if saying it too loud was dangerous. "You need to stay as far away from Ben Folger and his house as you can. And you should tell your brothers and sisters to stay away, too."

"If I told my brothers to keep clear, they would be knocking on his door before I even finished my sentence."

DESPITE Jude's warning, I couldn't get old Ben Folger out of my head the rest of that day or the next.

If Ben Folger really was a hermit, then bringing him out of his shell after years of hiding away would be a big deal. Everyone would want to know how I did it.

Or maybe he really did torture intruders in his basement. If I was able to prove that, I would be responsible for putting him behind bars and saving the entire town!

TWELVE-YEAR-OLD HERO SAVES US ALL!

It didn't seem like I could lose . . . well, unless he captured and tortured me.

I pushed that thought out of my mind and pictured my mom wrapping me in a big hug, and my dad proudly ruffling my hair as reporters interviewed me. "We're so proud of you, Sunday," my parents would say. "Our daughter, the hero."

A knock at my door startled me. After tucking the pages of the manuscript underneath my pillow, I opened *The Mystery at Lilac Inn* and pretended to read. "Come in."

The door creaked open and there was Bo, standing in the dark stairway.

I set the book down. I hadn't seen him much since this morning, and the sight of his messed-up hair, small bare feet, and dump-truck pajamas made me smile. "Bo? What are you doing still up?"

He rubbed his eyes and wrapped his blanket around his head. "CJ is snoring so loud I can't stand it, and Mom told me that unless I'm bleeding I can't come into her room 'cause Henry'll wake up."

I scooted over and flung back the covers. He grinned and dove in beside me, squinting his eyes closed, though I knew it would be a while before he fell asleep. I picked up the book and skimmed through the words. I was glad he was tucked in next to me, but there was a tiny part that was annoyed. With Bo here, I wouldn't be able to read more of the mysterious manuscript until tomorrow.

"Sunday?"

I sighed. "Yeah."

"I can't fall asleep."

"You haven't even tried. You just came in a minute ago."

Who was I kidding? There was no way he was going to fall asleep with the lamp glowing. I set the book down on the nightstand and flicked off the light. Then I carefully pulled out the manuscript pages from underneath the pillow and slid them under the bed. In the morning, I'd hide them under the mattress again.

Bo cuddled up next to me and I could faintly smell the toothpaste that he'd gotten in his hair before bed.

Bo yawned. "Will you tell me a story, Sunday?"

I closed my own eyes and told Bo about what I'd just read. Lilly and the boy, Mark, were becoming friends. She had just dared him to eat a dog biscuit, which he had done, throwing up afterward.

"Gross," Bo whispered. His voice was soft and I could tell that he was slipping off to sleep. I liked remembering the story even if I couldn't tell it with the same beautiful words and images that I had read. I told a little more. How Lilly had hidden in the woods away from her dad, who wasn't a very good dad and had yelled at her something awful.

"She was crying all alone by a tree. Crying until no more tears came out. Crying until her nose and eyes were swollen and her stomach ached. When she finally went home, she made herself a peanut butter sandwich, slipped quietly into her room, and fell asleep. When she woke up in the morning, there was a little flower on her windowsill."

I stopped and listened. Bo's breaths were even and deep. Tucking the covers higher underneath his chin,

I glanced out the window at the sky dotted with stars, closed my eyes, and drifted off to sleep, too.

After lunch the next day, I helped Mom wipe down the bookshelves and stain the desks that Dad had sanded smooth. Dad was busy with another desk, and Jude sat at the new computer, helping Miss Jenny install programs and get the library's Internet service up and running.

"The Internet's working now," he told her. "When the new cataloguing system arrives, I can help set it up on some of the other computers for you."

"That would be really helpful."

Dad walked over and watched Jude click away on the keys. He put a hand on his shoulder, then rubbed his hair. "Thanks for all your help."

I could tell that Jude was surprised by the gesture at first, but then I worried that if he smiled any wider he might strain his cheek muscles.

"Sunday," Mom called, holding out a book. "We must've missed this one when we were sorting. Have you read it?"

I set down my paintbrush on the drop cloth, walked over, and took the book from her hand. The paperback cover was worn around the edges with a small tear on the back. As I fanned out the pages, the musty smell blew across my face. Some of the pages at the beginning were starting to come loose.

I loved it already. *"The Life and Death of Birds?* I haven't read it, but I've heard of it."

"That was one of my favorites," Miss Jenny said, looking up from the computer.

Mom smiled. "I remember loving it, too. You know, the author lived here in Alma."

I glanced over at where the portrait now leaned against one of the walls. Dad had taken it down and covered it with a cloth so that it would be protected while we worked. "You mean the woman in the portrait?"

"Yep. Lee Wren," Miss Jenny said. "I would've loved to have met her."

Mom reached for her sandpaper. "Anyway, I know how much you like to read. You should try it."

I put the book in my backpack. "Cool. Thanks." My heart gave an excited skip. I wasn't sure if it was the idea of starting a new book or the fact that my mom noticed something about me. But I was already looking forward to cuddling under the covers and sinking into the pages.

At four o'clock, Dad made us all quit. Mom went back to the house to start dinner, Dad cleaned up, and Jude and I tried to decide what our next step was going to be. None of the authors we'd written to had sent a letter back yet, and though the thought of befriending Ben Folger tickled on the edge of my brain, I couldn't figure out where to begin.

I handed Jude a cookie and a glass of milk, then we went outside and sat on the porch stairs. I took a bite. "I think I need to talk to him."

"Who?"

I pointed across the field at the house.

Jude choked on a piece of cookie. After taking a swig of milk, he shook his head. "If you want to die."

"Come on, Jude. He can't really be dangerous. And even if he does have a sword in his cane—"

"A knife."

"Whatever. Even if he does, he's not going to hurt us."

"And what about the curse?"

I shrugged. "I doubt there is a curse."

"I don't think it's a good idea, Sunday."

Maybe it wasn't, but I had to do something to make my mark. Time was creeping away from me. And then there was the manuscript. There was no reason that the author couldn't be Ben Folger. And if that was the case I would have befriended the local hermit and discovered that he was also a really good writer.

"Well, I've got to try," I said, looking down at my cookie.

"I think I'll bring some of these over. Dad always says that nothing melts the heart like cookies on a plate."

Jude laughed. "But you have to have a heart to melt. And I don't think Ben Folger has one."

Ignoring him, I went inside, took out a paper plate, and set five cookies on it. Then I covered it with plastic wrap, ran a brush through my hair, and made sure that my brothers were occupied with something so they wouldn't tag along and get in the way. Luckily they were so busy making paper airplanes they didn't even hear me open their bedroom door and peek in.

"I'll be back in a little while, Mom," I yelled from the front door. "Come on, Jude."

"I don't know, Sunday. I really don't think it's a good idea."

"Fine, scaredy-cat. You stay here." I held the plate in front of me and started across the field.

"You can't go that way!" he yelled after me. "He'll see you coming."

"Well then, show me a better way. But with or without you, I'm going. So decide."

He groaned and caught up. "You're impossible."

I smiled, satisfied, and followed after him.

At first, I thought he was leading me on some sort of wild-goose chase. We walked downtown (in almost the exact opposite direction of Ben Folger's house) and said hello to Ms. Bodnar as she closed up the café.

We continued on in silence and finally came to a dead-end road. Jude stepped into the overgrown weeds that quickly turned into a forest of tall trees. It was getting darker by the second.

"Where are we going?"

He stopped and turned. "Ben Folger's," he whispered. "It's right through these trees. Unless you want to turn back."

I straightened, clutching my plate of cookies so that Jude wouldn't see the way my hands were shaking. "No, I'm fine."

"Now, be quiet. Who knows if he's lurking out here."

I held my breath and tried to step carefully, avoiding as many dried twigs and old leaves as I could.

Jude ducked behind a bush. "There it is," he whispered.

Clouds had moved in, and the sky had darkened even more. The windows looked black and the porch swing banged against the siding.

"What should I do now?"

He looked over at me. "How should I know? You're the one who wanted to come here and talk to him. And it doesn't even look like he's home."

"Maybe he isn't."

Just then a light flicked on in the front window. My heart raced. I found it hard to steady my breathing. The sound of the triangle clanged from across the field, making me jump. Mom was calling everyone in for dinner.

I didn't have much time. But what if he really did have a sword in his cane, or I did disappear after I crossed over to the other side of the hedge?

"Are you going or not? Dinner's probably ready at my house, too, and my mom is gonna kill me if I'm late."

"Maybe we should see if the curse is real first." I picked up a pinecone and tossed it over the hedge. Jude and I watched as it landed and rolled a few inches. I looked at him and shrugged. He picked up a rock and did the same thing.

Thud.

"Here goes," I whispered.

"I'll be the lookout."

I crawled the length of the hedge, one hand awkwardly holding the plate of cookies, until I could see the front door looming ahead of me. A solitary light glowed behind the closed blinds—the rest of the house was eerily dark. Nervously clutching a fistful of grass, I whispered to myself to stand up: "Come on, you can do this, Sunday. On the count of three. One. Two—"

Adrenaline rushed through my legs and arms, my toes and fingertips.

Jude whispered over to me. "Sunday?"

I turned to him. "I'm all right."

My heart sped up and my breaths came shallow and shaky. The door wasn't too far away, just down the stone walkway. But first I had to pass through the small white gate that was level with the thick hedge. I forced my foot forward one step, and then another. Holding my breath and closing my eyes, I pushed the gate forward and took a step onto Ben Folger's property. I opened one eye and then the other. I hadn't disappeared.

"I made it!" I whispered back to Jude.

There was no curse.

Turning back to the house, I clutched the paper plate, now sagging in the middle from the weight of the cookies, and started down the walkway to the porch, and then up three steps to the door. Everything would be fine. No one could resist chocolate chip cookies. Not even an old hermit who maybe ate stray cats and tortured intruders in his basement.

I knocked on the door, my heart doing flips inside me, my hands trembling. I tried on my best smile, the one I wore when I used to sell cookies for my Girl Cadet group.

The sound of footsteps shuffle-tapped closer.

The knob turned, and a sliver of dim light peeked out through the barely opened door. A blue, clouded eyeball magnified by glasses looked out at me.

"Well? What do you want?"

"Um," my voice squeaked. It took all I had to keep from sprinting back to my house. *Is he reaching for his cane?*

"I . . . I thought I'd bring you some cookies. They're, um . . . they're homemade. Chocolate chip."

The door didn't open any wider. The man behind it said nothing.

"I'm . . . I'm Sunday. Sunday Fowler. My family and I moved here for the summer. We're fixing up the library."

I thought I saw one bushy eyebrow rise ever so slightly. Still no answer.

"I thought you might like some cookies and–"

"Go away. I don't buy cookies from anyone."

"What? I wasn't–"

"I said, GO. Away. Get off my property." His voice was low, gravelly, and dripping with meanness.

"But–I just wanted to–"

"I said, get off my property! Now. If you don't–" The door opened wider, and Mr. Folger's voice grew louder. He took a step forward and held his cane in one hand. I watched in horror as he reached for it with the other hand, but didn't wait a second longer. My legs carried me off that porch and down the walkway, cookies flying off the plate. "Run, Jude," I yelled. "Run for your life!"

The only thing I heard over my own panting was, "I better not see you on my property again! Ever!"

Jude and I stopped when we reached the neatly clipped lawn of the library. I sank to the ground, trying to catch my breath. It sounded like Jude was about to have a heart attack right then and there.

"I told you," he said between gulps of air. "I told you he was nasty."

"You were right." I thought of Ben Folger's face, snarled up and mean as a badger, and cringed. Maybe befriending a hermit wasn't such a good idea.

"You could've gotten yourself killed, you know that?"

"Yeah, I know." I looked toward my house, the kitchen glowing warm and cheery. Dinner had started by now.

Jude must've been thinking the same thing.

"I gotta go, Sunday. My mom'll be wondering where I am and then she'll have Wally out looking for me."

I nodded. "See you tomorrow."

"See ya."

He disappeared into the gathering dark. It took another minute for my heart to slow back down.

Butters met me at the door, barking and wagging and slobbering. Mom's high-pitched laughter pealed from the dining room. That was good. At least she wasn't stewing quietly because I was late. I might as well come in on a high note. I found everyone digging into beans, rice, and tortillas.

"Sorry I'm late," I said, starting to take my seat next to Bo. Mom stopped me.

"Oh, Sunday. Before you sit down, could you grab the other jug of milk in the refrigerator for me?"

I forced a smile onto my face. "Sure." Mom and Dad always seemed to remember my name when they wanted me to do something for them.

She unscrewed the cap and poured Henry another glass. "So where were you?"

"I told you I was going out for a bit."

"Yes, but I rang the triangle. Didn't you hear it?"

I felt my cheeks fill with heat. "Yeah, but I was right in the middle of doing something."

Dad passed me the tortillas. "And what was that?"

"I was taking some cookies over to the man who lives in that house across the field."

CJ's fork dropped onto his plate with a loud clank. "You went over there? You know that guy's crazy, don't you? He eats raw animals and has a sword inside his cane, and the curse–"

"CJ," Mom said.

"But it's true. I met a kid named Parker today and he knows all about Old Man Folger. He said that when any-thing's thrown over the hedge–"

Mom sighed and set her glass down on the table with a loud thud. "I said stop."

CJ sulked and mumbled a quiet "–it disappears."

"He's probably just a lonely old man who doesn't want

kids prowling around his property and bothering him. I think that was very kind of you, Sunday, even if you were late for dinner."

Across the table, Emma and May looked at each other and rolled their eyes.

"Guess what I did, Sunday," Bo said. He scooped a pile of rice and beans onto his fork but it plopped back onto his plate before reaching his mouth.

Henry broke in, spewing bits of rice onto the table. "We made paper airplanes and then . . . and then we set them on fire," Henry said. "They went *whoosh!*"

Mom's fork dropped to her plate with a tinny clank. "You what?"

CJ knocked Henry hard with his elbow.

"Ouch! Mom, CJ hit me."

"Sunday," Emma said, "could you pass the rice? You're hogging it all."

"Henry," Bo whined, "I was gonna tell Sunday, and then you cut in."

"Did not."

"Did too."

"Boys, stop," Dad warned.

"Can someone take me driving tonight?" May asked. "I think I should get used to driving in the dark."

"Just a second, May." Mom's stare was fixed on CJ. "What is this about fire?"

CJ, both cheeks stuffed, shrugged. "Nothing," he mumbled. "We were just playing around."

Mom took a sip of her water. "Playing around? After dinner, you will scrub every toilet until all thought of playing around with fire is removed from your mind."

"Ah, Mom," CJ whined, "I won't do it again."

Henry wiped his mouth on his sleeve. "CJ, does that mean we can't try and melt some of my army guys tonight like you promised?"

Mom closed her eyes. "I think you need to start on the toilets now, CJ."

My brother picked up his plate and slumped off to the kitchen. "It was just an idea. It's not like I actually–"

"Go!"

And that pretty much signaled the end of dinner. After we all cleaned up, I took my ice cream sandwich out on the porch and sat on the steps. The night was warm, the crickets were starting up their songs, and, one by one, the fireflies blinked in the dark. I licked a drip of ice cream and looked out over the field toward Ben Folger's house. A single light shone out from an upstairs window.

I popped the last piece of soft chocolate cookie and vanilla ice cream in my mouth and stood up. At almost the same time, the light in the window flicked off.

I wondered how to befriend someone like Ben Folger.

And if I even should.

~~~~~

Though I had *The Life and Death of Birds* waiting on my nightstand, I found myself completely sucked into the manuscript, reading until my eyes burned.

Just as I was about to flip off the light, Bo turned the doorknob and came into my room.

"Can I sleep in your room, Sunday?" he asked.

"Sure." I flung back the covers, and he tucked in next to me.

"Tell me more of that story," he said through a yawn.

I yawned, too, and flicked off the lamp. "I'll try my best to remember it all, okay?"

"Okay."

"You know how I told you that the girl, Lilly, and the boy, Mark, became friends?"

"Yeah. But you never said how."

"Well, her dad gave her some money to buy food at the store. But when she got there, she saw a pen and tablet of paper that she wanted so bad she could hardly stand it."

"Like the time I needed to buy that orange car at the toy store, so I cried and cried and cried."

"Sort of. Anyway, she loved to write poems and write about her day and she thought it would be wonderful to write it all down on that pretty ivory-colored paper with that black-ink pen. So she bought a few of the supplies her dad wanted and spent the rest on that pen and paper. Then she went home."

"Uh-oh, did her dad get mad?"

"Oh, yeah. He was so mad he started throwing stuff and saying all kinds of terrible things. But then who should show up but Mark. He knocked on the door and said that Lilly had forgotten her other bag of groceries. She must have dropped her list because everything they needed was inside the brown paper bag."

"So he told a lie?" Bo sounded amazed.

"Yeah, I guess he did. But he did it because he wanted to help her. Protect her in a way."

"Then what happened?"

"They were best friends. Eventually she moved in with her aunt and uncle because her dad went to jail."

"I'm glad."

"Me, too. She told him how she wanted to be something big when she grew up. Something that would take her away from their little town. Mark said he'd like to stay right where he was and have a family and a dog and maybe work in a bookstore.

"They stuck together for the most part. Mark was quiet and didn't have too many friends. Everyone loved Lilly, but she liked spending most of her time with Mark. In the fall, they went to the same school and things were pretty much the same. They did everything together. Then one winter, Mark got really sick."

"Did he throw up?"

I shrugged. "I'm not sure. Probably. Anyway, he got really sick and went to the hospital. Every night, Lilly would write a story for him. Sometimes they were short little stories, and other times she would write longer ones, adding a bit to them every day. Then, after school, she would walk to the hospital and sit in his room and read to him."

"Would you write me a story every day if I was in the hospital?"

I didn't like thinking of Bo in the hospital. "I'm not a good writer. But I'd come and read to you every day."

"Okay."

"Finally Mark got better and went home. And you know what the very first thing that they did together was?"

"They ate ice cream?"

"Nope. They went down to the creek where they first met and talked and talked and talked."

"I would've had ice cream."

"Yeah." I couldn't consider Jude my best friend since I hadn't known him that long, but I thought it would be exciting to meet somewhere and talk. Maybe we'd eat ice cream, too, though it would probably be organic and taste like gerbil food.

Bo yawned, then nudged me a little with his shoulder. "Then what happened?"

I answered his yawn and closed my eyes. "Why don't I tell you the rest another time?"

Bo didn't object, and within seconds the room was filled with his gentle breaths. I thought back on the chapter, smiling to myself as I remembered the last sentence: "But no matter what happened throughout each and every day, whether they fought like siblings or spent the day in laughter, Lilly always awoke the next morning with a single yellow daisy sitting on her windowsill."

FOR THE next few days, Jude and I worked a little at the library each morning, helping stain or sand or sweep or wipe something down. In the afternoons, we talked to people in town to see if they could've written the manuscript. We had zero luck. The barber had never set foot in the library, the real estate agent didn't have enough time for reading or writing, and the two teachers we met said that they loved to read and would love to have an author come to their school if we knew of any.

It was time to think of other options.

"Hey," Jude said one afternoon. "Why don't we try and bake a huge chocolate chip cookie—one big enough to be written about in the newspaper?"

It wound up burning to a crispy black circle and setting off the fire alarm. Another time, I tried to jump rope for an entire afternoon. I had to quit after fifteen minutes to stop CJ from spray-painting his initials on the side of the garage. But the old house across the field kept grabbing at my attention, and as time passed, I thought how silly I was to run away.

Ben Folger was the answer, and Jude was just going to have to be okay with that.

The next morning I looked out the window and found Jude sitting on the porch with Henry. A plate of donuts sat between them. Butters wagged her tail, watching for crumbs. "What time did you get up?" I called down.

Jude jumped at the sound of my voice and looked up. "Oh, hey, Sunday! Your dad got donuts."

Henry held up fingers covered in chocolate. "Look!"

"I see," I said. "I'll be down in a minute."

I slipped on my shorts and a T-shirt, then jammed my feet into my sneakers and grabbed my backpack, a notebook, and a pen that I hoped worked.

I was going to do some snooping about Ben Folger. Maybe he was in the newspaper a long time ago or someone in town knew more about him.

Downstairs, I caught Bo carefully eating the frosting off of every single donut. Mom looked up from her computer and smacked his hand gently as he reached for another. "No way, mister. You decapitate another one and you'll find yourself eating a plateful of broccoli for lunch.

Your dad must have been out of his mind to think that two dozen donuts were a good idea."

Bo slumped down, crossed his arms, and stuck out his lip in a pitiful pout. When Mom wasn't looking, I handed him half of a donut and winked. He grinned and scrunched up his face, trying to wink back, though it was more of an exaggerated squint. I picked out a chocolate-covered donut that only had a single finger swipe through the top and joined Henry and Jude on the porch.

"Hey."

Jude licked off his fingers. "Hey."

"I didn't think that donuts were on the food pyramid," I said.

Jude shrugged and took the last bite of donut that Henry held out to him. "Sure they are. Under breads and sugars. I'm just helping make the pyramid complete."

I dropped my backpack and sat down. The morning was crisp and clear with only a few clouds floating across the blue sky. Two squirrels taunted Butters from their post on a nearby branch.

Henry crawled onto Jude's lap and leaned his head against his shoulder. Jude looked at me and smiled like he'd just won the lottery and had his picture in the *New York Times*. Henry must not have slept well if he was already tired. That, or the sugar just hadn't kicked in.

"Pony ride!" Henry yelled, suddenly sitting up straight and clapping his hands.

And . . . cue sugar craziness.

Jude got his legs moving, and Henry bounced up and down on his knee.

"Now he's never gonna leave you alone," I said, taking a bite of my donut. The chocolate was melting between my fingers and I licked away the sweet stickiness.

"I don't mind."

I shrugged. "Is your mom at work already?"

"Yeah." *Bounce, bounce, bounce.* "She goes into the bank early on Mondays. Wally dropped me off a little bit ago."

"And how was that?"

Jude shrugged and continued to bounce my giggling brother. "Same as always. Trying to be my best friend."

"You could give him a chance, you know."

He stopped and glared at me. "Yeah, maybe when you start liking your family."

"Sunday likes us," Henry said, and nudged Jude to continue. "Keep bouncing."

Jude started back up again. I decided to drop the subject. It wasn't worth it. Being completely forgotten by your family was way different. "Hey, do you know where there's a computer I can use? I want to look up something on the Internet."

Jude's leg stopped bouncing, and he set Henry on the ground. "You don't have one here?"

"We do, but it's my mom's and she's using it right now. At the library we might get stuck stacking books or sweeping and I want to do more investigating."

Jude got up and brushed off his shorts. "We can go to my house then."

"Can I come? Can I come? Can I come?" Henry jumped up and down in front of us.

"Not right now, Henry," I said. "We have to do something by ourselves. But we'll be back later, okay?'

He plopped himself down on the stairs and stuck out his lower lip. Butters sat herself conveniently next to his cheek, licking at his face and hands.

Jude bent down. "Hey, Henry? Why don't we go inside and get another donut? How does that sound?"

Henry looked up, brown eyes sparkling. "Okay." He stood and grabbed for Jude's hand.

"Hurry up," I called after him.

Mom came to the door with Bo trailing behind her, a circle of chocolate around his mouth. "Emma, where are you going?"

"That's Sunday, Mommy," Bo said, and laughed.

"Sorry, Sunday. Where are you going, sweetie?"

"Just over to Jude's house for a bit. Is that all right?"

Bo pushed through the door. "I'll come, too."

"No," I said a little too loudly. It was nice having Bo as my shadow some of the time, but not right now, not when I was trying to learn more about Ben Folger.

He frowned and his eyes filled with tears. "Please, Sunday? Please? I won't get in the way."

"Maybe next time, okay?"

Mom picked him up and gave him one of her squeezer hugs, the sort that takes the breath right out of you. He laughed. "Besides," she said, "I need you here to help me today." She winked at me. "Just be home for dinner."

Jude came back out on the porch with another donut in his hand. This one had the entire top eaten off of it, but he didn't seem to mind. He smiled and followed me down the stairs. "I guess Emma isn't up yet."

I walked faster, jealousy nipping at my heels. "Nope. She sleeps most of the day. She's almost like a zombie and looks like one when she wakes up. It's pretty gross."

13

JUDE'S house was on the other side of Main Street. It was painted bright white, and a small fence circled a yard that was cleaner than any of our rooms. The inside was even neater. There were no magazines, paper airplanes, toys, tools, peanut butter smears, or bits of dried browned apple left on the end table. I kept my hands to my sides like I was on a field trip to a museum.

"My mom likes it clean, and when Wally's around he picks up around the house, too."

"That's nice of him."

"Yeah, but now it's *too* clean."

I followed him down a hallway. Jude's room was slightly better. His bed was crisply made, like a hotel bed, and there wasn't anything on his floor. The books on the bookshelf were like soldiers all in a row, and the mirror had no fingerprints or dog-nose smudges. But there was a shirt hung over the frame of his bed and a poster of a surfer careening down a wave, loose on one corner.

"All right," Jude said, sitting down on a spin-ny chair, pulling out the keyboard, and clacking away. "What did you want to look up?"

"Is this your own computer?" There were only a few things that were actually mine. The rest fell into three categories: things I had to share, things I had been given as hand-me-downs, or things I was allowed to borrow.

He nodded. "I got it from my grandparents last Christmas. I want to be an architect. You have to know how to use a computer if you're going to do that."

The book *Hoot*—one of my favorites—sat next to a framed picture of Jude, slightly younger, on the desk. He stood on a surfboard in a bathing suit and surf shirt, though the wave was only a giant cutout, and the board was a sleek plastic. "I take it you like surfing, too?"

He shrugged. "Yeah. I've never done it, but Mom promised me that someday we'd go someplace where I could learn."

"Cool."

"Now, what did you want to look up?"

"Type in the *Alma Gazette*."

"The newspaper? Why do you want to look at that?" He tapped at the keys without even looking at the letters and hit ENTER. A list of websites filled the screen.

I shrugged. "I just want to see if there are . . . any old newspapers that mention . . . Ben Folger."

He whirled around. "Sunday, are you serious?"

"Wait, before you go crazy. I really think that maybe if I befriend him . . ."

"What?!"

"Or if I have proof that he's a criminal, then . . . this could be my chance to do something to get noticed."

We stared at each other in silence.

"Come on, Jude, please. We tried baking a giant cookie. I tried jumping rope. My mom and Miss Jenny are planning a reopening party, and I have no more leads on the manuscript. Just search Ben Folger's name. Maybe nothing will come up. But if there is something, then we could be heroes. Think about it."

He shook his head and muttered, "Think about getting killed."

"Please."

"Okay, okay." He clicked on ARCHIVES and then typed BEN FOLGER into the search box.

I smiled when a series of articles popped up.

LOCAL LIBRARIAN WINS GRANT FOR TOWN LIBRARY

LIBRARIAN STARTS UP READING PROGRAM FOR KIDS

FUND-RAISER TO BENEFIT LOCAL LIBRARY

LIBRARY TO HOST FAMOUS AUTHOR LEE WREN

"You never told me he was a librarian," I said, knocking Jude with my elbow.

He shrugged. "I didn't know he was."

"Do you see what this could mean?"

"That crazy Ben Folger used to be crazy Ben Folger, the librarian?"

"No, Jude. He was a librarian. I found the story in the library. That means he could've written the story I found."

The headline flashed in my head:

LOCAL RECLUSE WINS PULITZER PRIZE FOR STORY HE HID AWAY. TWELVE-YEAR-OLD GIRL HONORED FOR THE DISCOVERY.

Jude clicked out of the window and slid the keyboard back under the desk. "No, I don't think so."

"Well, he could have."

"Yeah, but you said my mom could have, too."

I straightened my shoulders. "And I still think she might have. But it's okay to have more than one potential person."

Jude spun the chair around and around. "I guess you're right. But Ben Folger—it's just not—"

"It is possible," I interrupted, plopping onto his bed. "But since we're at your house, why don't we search for clues and see if your mom was the author?"

"Okay. What should we look for?"

"Well, I guess anything that she's written."

I followed Jude into the bedroom across the hall. Like his room, everything looked as if it been washed, dried, and ironed to perfection. A long-stemmed rose in an elegant glass vase sat on the nightstand. I bent down and sniffed the petals, the sweet scent reminding me of the rose Dad gave my sisters and me each year on Valentine's Day. "Did Wally give her this?"

He turned and rolled his eyes. "Probably."

"That's sweet."

"I guess. Now, help me look."

I glanced around the room but other than her dresser drawers, which Jude was opening and closing, I couldn't see any places to hide something. There were no dust bunnies under the bed, and her closet held neatly hung clothes and shoes sitting side by side.

"Here's something," Jude said, pulling out a few pages from the nightstand drawer. "'The Modern Professional,'" he read aloud. "'Chapter One. Clothes. If someone wants to become a secretary someday, he or she needs to make sure to have nice clothes. What are nice clothes? For a woman, they are: skirt (not too short but not too long, either), high-heeled shoes, nylons, and a nice blouse. Jewelry is always an option. Maybe some nice pearl earrings. For a man, they should be—'" Jude stopped reading and looked up at me with a smile. "I love my mom, but from what you've told me about the story, I don't think she's the one who wrote it."

I shrugged. "Yeah, I don't think so, either. But who knows, maybe there are people out there who want to read about what to wear if they ever start working at a bank."

Jude tucked the papers back in the drawer. "I guess this means you want to search Ben Folger's house?"

I grinned. Even though we had only known each other for a little while, Jude already knew me well enough to know that's exactly what I was thinking.

"Before we go waltzing up to the local lunatic's house, which, by the way, we probably won't ever return from, and ask if we can look inside for clues about a story he might have written and locked away in the library, I think we should ask around about him."

We stood on the corner of Main Street. I pretended I didn't hear a word Jude said. Every day that I spent not trying to make my mark was another day that I remained just one-of-the-six. Hermit, lunatic, or writer, I needed to find out something about Ben Folger.

"So, do you have any idea who we can to talk to?"

Jude sighed and started down the sidewalk toward the thrift store. "We'll talk to Muzzy first. She knows almost everything that goes on in Alma."

We pushed through the door, a small bell dinging above our heads and announcing that we had arrived. The store was filled with everything you could think of. Old dishes, scuffed shoes, used clothes, scratched furniture, unpolished jewelry, and worn books. I'd started on

The Life and Death of Birds but couldn't bring myself to turn down a copy of *Princess Academy* for fifty cents. I unzipped my backpack and fished out my loose change. Two quarters, two dimes, and one penny. After grabbing the book off the shelf and tucking it under my arm, I smiled and reached for an old belt with the name JOHN pressed into the leather.

"Muzzy? Papa Gil?" Jude called out.

We heard the big dog before we saw him, his bark echoing from the back of the store. Then there was a clatter of nails on wood and he came bounding toward us, all fur, paws, slobber, and tail.

"Oh, Mr. Castor," a woman said, fluttering out from the back. "Down, Mr. Castor. Down." She had short white hair and pointed ears that reminded me of a fairy.

Mr. Castor didn't listen. Instead he jumped up, put his heavy paws on my shoulders, and licked my cheek. I gently pushed him off, wiped the slobber on my T-shirt, and scratched his ears.

"Hi, Mr. Castor." His tail swooshed back and forth, swiping pens and pencils and papers off one of the displays.

"I'm sorry," the woman huffed, tugging at Mr. Castor's collar. But she might as well have been a flea trying to pull a tractor. She gave up and wiped her forehead. "He just gets so excited, and he's still just a puppy."

I raised my eyebrows. If he was a puppy, I could hardly

imagine what he'd be like when he was full grown. He was already the size of a small polar bear.

The man I had seen walking up the library stairs a few days ago smacked red suspenders against his chest. "He's not a puppy, Joanne! The dog's about five years old."

"Oh, age means nothing," the woman said, brushing him off. "He's young at heart."

"He's young at something. Discipline maybe. Manners. All the characteristics that make it a joy to own a dog. Man's best friend, he is not."

"Hush, Gil," she said, then turned to Mr. Castor, who was gnawing on a table leg that looked to be about chewed through. "He doesn't mean it, Mr. Castor. You're a good boy."

The dog's tail thumped loudly on the floor, sending up tufts of snow-white fur.

The man rolled his eyes. "Well, now that Mr. Castor is occupied with destroying our business, we can find out what brings Jude into the store with a pretty young girl."

"Buying jewelry for your girlfriend?" the woman asked.

Jude's face turned the color of a red lollipop. "No. This is Sunday. She and her family are the ones fixing up the library this summer."

"Oh, yes," the man said, rubbing at the gray stubble on his chin. "I met your mom and dad and your sisters. Call me Papa Gil. It's nice to meet you, Sunday. Interesting name."

"Yeah," I said.

"Everyone names their kids something interesting these days," his wife said. "I've read about all sorts of names that were unheard of back in my day." She turned to Papa Gil. "I read the other day how someone named their child Rocket." She smiled. "Can you imagine?"

"I like it," Papa Gil said. "It has purpose. Maybe I'll start going by Rocket."

Muzzy shook her head and nudged him gently on the arm. Then she turned to me. "I'm Muzzy." She wrapped her arms around me, squeezing harder than I thought she could. "It's nice to meet you, Sunday."

Papa Gil squinted and glanced out the window at something, then smiled. "So what can we do for you two since you're not buying jewelry? Need any shoes?"

"Maybe a set of dishes?" Muzzy cut in, her face serious.

Jude nudged me forward. I felt my cheeks heat up. "I'm . . . well, Jude and I were wondering if you know anything about . . . about Old . . . I mean, Ben Folger."

Muzzy reached up to a shelf for a large basket overflowing with candy. "Oh, Ben, yes. Well, no, I don't actually. Not really. He keeps very much to himself and seems to like it that way, though I can't imagine why. I just love meeting people and talking with people and watching people. Though I suppose there are times when I—"

"Joanne, dear." Papa Gil gave her a look.

Muzzy smiled. "Yes, well. I've stood behind him in line at the grocery store a couple of times. I gathered from his cart that he eats quite a lot of deli ham, he loves mini chocolate cupcakes, and he eats an obscene amount of yogurt. I mean, I've never seen so much yogurt in all my life. It made me wonder if he has bad bones." She turned to Papa Gil, who was smiling down at her with the same puppy dog–eyed look I sometimes saw my parents give each other. "Isn't yogurt good for the bones?"

Papa Gil shrugged. "I'm not sure, dear."

"Anyway, he eats a lot of it."

Yogurt, ham, and chocolate cupcakes. Not much to go on.

"Do you know if he likes to do anything?"

Papa Gil shook his head no. "I wouldn't know about that, but he must like flowers. His yard is the prettiest in town. If I'm ever out by his house, he's always bent over one of the beds, or planting or watering."

"Yes, that's true," Muzzy said. "His flowers are the most beautiful I've seen. But what woman doesn't love flowers? I know I do, though Gil hardly gets them for me anymore." She said this last part under her breath but still loud enough for him to hear.

"I can't anymore, Joanne. That dog eats them. Remember the roses and the daisies and the gardenias? And don't even get me started on the potted plants I've brought home."

Muzzy held up her hand. "All right, Gil. I will never ask for flowers again."

"Well, if you do, I'll be sure to put them straight into Mr. Castor's bowl."

I knocked Jude with my elbow as he grabbed a Reese's Peanut Butter Cup from Muzzy's candy bowl.

"Well, I guess we should get going. Thanks for telling us about Mr. Folger."

"I'll let you know if I remember anything else. It was nice to meet you, Sunday." Muzzy smiled and held out the basket of candy to me. Besides Reese's Cups, there were other candy bars, little cupcakes wrapped in cellophane, packages of gum, and lollipops. I picked out a Snickers bar.

"Maybe you should ask them if they want some, too?" Papa Gil said, nodding to the window.

I turned around and saw the tops of three heads. One by one, they inched up to standing and there they were: CJ, Bo, and Henry, their noses plastered against the glass, making fog marks on the window. I inwardly groaned.

"Those are my brothers," I said.

Papa Gil motioned for them to come in. "Well, they must be pretty good spies 'cause they followed you two here and have been sitting outside ever since you walked in."

Anger bubbled up inside me. How long had they been trailing behind us? What had they heard? They couldn't know what I was doing or everything would be ruined.

As CJ, Bo, and Henry filed inside, Mr. Castor went through his scrambling, jumping, swooshing, slobbering, and chewing routine all over again. When the dog had settled down, Henry ran straight for Jude, locking his arms around his legs. Bo ran to me. CJ mumbled about how big Mr. Castor's poop must be, and picked up everything he could get his hands on, examining it, and then setting it back down.

I grabbed Bo and started for the door. "CJ, put that down. Come on, Henry. Bo. Sorry, Muzzy and Papa Gil."

"Oh, don't worry, and don't go yet. Let them each pick out a piece of candy."

Bo wriggled out of my grip and ran to the basket to join CJ and Henry, who were already pawing through it. Bo emerged with a Snickers bar, Henry with a pack of gum, and CJ with a lollipop.

"So," Muzzy said, selecting a lollipop for herself. "Tell me everyone's name."

"Bo."

"CJ."

"I'm Henry."

Muzzy and Papa Gil shook each of their hands. "It's nice to meet you. Come back real soon and visit."

My brothers grinned, and I could pretty much picture what each of them was imagining. Eating candy,
swimming in candy, pockets loaded down with candy.

"Sure!" they said in unison.

I herded everyone, including Jude, to the door. "Thanks
again."

"And tell your parents that we said hello."

"I will. Thanks."

The bell dinged above our heads as we all filed out
onto the sidewalk. I turned to CJ. "How long have you
been following us?"

He shrugged, unwrapping his lollipop. "I don't know.
Since you left. I can't believe you didn't see us."

Great. Just great. He'd probably heard everything.

The lollipop made a big lump in the side of his cheek.
He laughed. "So do you guys looove each other now?"

Jude and I both gave a hearty *no,* and I stomped off in
the direction of home. There were still things I needed to
find out, especially since I hadn't gotten anything useful
from Muzzy. But I couldn't do it with the Three Attention
Stealers at my heels. I turned around to say something
and saw CJ showing Jude how to stick his hands in his
armpits to make toot noises.

Even Jude had fallen under my siblings' spells. I
should've known. Well, maybe Mom could keep the boys
occupied at least for a little while. And May or Emma

could watch them for once. They always got out of helping.

Just then our van came squealing around a corner, hiccupped once, then stalled in the middle of the street.

May.

The back door opened and Emma jumped out, slamming it behind her. "Never again, May Fowler!" she yelled. Emma threw her backpack over her shoulders and stomped off down the sidewalk toward a large brick building.

I spied Mom in the passenger seat, her cheeks splotchy with bright red hives. May was attempting to restart the car, wiping her nose at the same time.

"Cool," CJ said, crunching down on his lollipop. "Did you see how she almost crashed? That was awesome."

I rolled my eyes and started toward home. "Come on. We'll go and see what Dad is doing at the library."

Jude caught up to my pace and smiled sheepishly. "I bet there's play practice today." He shrugged like he didn't really care, even though he obviously did. "Who knows, we might be able to talk to someone about"—he turned around and then whispered—"Ben Folger."

I kept walking. "I know why you really want to go." I looked down the sidewalk at the retreating figure of my sister, her hair bouncing on her back, always the picture of beauty. "You just want to see Emma."

"Ew, Jude likes Emma?" CJ laughed. "That's so gross."

"I like Emma," Henry said.

Jude's cheeks filled with red. "No. And she's not my sister, so it's not gross. And you have to admit, Sunday, that we might find someone there to talk to who knows hi–"

I covered his mouth with my hand and clenched my jaw. All three of my brothers surrounded us, itching to know our secret.

"Knows who?" Bo asked. He now had a chocolate mustache and beard from the Snickers Bar. "Do you like someone, Sunday?"

"No," I said.

"Yeah, 'cause she already has a boyfriend," CJ crooned. "Robo Matthews."

I felt my cheeks burn. Jude smiled smugly. "Really? Robo?"

Robo. The cutest boy I had ever seen. The name that I had scribbled in my journal a hundred times (and then erased). The boy who didn't know I existed.

"I do not like Robo!" I yelled. No girl in her right mind would ever admit a crush to her younger brother who still thought deodorant was a weapon.

"Oh, yeah?" CJ teased. "I saw a page of lovey-dovey drawings that proves it."

I swore on the grave of my goldfish, Goldie, who I won

at the town fair two summers ago, that I was going to wring my brother's neck right then and there. I lunged for him but Jude grabbed my arm and pulled me back.

"Oh, let it go, Sunday. I like Emma, you like a guy named Robo. Who cares?"

"I do not." My eyes stung and I wriggled out of his grip.

CJ started making kissing noises, which Henry thought was hilarious, so of course, he started in on it, too.

"Cut it out, CJ," Jude said.

Bo licked his fingers. "Yeah, cut it out. Sunday is sad."

Good old Bo. My anger fizzled down a little bit.

Jude pulled my arm. "Now come on, Sunday. Let's go and watch the practice. We'll see if someone there knows anything about . . . you-know-who. If not, we'll go."

I nodded, trying to ignore the "K-I-S-S-I-N-G" song that CJ was singing.

"Go home, CJ!" I yelled.

"No way. I'm coming with you guys."

Jude shrugged. "Fine. I guess you won't mind watching me kiss your sister?"

CJ's face turned pale, and he pretended like he was going to throw up.

Jude made kissing noises of his own, and CJ was off and running with Henry at his heels.

I smiled. "Thanks."

"Sure."

Bo put his sticky hand in mine. I looked down at him. "Why don't you go back with CJ?"

"I don't want to. I wanna stay with you. I promise I won't talk about Robo."

As sweet as he had just been, and as much as I liked it when he chose me over my brothers, I rolled my eyes at the thought of him tagging along. "Come on, Bo," I said, louder. "Go home. Jude and I have stuff we have to do."

"No. I don't wanna."

I groaned and dropped his hand. Bo's lip trembled.

If my parents saw me pouting like that they'd say I was acting like a baby. But if I pouted in the slightly more sophisticated way that Emma and May did, my parents would accuse me of trying to act older than I was.

Too young. Too old. I couldn't win.

"Oh, let him come," Jude said. "He won't get in the way. Besides, we might not even be there for very long."

Bo's face broke into a wide smile, and he grabbed my hand again, then reached for Jude's. He looked up at me, his brown eyes sparkling. "Do you love Robo more than me?"

I wanted to yell that if he wanted to live another minute he should never, ever, ever mention the name Robo again. But I stopped myself and sighed.

I remembered Bo's even breaths as he slept, cuddled up under the covers the night before. His small voice asking me if I could tell him a story. The way he'd told CJ to cut it out. I gave Bo a small smile. "No. I could never love him more than you."

The rehearsal for *A Midsummer Night's Dream* was uneventful. The director said he'd talk to us if we agreed to be Puck's fairy friends in the play, which we wouldn't. (Jude thought about it but said no when he saw sketches of what Emma had in mind for the costumes.)

All the other adults were busy with the sets, or working with the sound and lighting. When I saw a group of kids who looked around CJ's age, I almost wished that he and Henry had come along. If he made some friends, maybe he'd stay out of my hair more. But that would probably mean that I'd be on full-time Henry and Bo duty. Even though CJ was a pain almost every second of the day, he did entertain our brothers. I had to give him that.

We left the play practice with no more information than when we had started this morning, and Jude was more starry-eyed for Emma than ever before.

"I won't make fun of you and Robo Matthews if you promise not to make fun of me and Emma," Jude said. Bo ran ahead of us, jumping over the cracks in the sidewalk.

"Okay. But—" How was I going to explain that I didn't

mind that he liked Emma. I just didn't want to get left behind. "Just . . . when she's around, don't forget that I'm still there."

"Course. Why would I forget? We're friends. Besides, she hardly knows I exist."

"Ah, don't worry about it. She's just crazy about the play right now." I wanted to add that she was also a few years older than him but stopped myself. He knew that already. And really, it didn't matter.

14

A FEW mornings later, Jude was dropped off by his mom and Wally.

"I get off early today," Wally called through the rolled-down window. "Maybe you and I can practice our catching for the fair or go out for ice cream or something."

"Wally," Ms. Trist said. "He doesn't need all that sugar, and I know they don't use organic milk in that place."

Wally leaned over and kissed her on the cheek. "He'll be fine." Then he turned back to Jude, who was staring at his shoelaces. "What do you think?"

Jude shrugged. "If Mom doesn't want me to eat ice cream, I probably shouldn't."

Now Ms. Trist smiled. "Well, maybe just this once. You two go and have some fun."

After they left, Jude quietly sulked until the smell of Mom's waffles drifted out.

"Come on," I said, pulling on his arm. "You'll love my mom's waffles."

We each wolfed down two, put our plates in the sink, and then walked back outside. My sisters were upstairs fussing over their hair and clothes, and my brothers were just sitting down to eat their breakfast. Judging by how fast the boys usually ate and how quickly they'd be nosing around to see what Jude and I were up to, I figured we had about ten minutes. Eight, if CJ decided to have four waffles instead of his usual six.

"So tell me again, why are we sneaking down to the basement of the library?"

I shifted my backpack on my shoulders. "It isn't really sneaking if you're talking that loud, is it? Now, come on."

"No one can hear us over all that racket your dad's making outside anyway." At least he whispered this time.

"We can't take any chances. By the way, you have chocolate on your cheek."

Jude reached up and swiped the blob away, then licked his fingers. If his mom only knew all the nonorganic things he was eating every day when he came over, she'd probably choke on her arrowroot cookie.

Our shoes squeaked on the new floor as we made our way to the basement stairs.

"So what is this about?" Jude eyed one of the empty spiderwebs in the corner of the room.

"Looking around to see if we find anything else. Another clue to that manuscript. This is where I found it.

There could be other things that were hidden. You look in the boxes on the first two shelves. I'll look in the other ones. Since Ben Folger was a librarian, see if you can find anything with his name on it."

We sifted through dusty books and folders, but all we found were old tax forms, books, unused envelopes, and an occasional overdue notice.

"Have you looked in the place where you found the story?" Jude asked as he returned a box to the shelf.

"Yeah, but there wasn't anything else. Just some old—" I remembered the small stack of envelopes bound with a rubber band that I had tossed inside a cardboard box when I first found the story. I walked over to the box, still sitting on the table where I had first set it down. The envelopes—worn around the edges, their blue ink faded— sat on top of two old cassette tapes.

"What are those?"

I shrugged. "Not sure, but they were in the locked box with the manuscript." I pulled out the first envelope from underneath the rubber band and handed the next one to Jude. Inside was a handwritten letter. I read it aloud:

Dear Librarian,

It's a warm day here, but it's always warm, even when it's cloudy. I suppose it's the car exhaust and heat radiating from the brilliant buildings that had once captured me. Once? you ask. Yes. Once. I still love this place. How could anyone not love something as magnificent as the bustle of the city? But more and more I find that my heart is really back in Alma. With you. I don't know what you think of that, and I am almost afraid to ask. But I'm returning for a visit soon. Within the month, though I can't help wishing it were sooner.

Daisies and hearts,

Me

PS–I suppose you've heard that my father died two weeks ago. I did not go back for his funeral. I felt nothing. Is that wrong of me?

I stopped and looked at Jude. He shrugged and read his aloud.

Dear Librarian,

Today I took a walk in the park. To tell you the truth, I had not been to the park in a long while. I've hardly stepped outside, it has been so wet. I know you would remind me of how you made me dance in the rain with you when we were kids. Yes, though I blame you for the cold I got afterward. Do you remember how I couldn't sniff

any of the flowers I love so much for an entire
week? I'm finding that I miss Alma more than I
thought I would. It's come on gradually, this long-
ing for home, but I'm finding it harder to ignore.
Maybe I just miss you and our conversations.

Perhaps you could come and visit. It really
isn't as bad as you think, and I promise I
wouldn't make you go to a party or do anything
social. We'll stay inside and play crazy eights,
and I'll beat you as bad as I always have. Do
think about it.

Daisies and hearts,

Me

PS—Because of the city lights, I haven't seen
Orion's Belt in longer than I can remember. So
trivial a thing, but it makes me sad.

Jude flipped the letter over in his hand. "'Dear Librarian'
and 'Me.' Not much to go on."

A stampede of footsteps thumped overhead. The boys!
I folded up the cream-colored paper and slipped it back
inside the envelope. Then, grabbing the other three letters, I stuffed them into my backpack and zipped it shut.

"Sunday! Jude!" It was Henry.

"I bet they're down there," CJ said. "Maybe they're
making out."

"What's making out?" Bo asked.

"Kissing."

"Ewwww."

"We're coming up," I yelled, exasperated. I put the cardboard box back on the top shelf and thumped up the stairs, Jude at my heels.

I needed to get my brothers out of my hair. The problem was, if they knew I didn't want them around, then they'd only make sure to stay glued to my side. So I either needed to bribe them (I had ten dollars in my money jar), or make them so bored that they would leave us alone.

I decided to go with option two.

"What are you guys doing?" CJ asked. "You going downtown?"

Bo gave me a big hug, wiping his sticky face on my shorts, and Henry clung to Jude.

"Oh, nothing," I said. "Jude and I were maybe going to help Mom and Miss Jenny organize and clean up around here, and then we were—"

Jude cut in. "I thought we were going downtown—"

I jabbed him hard in the stomach.

"OW! Sunday! Why did you—?"

"Don't you remember how we were going to help out around here?"

He rubbed his stomach. "Oh, yeah. Help out."

CJ looked at me hard and stroked his chin suspiciously.

To be more convincing, I picked up a roll of paper towels and the cleaning spray Mom had left sitting on a window-sill and started wiping down the circulation desk.

"Hey, CJ, will you hand me that garbage can?" I asked, for added effect.

He plunked it down next to me and then started for the door. "Come on. Let's add booby traps to our fort and then walk to town and see if Muzzy and Papa Gil will give us candy." The word *candy* was all it took for Henry and Bo to follow after him.

Once the door closed behind them, I got down on my hands and knees and pulled Jude to the floor next to me. We crawled to a window and watched my brothers dis-appear into the trees. When they were a safe distance away, I grabbed my backpack, and Jude and I snuck outside.

"So we're going to do some more investigating?"

"Yeah." I pulled out the letters.

Jude reached for one. "But the letters really didn't tell us anything."

"I know. But we haven't read all of them. And besides, they were locked up with the manuscript in the library, so they probably belong to the same person."

He shrugged. "Yeah, maybe."

"The first thing we should do is try and find out who all the librarians have been. I think finding out who these letters belong to will lead us to the author of the story."

We had taken a right onto Main Street, and Jude automatically turned toward the crepe stand.

Ms. Bodnar greeted us with a wide, warm smile. She swiped a hand across her forehead. "Whew. It's as hot as Hades back here. How about a crepe? I have one hot off the pan."

Jude licked his lips and took the plate that Ms. Bodnar handed him, the blob of whipped cream sliding off the side of the warm, rolled-up pancake.

"We're investigating and wanted to know if you knew the names of any of Alma's librarians."

"Hmm. Well, I don't know them all, but a few."

She took out a piece of paper and began writing. "Well, there was my husband. Fanny Smith was after him. In my opinion, she's one of the reasons the library went downhill so fast. Miss Dunghop is the new librarian, but you know that. Before my husband there was Kimberly Nicolas. Cathy Carleton was also one for a little while, and I think old Ben Folger was the librarian, too. Then—"

"So did you know him?" I asked. "Ben Folger, I mean?"

Ms. Bodnar looked up from the paper and brushed a stray curl out of her face, leaving a floury streak across her cheek. "No, I don't think anyone really knows Ben Folger, at least not now. I heard he was a pretty good librarian, though. He mostly keeps to himself now, so it's hard for me to imagine him serving the public, but I guess once upon a time . . ." She handed me the piece of paper. "I'll let you know if I think of anyone else."

"Thanks, Ms. Bodnar. Come on, Jude." I pulled his elbow and started out of the café.

Ms. Bodnar nodded, wiping down the countertop. "Sure thing. Come back soon."

"Ben Folger's name mentioned again!" I said to Jude as we walked down the sidewalk.

"Yeah, but she was just listing off the names of other librarians, and we already knew he was one."

"I know, I know. But still, I think he has something to do with the story from the library. Maybe he's the Librarian in the letter." My heart sped up at the thought. "And if he is, I bet he's also the author of the manuscript."

"That's a pretty big jump, Sunday. Just because—"

A desperate voice called to us from across the street.

"Jude! Sunday!" It was Muzzy. She crossed over to us, wringing her hands. A leash dangled around her neck like a scarf. "Oh dear, what am I going to do?"

"What's wrong?" I asked.

She looked up and down the street. "It's Mr. Castor. I can't find him anywhere. You haven't seen him, have you?"

"No. But we'll help you look," I said.

Muzzy started down the street. "That would be so nice. I really don't want Gil to find out. He loves Mr. Castor, don't get me wrong, but I do admit that our dog is a bit difficult. And when he runs away, it's the worst."

"So he's run away before?" I asked.

"Oh, yes, Mr. Castor is always getting loose. He's so big, you know, and with the way he pulls, it's sometimes impossible for me to keep ahold of him. And you might not think it, but he's quick as lightning. Whipped right by me and out the door."

We continued down the street, yelling for Mr. Castor. And even though Muzzy had said that she couldn't find him, she seemed to be walking in a specific direction. We took a right, walked two blocks, then took a left, then a left again. Muzzy slowed down when we reached a small yellow house. The sound of jingling dog tags greeted us.

"Mr. Castor," Muzzy whispered.

Jude and I glanced at each other, wondering why in the world she was whispering and why Muzzy looked more worried than ever. It was as if she thought at any moment something might come out and pounce on her.

"Come here, Mr. Castor," Muzzy said again.

A big white furry head with a snout completely covered with dirt poked up from behind a bush. Mr. Castor cocked his ears, snuffled, and then disappeared again.

Jude and I started toward the bush, but Muzzy caught us both in a death grip. "No, don't! If he sees you coming, he'll run off again."

"Then how are we supposed to get him?" I asked, feeling silly for whispering.

Muzzy wrung her hands and bit her bottom lip. "I don't know. We sort of have to herd him back home."

"I have an idea." I set my backpack down and unzipped it. I always kept snacks handy. After digging around for a bit, careful not to hurt the letters that I had stuffed inside, my hand found the small crinkly package of peanut butter crackers. I pulled them out and opened the wrapper.

"What are you going to do?" Muzzy asked, then mumbled to herself, "If Mrs. Potts sees Mr. Castor in her yard again, she's going to be furious."

"Don't worry. I have a dog, Butters. She always used to run away, but I taught her not to with treats." I walked slowly to where Mr. Castor was snuffling around in a bush. "Come here, Mr. Castor," I said. "You want a treat?"

At first he ignored me, bounding away, tail wagging. He sniffed somewhere else, stopped, and then started flinging dirt behind him into a pile. I continued to call him, holding out the peanut butter cracker.

"Mr. Castor, come here," I said again. And just when I thought that maybe I was wrong and there was a dog on the earth that could resist peanut butter crackers, he dashed over. I grabbed his collar and walked him back to Jude and Muzzy.

Muzzy clapped her hands. "Oh, you're a genius, Sunday!"

She clipped the leash back on Mr. Castor's collar and smothered the dog with kisses and pats. "My poor, naughty Mr. Castor," she crooned, seeming to forget how nervous and upset she had been a moment before. "Now, come on, we have to get you out of here before she sees you."

I turned around and looked at the yard dotted with holes, mounds of dirt, and decapitated flowers. "So I guess he's come here before?"

Muzzy started down the street after Mr. Castor, who was pulling on his leash so hard he was almost choking himself. "Oh, yes, he always comes here. I don't know why, but at least I always know where to find him."

"And she gets really mad?"

"It's a pretty terrible sight to see. But he doesn't mean any harm."

"Maybe you should make sure he doesn't run away at all," Jude said. "Then you wouldn't have to worry about him getting stolen or hit by a car, and Mrs. Potts won't get mad at you."

Muzzy turned to me. "You seem to be very good with dogs, Sunday. Maybe you have some advice?"

"I don't know about that. But I love dogs, and I guess I've had enough practice taking care of my brothers, and sometimes they're worse than dogs."

"Well, if you think of anything let me know," she said,

stopping at the corner of a street. "My house is down this way. Do you two want to come in for a snack?"

"Sure," Jude said.

I grabbed on to his arm and pulled him away. "No thanks. We have stuff that we need to do. Remember, Jude?"

Muzzy said good-bye and then half jogged down the sidewalk toward her house, Mr. Castor leading the way.

The sound of the triangle clanged through the air just as Jude and I were walking up the driveway for lunch. We sat on the front porch thinking about what to do next. In my head, I went over the all the evidence we had:

1. Old letters and an old manuscript
2. They'd been locked up together inside the library.
3. The letters belonged to the Librarian.

I bit into my sandwich and stared across the field.

4. Ben Folger. He is a hermit. And he'd also been a librarian.

Surely there was a connection between him and the story I'd found. And even if there wasn't, there had to be a way to get him to talk to me.

"I think I have an idea," I said.

Jude had been busy seeing how many grapes he could stuff inside his cheeks. He gave a gurgled *wha?* and a grape shot out of his mouth, rolling into the dirt.

I ignored it and stared back over at the house across the field. "How do you like the idea of being a spy?"

Jude followed my gaze to Ben Folger's house, the rest of the grapes plunking out of his mouth. "No way."

I nodded. "Tonight."

15

"LET'S go through the plan one more time," I said, pacing back and forth across the porch. Jude had his head in his hands. "I'm going to sneak out of my house and go to yours. Then, I'll–" I waited for him to finish my sentence. He didn't, so I repeated it one more time, louder. "Then I'll–"

"Shine your flashlight in my window twice." His voice was muffled. I tried to ignore his lack of enthusiasm.

"Then we'll creep over to Ben Folger's, peek in the windows, and see if we can find out any information on him that will help us–" I stopped again and waited for Jude.

"Bring him out of hiding," he said robotically. "We can't break into his house. You know that, right?"

"I already told you, we're not going to break in."

"Well then, why are we going over there?"

"To get information."

"Like what? It's not like we're going to look in and see

a sheet of paper lying on his coffee table that says 'I wish someone would befriend me' or 'I wrote the letters and story that were locked up in the library.'"

"I know that. But we can get a peek inside his house. Maybe it's full of cats, or maybe we'll find him playing a piano. You know, reconnaissance. That way, when we go over to see him again, we'll be able to talk about something that interests him."

"Fine," Jude said. "But just know that I don't think this is a good idea."

"Fine."

"Fine." And he stomped off to his house.

"Be ready!" I yelled after him.

Of course the one night that I wanted everyone to go to bed early had to be the night that Mom and Dad decided to grab pizzas and have a family movie night.

The movie started, but I didn't hear two words of what was going on. My mind was running through the plan again and again. I was itching to get moving.

Finally when the credits rolled and Mom sent my brothers off to take baths, I scurried up the stairs and closed the door behind me.

Below I heard the water running and Henry crying about having to go to bed.

Jude and I had read each of the letters a few times and gathered this much:

* "Me" and "Librarian" were friends.

* "Me" lived in New York City but had lived in Alma once and wanted to go back.

* "Me" sounded like a girl.

* They knew each other when they were kids.

* They hadn't seen each other in a long time.

* "Me" didn't go to her dad's funeral.

* "Librarian" still lived in Alma.

* And it sounded as if "Me" liked "Librarian" the way I liked Robo Matthews and Jude liked Emma.

Not a lot to go on.

I glanced at the clock beside my bed. Nine o'clock.

Laughter erupted from the bathroom. Setting the letters aside, I pulled out the manuscript:

By summer, the glow returned to Mark's face and strength, slowly, to his limbs. Though his mother and father refused to let him outside for long, he and Lilly managed to enjoy the summer.

It was Lilly who found the place that would be forever theirs.

"You need to open the window a little," she said, twisting the handle and allowing the sounds and smells of summer in. "If not, you'll suffocate in here."

It had been looking out the window at the orange sunset that drew her attention to the small piece of roof outside Mark's window, just wide enough for two friends to sit on. The oak in front of his house had a limb that would drop her right onto the ledge.

She did not tell Mark her idea, not wanting to fail in front of him. Failure had never been acceptable to Lilly, and she didn't plan on starting now.

Later that evening, after she had stayed for dinner she returned home. Though not for long. She waited until her aunt and uncle left for their bowling night, then secreted away the old astronomy book they kept in the basement. The cover was ripped and pages were missing, but she loved to look at it. Mark had recently read a book about space.

"I'm going to learn all the constellations," he told her one day. "That way I can navigate using the stars, and when you and I go somewhere we'll never have to worry about being lost."

Lilly tucked the book under her arm. They would start learning that night.

Even though the air was warm, she filled a large thermos with watery hot chocolate and carried the book over to Mark's house.

She shined her flashlight in his bedroom window

twice—their signal to each other—and moments later, Mark appeared at the glass.

"What?" he whispered.

"I'm coming up, but I can't carry these up the tree. Do you have anything you could lower down?"

Mark disappeared inside his room, and Lilly watched as a small light flicked on and his shadow moved across the curtains. She knew he would come up with something. He always did.

He came back, and soon she, her book, and the thermos were sitting on the little ledge.

Mark stuffed a blanket out the window for them to sit on. "We should do this every night."

Lilly smiled, pleased. "We will. Now, hurry up and open the book. The sky is clear, but you never know when clouds are going to start moving in."

They found the North Star, Cassiopeia, the Big Dipper, and the Little Dipper. But Orion's Belt was their favorite.

Lilly searched the sky. "Where is it again?"

Mark leaned in closer, so close that she could smell the shampoo in his hair. She looked at him, her heart thudding harder in her chest.

He pointed up at the sky. "Right there."

She followed his finger and nodded. "I see it."

She got up, reaching for the now-empty thermos. "I better go. I'll see you tomorrow."

Every night after that, they met out on the small space right below Mark's window. And each night they searched the sky for Orion's Belt.

At first, Lilly spent a long time staring at the blackness, frustrated because all the stars looked the same. But each night Mark calmly pointed it out. Eventually it became like a familiar friend.

Lilly searched for it in the sky every night after.

Orion's Belt.

Orion's Belt.

Where had I read that?

In *The Life and Death of Birds? Princess Academy?* No. I grabbed for the letters, sifting through the envelopes until I found the one that Jude had read aloud. Skimming it, I came to the PS—*Because of the city lights, I haven't seen Orion's Belt in longer than I can remember. So trivial a thing, but it makes me sad.*

Orion's Belt mentioned in both the letter and the manuscript! That had to be a connection. I couldn't wait to tell Jude.

Complete darkness had overtaken the sky, and I ran to my door, pressing my ear to the wood.

No noises. No footsteps.

Of course, Mom and Dad and my sisters were still up, but for the first time in my life, as I slipped out the door, I silently prayed that I would be invisible. Just for tonight.

"Ouch." I brushed away the sharp branches and found a more comfortable spot. Ben Folger's house was dark except for a light on the second floor. Jude was in the bush next to mine. I couldn't see him, but I could hear his heavy, nervous breathing. Mine wasn't much better. I pointed my flashlight at the ground and clicked it on and off.

"Did you bring the binoculars?" I reached out blindly and grabbed hold of the cold, heavy glasses. "Thanks."

"We just gotta be careful. They're Wally's."

"Don't worry. Did you go out with him for ice cream?"

"Yeah."

"And how was it?"

"Same as always."

Wow, wasn't Jude Mr. Talkative tonight? "Aaaand, what does that mean?"

"Oh, you know. Ice cream, playing catch, saying he's proud of me and loves my mom. Stupid stuff like that."

"That doesn't sound stupid."

He sighed. "You wouldn't understand. Wally is a dork who is just trying to trick me into liking him. He doesn't know how to fix up houses or sand floors or remodel or anything like that. Not like your dad. Your dad is cool and loves your mom. You can tell he loves all you guys."

"Oh, just like how Wally is with you and your mom? Besides, Wally can fix cars. My dad can't do that." I knew as soon as the words came out of my mouth that I probably shouldn't have said them.

"Look, Sunday, I didn't come out here to get a lecture."

I reached out into the darkness and felt for his arm. "No, wait. You're right, I don't understand, just like you can't understand what it's like to be the middle-of-the-middle child. Sorry."

"It's fine."

"But from the little I've heard about Wally and the few times I've seen him, he seems like he's a good guy. Maybe he really does love you and your mom."

Silence.

"Jude?"

The bush rustled beside me. "Yeah, I'm here. Let's stop talking about it, okay?"

Just then a light flicked on in the front window, and Ben Folger walked across the room and disappeared. He was probably sitting down in a chair or something.

"There," I said. "We'll be able to see inside and now we also know where he is."

"So what do we do?"

I tried to judge the distance to the nearest window but couldn't see a thing in the dark. "I think we need to run to that window over there and—"

A twig snapped somewhere behind us.

"What was that?"

I searched the darkness. Thick clouds had moved in, covering the moon. "Hello?" I whispered.

Nothing.

Then another snap followed by a shuffle. Clicking on my flashlight, I pointed the beam toward the noise, again finding nothing. "It's probably a squirrel," I said.

Jude shifted, rustling the leaves. "I think we should go. What if it's Ben Folger?"

"It can't be. We just saw him walk by the window."

"I can't decide which is better. Ben Folger behind us, stalking us in the woods, or Ben Folger waiting for us ahead. I bet he has his cane ready."

I looked toward the house again. If we were going to look in the windows, we might as well do it now. "All right, Jude. On the count of three, we'll run to the window."

"I can't believe we're doing this. You know if we get caught he might—"

"He's not going to kill us," I said, finishing his thought. "Besides we already proved there's no curse on his yard. Ready? One." My heart thunked heavily in my chest. "Two." I took a deep breath in and closed my eyes. "Three."

I bolted from the bush, Jude panting behind me.

When we'd crossed the yard, I flung myself underneath the window, plowing through a bed of soft dirt. Jude did the same, and we looked at each other in the dim glow from the window. We sat, catching our breath, staring into the darkness. My house sat in the distance, a few lights still on.

I prayed that Bo wouldn't try to come into my room.

"So now what?"

"Well," I whispered. "We'll turn around and peek into the window. I'll use the binoculars to get a good look at everything across the room, and you try and get a good look at things close by."

"And don't get caught. You forgot that."

"Of course. We can't get caught."

I slowly turned around and peered over the lip of the window into the lighted room. It didn't look like the home of someone who ate raw squirrels and tortured people in his basement. A dusty piano stood against one wall with a piece of music sitting above the keys. There was an old couch, a small rug, and an even smaller TV that sat on a rickety metal tray table. The TV was mostly covered by small green plants, and I got the idea that he probably didn't turn on the television very much. On the other wall was a humongous bookcase. The spines were neatly arranged—like a small library. He had been a librarian, so obviously he loved books. That was something I could definitely talk to him about. I continued my spying, looking for photographs, but saw only paintings hanging on the walls. Ben Folger got up from a chair and walked into the kitchen and then back into the living room. I ducked down more.

"What?" Jude whispered. "Did you see something?"

I waved him away and watched the old man. He went to the bookcase, selected a book without even looking, and then sat down at the small wooden dining table.

"Sunday, what is it?"

I brought the binoculars up to my eyes and peered through them into the room. "Just a second. I can almost make out the title of the book he's reading—"

A small voice called from the woods, followed by a lot of scuffling. "Wait! I'm scared!"

"Sunday," Jude said, tugging on my arm. I had already turned toward the voice. "I think someone's out there."

Another plaintive whine. "CJ, I want to go back."

No way. They wouldn't. They didn't.

But they did. The three forms of my brothers emerged from the woods and dashed toward us.

No, no, no.

"What are you doing?!" I stood up all the way and let the binoculars drop from my hand. They clunked loudly against the windowsill. I ducked back down just as I saw Ben Folger's head whip around to the window.

"He saw us. Run," I half spoke, half whispered.

I whisked Henry up into my arms and we all dashed for the field, pumping our legs harder when we heard Ben Folger's screen door slamming and his angry voice yell out. "Stay away from my house!"

We all dropped to our knees when we reached the other side of the field.

I tried to catch my breath for a second before I laid into my brothers. "You just ruined everything! What were you thinking?"

CJ glanced up at me and shrugged, his words coming short and ragged. "Same thing you were thinking."

"Well, you weren't invited!"

Jude grabbed of my arm. "Sunday, just let it go."

I jerked away. "No, I won't let it go!" I turned to CJ. "You ruined everything. And you almost got us caught! He didn't know we were there, but now he does, and it won't take him long to figure out it was us and then he'll call the police and haul us off."

"But I don't want to go to jail," Bo sniffled.

"Well, you should have thought about that before you tagged along uninvited," I snapped.

CJ slung his arm over Bo. "Ignore her, Bo. They won't come for us. And I wouldn't let them haul you off to jail anyway."

Bo swiped the tears that had started to drip down his cheeks. "Promise?"

CJ nodded, stood, and then pulled Bo to his feet. "Promise. Come on, Henry. Let's go back inside. Let's leave Sunday and Jude *aloooone.*"

I watched my brothers leave, feeling a little jealous seeing Bo's hand tucked into CJ's. If they hadn't messed everything up, I wouldn't be so mad.

"I gotta get going, Sunday," Jude said, brushing off his shorts. "I'll see you tomorrow."

I stomped toward the house. The night had started full of promise. Now I felt like I'd swallowed a big rock.

"Sorry it didn't work out," Jude whispered. "We'll find out more tomorrow."

A soft *yeah* was all I could muster.

16

THE NEXT morning was cloudy and wet, mist hanging over everything like a blanket. Even though I'd stayed up late reading *The Life and Death of Birds*, I couldn't sleep. I kept thinking that Ben Folger was going to appear on our doorstep at any moment.

Bleary-eyed and annoyed, I walked into the kitchen and found my three brothers huddled over bowls of cereal, drips of milk splattered across the table.

Bo smiled and skipped over to me, hugging me tight around the waist. "'Morning, Sunday," he said.

Feeling his wiry arms around me and seeing his hair stuck up in every direction made it impossible to hold on to my anger. I squeezed him against me. "'Morning, Bo. Where's Mom and Dad?"

"Mom went to get more cereal with May," CJ said, peeling an overripe banana. "May is probably crashing the car right now. I think Dad's at the library. You should be thankful we came last night. We saved you from being murdered."

"What? CJ, if you think—"

The screen door opened and Jude waltzed in, taking a seat next to Henry. "'Morning," he said, smiling.

Henry abandoned his cereal and plopped himself into Jude's lap. "Last night was fun, wasn't it?"

Jude looked at me warily.

I shrugged and sighed. There wasn't much we could do about it now. If we got caught, we got caught. "It was, Henry, wasn't it? But I don't think we'll do something like that ever again, okay?"

Everyone nodded except CJ. I knew he would gladly relive last night if he could.

Mom and May returned, and Jude and I managed to slip outside while CJ, Bo, and Henry gorged themselves on more cereal, eating bowl after bowl and betting each other on who could eat the most.

We crept down the porch stairs, avoiding the creaky second step, and went to help at the library. I filled Jude in on what I'd read of the manuscript the night before.

"Orion's Belt. That means the manuscript and the letters probably belong to the same person. I bet as I keep reading I'll find even more evidence."

"Cool. So after our near-death experience have you given up on befriending Old Man Folger? Or at least that he wrote the story?" Jude asked. He kicked at a stray pinecone, causing a squirrel to skitter up a nearby tree.

I shrugged. "I don't know." I hadn't thought that becoming friends with Ben Folger would be this hard or this scary. In *The Secret Garden*, it had been pretty easy for Mary Lennox to befriend Colin. But Colin was a cranky boy, not a grumpy potential murderer.

Nothing could have prepared me for what happened an hour later when I saw Ben Folger walking toward the library stairs. Plain as day.

My fingers froze around a new copy of *Charlotte's Web*.

He knew! He knew that Jude and I had been at his house the night before.

And now he was coming for us.

My legs went noodle-y, and when I reached for Jude's arm, all that came out was a high-pitched squeak.

"What?" he asked, looking up from the book he was helping catalogue into the computer.

I think I motioned to the door, but I wasn't sure. I followed Jude's gaze out the window.

Footsteps *tromp-scuffle-tapped* up the library stairs.

Jude's eyes grew wide, and he squeezed my hand so hard I thought he was going to break one of my knuckles.

Ben Folger. I had definitely seen right.

"Hello?" His gruff voice broke the quiet.

I couldn't move. I wanted to, but I couldn't.

Mom, kneeling beside a box of books, turned and flashed a warm smile. "Hello."

Miss Jenny stood up, her chair screeching on the newly finished floor. "I'm sorry, but the library isn't open just yet. We're doing some renovations. We'll be having a reopening party in about two weeks if you want to come back then. Otherwise, the library at the high school is open for the community."

My noodle-y legs melted beneath me and I ducked down farther, wishing the stack of books was taller so that I could hide behind it.

Ben Folger nodded and kept his eyes cast down to the floor. Sweat gathered on his forehead, and he rubbed his hands on his dirty jeans. He looked more nervous than a squirrel trapped in a doghouse. "I used to be a librarian here, years ago. My name's . . ." He coughed into his hand. "My name's Ben Folger."

Miss Jenny smiled again. "Oh, hello, Mr. Folger. Yes, of course. I'm Miss Dunghop, though please call me Miss Jenny. And this is Mrs. Fowler." She gestured toward Mom, who stuck out her hand as well.

"It's very nice to meet you. My husband is the one outside with the sander." Mom pointed over at me, revealing my pitiful hiding spot. "That's my daughter Sunday and her friend Jude."

An awkward silence hung in the air.

"Is there something I can do for you?" Mom asked.

He ran his thick hands through his white hair. "I've seen a lot of kids running around here."

"Yes," Mom said a little more warily. She shot me a what-has-CJ-done-now look, then turned back to him. "I hope that my son CJ hasn't been bothering you."

Ben Folger's ice-blue eyes landed on me. He knew it was me who had been at his house. My stomach twisted. "No, no, ma'am. But some sort of animal got into my flower bed last night and trampled my daisies. I was wondering if maybe I could borrow two of your kids for a few days to help me fix the damage? They'll be turning and tilling the soil in the old flower bed and helping me start two others. What with my arthritis and hip, I can't do nearly as much. I'll give them lunch and won't keep them too long. I'd . . . I'd really appreciate it."

Jude knocked me hard with his elbow and I winced.

Please say no. Please say no, I wished. But wait. This is what I wanted, right? A chance to talk to Ben Folger. He obviously knew that it was me in his garden last night. He just wasn't telling. Was he going to take us over to his house and make us dig up the old bones he'd buried? Or maybe—I gulped—we would be forced to dig graves for new bones.

"Sunday?" Mom said, interrupting thoughts of being forced to eat a dead squirrel.

"Yeah, sorry. What?"

"How about it? Why don't you and Jude go over and help Mr. Folger? I think Miss Jenny and I can handle the rest of the cataloguing for today. Jude, I'll let your mom know and come and get you if she says no. Sunday, I want you back in time for dinner, okay?"

"Thank you," Ben Folger said, and then tromped out the door. "Follow me."

I turned to Mom with a "now what?" look on my face, and she gestured for us to scoot out the door after him. "You two behave and be polite," she whispered.

Jude and I walked side by side, following ten steps behind the old man. Even though he had his cane, he didn't seem to have any sort of arthritis or hip problems that I could see.

"What'll we do now?" Jude whispered. "He's gonna kill us. I just know it."

"I don't think he will," I said, sounding braver than I felt. "Besides, my mom knows where we are, and I can scream real loud if I need to."

CJ, Bo, and Henry saw us and huddled together by the old oak tree to watch us pass. They stared at Ben Folger, who didn't give them the time of day.

"You're not really going to go with him, are you?" CJ asked, following behind us.

"We have to," I said.

"But, Sunday," Bo whispered, grabbing my hand. "He'll kill you or make you eat raw meat."

CJ laughed grimly. "That's just the beginning."

"Shh, CJ. You're scaring Bo and Henry." I pried my hand out of my little brother's small-but-firm grip. "Don't worry, I'll be back before dinner."

I think. Gulp.

CJ pulled Henry and Bo off to the side, placing his hand over his heart like a salute.

"Can I have your iPod if you don't come back?" he called after me.

I turned around and glared, then continued on. Ben Folger didn't slow for a moment. Jude and I looked at each other. I wanted to reach for his hand but couldn't bring myself to do it. I felt like Dorothy going to get the broomstick from the Wicked Witch of the West. Eating raw meat and/or dying in a damp, dark basement was *not* my idea of making my mark on the world.

Ben Folger waited for us by the flower bed where we'd crouched in the dark the night before. Our footprints were still visible in the soil and there was a sad, trampled patch of flowers, broken and torn at their stems.

"Before I feed you raw squirrel, I might as well get some work out of you," he said gruffly, handing me a trowel and Jude a small spade. "When you're done fixing this bed, you can add two new beds on either side of the walkway. Turn the soil and then till it. What you don't get done today, you can do tomorrow, and the next."

Jude and I both nodded, then watched as he walked up the stairs to his house and opened the door. He turned around just before he disappeared inside. "Well, what are you waiting for?"

Jude and I tilled and shoveled and tilled and shoveled till I thought my arm was going to fall off. Sweat slid down my forehead and dripped into my eyes.

After what felt like forever, Ben Folger came out, leaving behind two glasses filled with bright pink liquid and two paper plates with a sandwich on each.

"Eat," was all he said, then disappeared inside again.

Jude and I set down our shovel and tiller, washed our hands and faces with a nearby hose, and then sat down in the grass with our lunches. We looked at each other.

"Do you think it's safe?" Jude asked. A fly landed on the plate and he brushed it away. His stomach grumbled.

Would I know the smell of dead squirrel or poison? I shrugged and picked up the sandwich, bringing it to my nose. Peanut butter and jelly. Grape. I guessed it was non-organic peanut butter. "It smells okay."

Jude sniffed the liquid in the cups. "Poisoned, I think."

Our stomachs grumbled again.

"I don't think he'd risk poisoning us, and it's definitely not raw squirrel." I picked up the sandwich, sighed, closed my eyes, and took a bite.

I chewed and swallowed, chewed and swallowed. It was a pretty good sandwich. Actually it was probably the best peanut butter and jelly sandwich I'd ever eaten. Jude licked his lips as he anxiously watched me eat, like any moment I might drop dead right in front of him.

I shrugged. "It's really good."

That was all the encouragement he needed. He grabbed his sandwich and devoured it in a few bites.

"You're right," he said, his voice sticky with peanut butter. "It's really good."

I picked up the glass. "This is probably pink lemonade." I took a swig, my cheeks tightening and my lips puckering at the sour sweetness.

"What?"

I took a smaller sip, feeling the grains of sugary powder on my tongue. "It's tart. I think he just put in too much lemonade mix and not enough water."

Jude looked up at the house. "Or it's poisoned."

"It's not poisoned, Jude. My mom said he was probably just a lonely old man."

"A lonely old man who poisons kids with lemonade."

Jude was hopeless. I drank the rest just to prove that nothing was wrong with it and took my plate and glass to the porch. "Now, hurry up. I want to finish one side of the walkway and then we can talk to him about . . . something."

Jude nodded, brought the glass to his lips, and barely let a dribble touch his mouth. Then he set his plate and glass on the porch as well, licking a blob of peanut butter off his finger.

Tilling and shoveling a brand-new bed along the walkway was a lot harder than redoing the two beds underneath the windows. We barely finished the first when Jude checked his watch.

"We should probably go now, Sunday," he said, swiping a hand across his forehead. "It's almost five."

I stood, my back and neck and arms and legs and everywhere in between stiff from being hunkered over the ground for most of the day. I dusted my hands on my shorts. At some point, Old Ben Folger had snuck out to grab the paper plates and glasses and then snuck back inside.

I set down my shovel against the side of the house. Though my heart was beating fast inside my chest, I wasn't about to give up the opportunity to talk to him. I couldn't.

"Sunday? What are you doing?" Jude whispered loudly, his hair wet with sweat and his face streaked with dirt. "Let's just go."

"I've got to talk to him, Jude."

Before I lost my nerve, I walked up the path to the steps.

"Sunday," Jude said, "I don't think you should."

I stood up tall and rapped hard on the door.

Footsteps scuffled along the floor, then the curtain on the door was pulled to the side and Ben Folger's sour old face peered out at me. He let the curtain fall and opened the door.

"Yes?" his voice was quiet, but I could tell that he wasn't too pleased I was standing there.

"Umm . . . " I realized I should've prepared something to say. He started to shut the door, but I pressed my hand against it. "Thanks for the sandwiches."

He nodded. "You're welcome. I'm . . . I'm not used to making lunches for kids."

"It was good. And we finished tilling one of the new flower beds. And—" *Think, Sunday, think.* I peered behind him into his house and noticed the bookshelf I had seen last night. "Books!" I blurted out.

"What?"

"Um . . . I see you like books. I do, too. I read all the time. I even won a contest in my school for reading the most books. I'll probably win this summer, too. Since we've been here I've already read *The Secret Garden* again, a Nancy Drew book, and *Princess Academy*."

"That's nice."

"Could I . . . could I look at them?" *Did I really just say that?* I must've, because there he was, opening the door wider so I could come in.

"I suppose. Just be careful."

I gulped, turned to look at Jude, whose face was pale, and then stepped inside. It smelled like pine trees and cinnamon. I walked past the piano and the small table where a cup sat alongside an empty cellophane wrapper. Maybe he'd just eaten one of the chocolate cupcakes that Muzzy said he liked. There was also a book, flipped over with a small bookmark sticking out from the top of the pages.

I recognized the back cover because it was the same as the one that sat on the nightstand in my room. Lee Wren's *The Life and Death of Birds.*

"I just started reading this book," I said, reaching for it. Ben Folger rushed forward and grabbed it.

I jerked my hand away. "Oh, sorry."

His wrinkled cheeks flushed red and he looked down at the book, tucking the bookmark inside the pages so that it disappeared. "I . . . don't want to lose my place."

I could tell he was embarrassed. "I'm the same way. I hate it when my brothers lose my place."

He didn't look up but nodded with a hint of a smile.

"I like the book so far. What part are you on?"

His smile grew. "When Hunter's father finds the bird in the backyard."

I nodded. "Hmm, I'm not there yet. I'm only on chapter two, when Aunt Sierra arrives at the house."

Ben Folger gave me a quick smile. Without the scowl plastered on his face, he looked almost kind. Sort of like a face that loved stories like I did. And one that I bet had stories to tell.

The dinner triangle clanged from across the field. My mom had been forgiving the other day but probably wouldn't be a second time.

"Sunday!" Jude called from the doorway.

"I'm coming." I turned to Ben Folger. "I better go."

"Yes," he said, and followed after me to the front door. "I'll see you both tomorrow."

Jude and I walked quietly down the walkway and out of the gate. From there, we burst into a run, dashing through the tall weeds in the field and flushing out a flock of small blackbirds.

"So what in the world did you do in there?" Jude pushed out through gasps of air. "See any bones?"

"No. I talked to him about books," I said. "He's reading the same book I am right now, isn't that crazy?"

"He's crazy."

We stopped in front of my house. "He isn't," I said.

"And I'll prove it to you. Tomorrow we'll both go in and talk to him. Unless you're scared."

Jude started off toward his house. "I'm not scared. I just have more brains than you do."

I laughed. "Tomorrow, Jude!"

Bo dashed out from behind the house and wrapped his arms around my waist. "Sunday's here. See, CJ! I told you she'd make it back alive."

"Of course I'm alive," I said.

He pulled away and grabbed on to my hand, leading me into the backyard. "CJ was making a grave for you."

"Really?"

"Henry and me were in charge of taking away the dirt."

We reached CJ, who was streaked with mud and looking a little disappointed to see me.

"I told you," Bo said. "And look, Sunday, I picked that piece of wood for your gravestone."

"Don't worry," CJ said, digging his shovel into the ground again. "I was gonna write something nice."

I examined the large hole—more deep than it was long. "Wow, thanks, CJ." I let the sarcasm drip off my words.

He shrugged and pressed the shovel into the earth. "Sure thing."

"You know you still have a lot of digging to do, right? I mean, no one can fit in there."

"Well, I thought that maybe we'd bury you feetfirst. You know, have your head sticking up out of the ground. It would completely freak people out."

I rolled my eyes. "Come on, guys. Mom rang the triangle a few minutes ago. If we don't hurry, we'll have more graves to dig."

After dinner, standing on the porch, I found myself torn between sneaking away to my room to read or dancing around in the cool grass, catching fireflies.

"Come on, Sunday," Bo said, pulling me down the stairs. "Let's see who can catch the most."

I glanced up at my bedroom window imagining myself sinking onto my pillow, book in hand, surrounded by nothing but quiet and words. I sighed. I didn't want to dash around in the dark right now. It seemed . . . silly.

I started to sneak away, unnoticed by Bo, who I could barely see in the deepening dusk, when a firefly blinked in front of my eyes. Smiling, I reached for it, plopping it into my jar as I had done every summer since I could remember. "I caught one!" I called out.

But watching the bug crawling up the sides of the jar didn't feel exciting like it had every other summer when

I caught fireflies. Instead of placing my hand protectively over the lid, I watched as the small bug perched on the lip of the jar, spread its wings, and then buzzed off. I followed it for a moment as it blinked once or twice more until it blended in with the rest of the flashing lights.

The screen door creaked, and Mom and Dad walked out, sitting on the stairs with steaming cups of coffee.

My brothers' giggles and shouts echoed around me as I stood once more in that unfamiliar place between too old and too young. After a few more moments, I slipped away into the house and up to my bedroom.

Picking up *The Life and Death of Birds*, I went to the window and looked out, my brothers' shadows dancing and the fireflies blinking around them. I plopped onto my bed and let myself drift into the pages.

17

"SO," Jude asked the next morning. "Any letters from the authors yet?" He was pouring syrup on a small stack of pancakes slathered in butter, even though he said he'd already eaten gluten-free granola and homemade nonfat sugar-free yogurt before coming over.

I shook my head, flipping through the *Alma Gazette*. "Nope. They probably just need more advance warning."

He mumbled through a bite of pancake.

"When you finish eating, we should head over to Ben Folger's house." I'd just gotten to the part in *The Life and Death of Birds* where Hunter went against her aunt's wishes to take care of the injured bird, and I wanted to see what Ben thought about it.

Jude looked out at the gray sky and the puddles that were starting to form in the grass. "I don't think we'll be able to work in the rain."

"I think we should go over and at least ask."

Jude stuffed another bite in his mouth and shrugged.

My eyes landed on a short article on the fourth page of the paper. "Hey, look at this." I turned the paper toward Jude and pointed at the bold title: ALMA LIFE. "It says it's by Joanne 'Muzzy' Hopkins."

Jude stopped mid-chew and squinted his eyes at the paper. "Wow, I never knew she wrote for the newspaper."

I read the article aloud, hoping to find a clue:

"'Monday was a sunny day, though a few clouds passed over in the mid afternoon.

'Mrs. Fielding's son, Aaron, who has been in California for the past two years, came for a long-awaited visit. To celebrate, she made one of her delicious apple pies, which was always Aaron's favorite. It's good to see Aaron applying himself, as I'm sure Mr. and Mrs. Svently still remember the year he put toilet paper in their maple tree. In other news, Mr. Goldfine, an English teacher at Alma Area High School, has finally decided to cut his long braid and donate it to an organization that makes wigs. Scott O'Deary has informed me that because of the recent aches in his knees, we are in for a low-pressure system. Until next week, keep smiling.'"

Jude laughed. "Was that it?"

I looked up. "Maybe she wrote the story I found?"

"No way, Sunday."

I licked the blob of syrup hanging off the end of my fork and shrugged. "Well, it definitely doesn't seem like the same writer, but who knows? Maybe she's brilliant and undiscovered." I ignored Jude's snort. "Besides, we need to check out all the possibilities."

By the time we finished with breakfast, the rain was just a drizzle. Jude and I started across the wet field.

Ben Folger must've been watching for us, because he stepped out onto the porch just as we pushed through the front gate. Jude sucked in his breath.

"Relax," I whispered. "If he was going to kill us he would've done it yesterday. We're fixing his flower beds."

"Yeah, that's probably where he's planning on burying us. I thought I found a cat bone yesterday."

I rolled my eyes and glanced at our work. The dirt was a deep chocolate brown, rich and healthy looking. I imagined deep green leaves poking out from the surface.

"It's raining," Ben Folger said from the porch.

"Yep," I said.

Jude didn't say anything, but I felt him step closer to me, his arm brushing against mine.

Ben Folger took his glasses off and wiped them on his plaid shirt. "I don't think it'll last much longer. I suppose you should come inside and wait it out."

I said "All right" at the exact time that Jude said "No thanks."

I glared at him. "Jude," I said through clenched teeth.

Ben Folger turned and stepped inside. "It's up to you."

I reached for the door, catching it just before it closed, and then stepped inside. Jude stood on the other side of the screen. I motioned him with my hand. "Come on."

He rolled his eyes, opened the door, and followed me into the living room. Ben Folger was nowhere in sight, though I heard a cabinet being opened and closed, and the sound of glasses clinking together.

"Sit anywhere," he called out.

"I'll sit here, next to the telephone," Jude whispered. "That way I can dial 911 in case he turns on us. You sit closest to the door and make a run for it if he does."

It was my turn to roll my eyes at him. "Jude, you're being ridiculous. How many times do I have to tell you that he isn't going to kill—"

The whistling of a teapot interrupted our whispering.

"I'm just saying that we should be prepared." He sat next to the telephone, resting his hand on the small end table so that his fingers brushed the phone's base.

I walked around the room, my eyes settling on a stack of records on top of the cluttered piano—something I hadn't seen since I was probably Henry's age, standing in front of my grandparents' record player.

"Have you ever listened to a record?"

"What?!" I jumped at the sound of Ben Folger's deep

voice behind me, the record sleeve clunking to the floor. "I . . . I'm . . . I'm sorry," I said. "I–"

He waved his hand and picked up the record. "Please, it's . . . it's okay."

He smiled as he looked down at the record.

"It's just about finished raining out there," Jude said, standing. "Come on, Sunday. I think we better–"

Ben Folger went to the record player. As he busied himself with clearing it off, I grabbed Jude's arm.

"What's he doing?" he mouthed.

"I don't know," I whispered back.

"Well, I think we should make a run for it."

"No. Don't run." Ben Folger turned around and held out the record. "This was always one of our–one of my favorites. I haven't listened to it in years."

He sat down as the needle skimmed the record, crackled, and then filled the room with music.

"I'll go and get our hot chocolate. I know it isn't lunchtime yet, but I made brownies this morning. I've never tried to make them before, but they seem to have turned out. Maybe you want to try one?"

That was all the persuasion Jude needed.

Ben Folger handed me a steaming mug.

As he set the plate of brownies and three plates onto the coffee table, I couldn't help but wonder how relaxed, yet awkward, he seemed.

Jude reached for one of the dark chocolate squares and took a generous bite. Clearly he wasn't worried about being poisoned anymore.

I did the same. "These are really good."

"Sure are," Jude mumbled.

Ben Folger took a sip of his hot chocolate, looking pleased.

"I'm on chapter six in *The Life and Death of Birds*," I said, hoping to get him talking.

"And what do you think?" he asked.

"I really like it. The main character, Hunter, is funny and I like how the book has a little bit of everything in it: mystery, funny lines, and sad parts."

He nodded and smiled. "Some say it's the best book written this century. I've read it ten times."

"Ten times?" Jude said, reaching for another brownie. "I don't think I could ever read a book that many times."

Ben Folger nodded. "I never thought I would, either. But Lee Wren was brilliant."

I'd been waiting for the chance to ask him about the manuscript in the library. This seemed like as good a one as any. "Do you like to write, Mr. Folger?" I asked.

He shrugged. "I do."

I looked at Jude, but he was too busy dabbing at the crumbs that had fallen onto his shirt to notice. "Really?"

"Yes, but I've only written boring things like grants and

library articles. Nothing like this." He reached over and picked up his copy of *The Life and Death of Birds.*

My excitement deflated. So he hadn't written the story.

"I recognize that cover," Jude said, pointing at the book Ben Folger held out. "My mom has it at home; I think she really liked it."

Ben Folger blew across his hot chocolate. "Is that so?"

Maybe Ben Folger had been the person who got Lee Wren to come in the first place since he was a librarian. I think I remembered that headline in the newspaper articles we looked up. "You probably met her before, right?"

He nodded, stood up, and turned to the record player. "I did." He lifted the needle, bringing the room into silence except for the hum of the air conditioner. "She was . . . she was wonderful," he said.

"What was so wonderful about her?" I asked.

Instead of answering, he glanced to the window, where the rain had stopped. "Actually, it's looking pretty muddy out there. Not good for yard work. Maybe you can come back tomorrow morning."

"Are you sure?"

"Yes."

I sighed and set my mug down on the table. He was done talking and I didn't want to push him. "Thanks for the hot chocolate and brownies."

Jude stood up. "Yeah, thanks."

Ben Folger didn't turn around, but I saw his head nod ever so slightly.

Jude and I left, letting the screen door close behind us. The air was muggy and the gray clouds were spread across the sky.

"Well," I said, "I guess he wasn't the one who wrote the story from the library."

"Yeah."

"But you have to admit he isn't going to kill us."

Jude shrugged. "I guess. But he could just be waiting until we let our guard down. Or fattening us up like the witch in 'Hansel and Gretel.'"

I rolled my eyes and closed the gate behind us. "You're hopeless."

18

THE NIGHT was hot. I lay on my side on top of the blankets with the manuscript beside me. The fan blasted just inches away from my bed. I reached over and took a sip of water, turning the page:

They loved all the seasons of the year. The apple cider of fall, the smell of pine in winter, the puddles in spring. But summer—summer seemed made just for Lilly and Mark—forts and ice cream, fireworks and fireflies. Lilly opened her eyes, glanced over at the daisy on her windowsill, dressed, and raced over to Mark's house. He was always up early, at least always earlier than her.

But the summer before they began seventh grade was the most wonderful.

On the Fourth of July Lilly remembered first seeing Mark differently—his face lighting up under the glow of fireworks. She didn't mean for her cheeks to blush so deeply, nor for her heart to dance in staccato beats.

<u>But it did.</u>

It was like the author had been there with me when Robo Matthews first said hi to me in the hallway. I had felt the staccato beat of my heart, and my cheeks filled with heat just thinking about it—even now. I couldn't help but smile. My eyes drooped and I yawned, flipping to the next page. I felt like I'd hit a dead end. And even though I'd spoken with Ben Folger, he was by no means befriended yet.

There was a knock on my door. Probably Bo. "Just a second," I said, and quickly reassembled the manuscript and slipped it under my pillow.

I grabbed Lee Wren's book and opened it to a random page. "Come in!"

The door opened and Emma stood in the doorway, her hands filled with fabric. She had never ventured up here—neither had May—so it surprised me to see her now.

She dropped the bundle of fabric on my bed. Her cheeks were flushed, there were hives dotting her neck. "You have to help me, Sunday. Please, please, please."

I pulled out a piece of olive-green fabric. It was a sort of skirt thingy. "Help with what?"

"All the fairies in the play are tiny like you. May's

you-know-whats are beyond huge, so she's no help. Could you try them on for me? The director wants to see some of the costumes tomorrow and they need to be right."

I shrugged. "Sure."

I barely had put on an outfit before she stuck me with pins and threw another one at me. Still, it was fun. We giggled at some of the pieces that were beyond help, while other things I tried on were close to perfect.

When I had the last piece on—a toga-looking dress that was meant for one of the queens to wear—Emma walked me over to the mirror on the closet door. She pulled my tangled hair off my neck. "You look real pretty, Sunday. You have a long, slender neck, not like the rest of us, and I think your eyes are a darker shade of brown. And wow, I only wish my eyelashes were as long as yours."

"Really?" I laughed, feeling my cheeks redden at the compliment. Sure, my parents said I was beautiful, but parents have to say that sort of stuff. I stretched my arm around my back and reached awkwardly for the zipper. "You know, Emma, you're really good at this."

She helped me step out of the robe-dress-toga thing and laid it on top of the others. "You think so?"

"Sure."

Gathering up the garments in her arms, she sighed. "I hope you all come to the show."

"Of course. Why wouldn't we?"

"Oh, you know. Everyone has their own stuff going on, and sometimes I feel like it's easy to get forgotten in the middle of everything."

I swear it took all the muscles in my face to keep my jaw from dropping open. A small laugh escaped. "You? Forgotten? That would be impossible." I shook my head. "No, I wouldn't worry about that."

She smiled and turned, opening the door. "Well, I gotta try and fix these tonight. It's going to be a late one." She stopped and turned. "Thanks, Sunday. It was fun."

The door closed behind her, and when the sound of her footsteps disappeared, I walked to the mirror.

But she was right, it had been fun.

The next day, just as Jude and I tilled the last bit of soil in one of the flower beds, the screen door opened.

"Lunchtime," Ben said through the screen. "If you like, you can eat in here."

We set down our tools, brushed our hands off, and followed him inside. The table was set with three bowls, steam rising off them, and three plates with grilled cheese sandwiches cut into triangles. My stomach grumbled.

Once we had scrubbed off the dirt that was caked under our fingernails, Jude and I sat down on either side of the small table, and the three of us dug in. It was tomato soup, mozzarella cheese already melted into the rich, creamy red. The smell reminded me of when I had been sick last year.

Everyone else went to school except, of course, Henry, who hadn't started yet. But Mom had sent him over to one of his friend's houses for the day.

I lay on the couch, my nose red and stuffed up, my throat scratchy, and my head aching. I remember how Mom covered me up with a thick red blanket and sat down on the couch so that my feet were resting on her lap. We watched the cartoon channel together, her hand on my feet. I must have fallen asleep, because the next thing I knew she was gently pushing my hair away from my eyes and whispering my name.

"Sunday? Wake up and try to eat something, sweetie."

I sat up, trudged over to the table, and sat down next to Mom. I sipped my tomato soup as she told me about the day I was born. I'd heard it before, but usually it got mixed up in the jumble of prying questions from my siblings, who wanted her to tell their stories. She still didn't get to finish that day because Dad had walked in, his clothes and hair white with dust.

"I came home for lunch to see how my Sunday was doing," he said, kissing my forehead.

"I'm okay."

We ate lunch together, just me and my parents. After

I was done, I slept until my brothers and sisters came home. Even though I had been sick, I loved that day.

A loud slurp from Jude brought me back to the present.

"So," I said, "how is your day going?"

Ben took a bite of his grilled cheese sandwich. "Fine."

"Good."

Silence.

The rest of lunch was similar. I asked generic questions, Ben gave convenient, one-word answers, and after the plates were set in the sink I was no closer to befriending him than I was before lunch.

I needed to find something that he'd want to talk about. I needed to switch strategies.

"Thank you for lunch," I said, walking casually around the room. I looked at the various small pictures I hadn't seen the other day. One was of him standing in front of the Eiffel Tower in Paris, another was a picture of a big ornate clock I didn't recognize, and a third was a picture of him waving from in front of the Taj Mahal.

"Is this you in all these pictures?" I asked, though I already knew the answer was yes.

Mr. Folger nodded and smiled slightly.

"Which one was your favorite?"

"India." There was no hesitation in his voice. "There's a magic in India that you can't really explain. The colors, the people, the beauty, the ugliness—all of it mixed together."

Encouraged that he was talking more, I asked, "Can I look at your books again?"

"Anytime." I heard the chair squeak across the floor. "So, what grade are you two in?"

Letting Jude answer, I bent down, my eyes scanning the very bottom shelf until they landed on a long white book with a spine that read: ALMA AREA HIGH SCHOOL 1962

I turned my back toward the table and pulled the book from off the shelf. Flipping quickly through the black-and-white glossy photos of girls wearing dresses and bobby socks and boys in shirts and ties, I reached the section where the individual senior pictures were. There was Ben Folger, smiling into the camera, his hair rich and dark and his smile warm yet serious.

"What are you looking at, Sunday?" Jude asked.

I jumped a little and turned the page quickly. "Just some books." I pulled another down from the shelf, looking at it briefly, and then put it back.

As Jude launched into a description of my mom, dad, and each of my siblings, I flipped through the candid shots, slowly this time, trying to spot Ben Folger again.

I found him on page 75.

At first I had turned past it, but Ben Folger's wide smile—the one I had only seen once or twice—was unmistakable.

The caption was simple. "Friendship: longtime friends

and fellow seniors LEE WREN and BEN FOLGER get some laughs in the school library, where the two of them volunteer."

Lee Wren? *The* Lee Wren?

I glanced behind me at Ben Folger and then back at the yearbook picture one more time. He and Lee Wren were standing in front of a circulation desk in a library, a stack of books piled to one side. They were both smiling warmly into the camera, their faces leaning in toward each other.

I flipped to the W's. "Wagley, Whanter, Wistorn, Wolf," I whispered. "Wren, Lee."

She looked a little like the picture hanging in the library: the same smile, the same full cheeks, the same arched eyebrows, but her hair was long and pulled off her face, and there weren't any wrinkle lines around her smile or on her forehead.

Ben Folger obviously had known her better than he was letting on.

"So," I said, hoping to sound casual. "I read more of *The Life and Death of Birds*. I wish I had gotten to meet Lee Wren."

Ben Folger gave a "Hmm."

He wasn't taking my bait. I was just going to have to ask. "You knew Lee Wren, right, Mr. Folger?"

He swallowed and nodded.

"I'd love to hear about her."

Ben walked into the kitchen and came back with a plate of cookies. "I bought some cookies at the store yesterday. Would either of you want any?"

Jude's eyes lit up. "Yeah, sure."

Ben set the plate down, reached for a cookie, and took a big bite.

"Please," I asked. "I really like her book and since she lived here and you knew her could you just tell us any little thing that you know?"

Ben dabbed at his mouth. "When she came to town she was professional and kind, and everyone loved her appearance at the library. But she kept to herself." He got up and walked to the window. "That's about all."

"You didn't know her better than that?"

He turned and looked at me, his glance moving from my face to the yearbook in my lap. His shoulders slouched a little. "I knew her in high school. But . . . that was a long time ago."

It was the first time—seeing him standing there looking at me—that I understood what my mom had said: maybe he was just a lonely old man.

He wasn't a killer. He didn't eat raw meat, and there wasn't any curse. He even seemed to like having Jude and me over, though he was out of practice when it came to having company. Maybe that was it. He was lonely and out of practice. Anyone would be. He lived in this house all by himself. No neighbors. No pets.

Maybe he just needed a friend.

"Did she write any other books besides that one?" Jude asked, interrupting my thoughts.

"No, that was her only published book." He said it matter-of-factly.

"Really?" I didn't try to hide my disappointment. "I was looking forward to reading another one by her."

"The whole world felt that way." Ben picked up the plate of cookies and started toward the kitchen. "I'm getting a little tired now. Why don't you two finish up out there? I think you'll be done by the afternoon."

I echoed Jude's thank-you and followed him to the door.

Lonely. Out of practice. Need to get around people.

I turned. "Mr. Folger? Ben?"

He stopped, the cookie plate still in his hands. He did look tired. "Yes?"

"Do you want to come to my house for dinner tonight?"

He looked surprised and a little confused, and I thought he was going to say yes. But, just as quickly, he shook his head no. "I don't think so, Sunday. Thank you. I'm . . . well, I'm just a bit too tired, and I don't think–"

I wasn't going to let him back out so easily. "My mom

is a really good cook. I don't know what she's making yet, but she always makes enough, and I"–I tried to slow myself down–"I know you'll have fun."

"That's very nice, but no thank you. I'm going to lie down. You two better get busy."

I grabbed Jude's arm as soon as the door closed behind us. "Will you start on the flower bed? I'll be right back."

"What are you going to do?"

"Ask my mom to call him to come over for dinner. I think he'll come if she asks."

Jude shrugged. "Okay. But hurry back. My arm is about to fall off as it is."

I dashed across the field. Mom, who said, "Why of course. Invite Jude as well. Now hand me the phone," turned to Miss Jenny and asked her if she'd like to join us for dinner, too. It was turning into a regular party.

I rushed back over to Ben's house and helped Jude finish up the flower bed. "My mom said you could come. I think she's going to call your mom and ask."

We finished the flower bed an hour later. After we put our trowel and shovel on the porch and washed our hands, I knocked on Ben's door.

"We finished the flower bed."

"Is that so?" He stepped out and looked at the freshly tilled soil. "Very nice."

"It was actually sort of fun," I said.

"It looks like I'll be seeing you two sooner rather than later. I think hamburgers and hot dogs are on the menu?"

I grinned.

"Cool. I'm coming, too," Jude piped in.

"I'll see you later on then." Ben walked back inside his house. "Thank you."

Jude and I bounded off the porch and across the field.

"He'll kill us all!" CJ said, grabbing ahold of his neck as if he couldn't breathe.

Mom sighed. "CJ, will you stop. He is not going to kill anyone."

"Yeah, he hasn't killed Sunday yet, right, Sunday?" Bo said, squeezing my hand.

I nodded. "He's really nice."

"And he makes really good brownies," Jude said.

CJ stuffed his walkie-talkie in his pocket and huffed. "Well, I'm going to carry this around with me. I have the police radio on station three so I can—"

Mom held out her hand. "Hand it over."

"But, Mom."

"I told you before, do not try and listen in on people, most of all the police. You could get in serious trouble."

"We'll all be in serious trouble if I don't keep it close. Besides, I promise I'll only listen a little bit."

"Hand. It. Over."

He plopped the walkie-talkie into Mom's hand, then slumped off outside. "I never have any fun."

Ben Folger arrived ten minutes before dinner carrying a small bouquet of flowers. He looked kind of uncomfortable in his button-up shirt and wrinkled pants, and smiled nervously.

"Hi, Ben," I said, leading him up the stairs to the house. "My mom's inside."

He coughed into his hand. "Oh, okay."

"You look nice."

He laughed a little bit and leaned down. "I haven't worn these pants or this shirt in over ten years."

I grinned but didn't mention the fact that I could tell.

Mom greeted him as soon as we walked through the door. "Thank you so much for coming, Mr. Folger."

"Call me Ben, please." He held out the bouquet of flowers to her. "Thank you for the invitation."

"Hi, Ben," Jude said, staggering toward him—Henry clinging to his right leg.

"Hello, Jude. It looks like you have a stowaway."

Henry tucked his head out of sight.

"That's my youngest brother, Henry. This is Bo," I said as Bo rushed up and pressed himself against me.

"Hey." CJ walked over and gave Ben a good look up and down. "Can I see your cane?"

"CJ!" I scolded.

Ben handed my brother his cane. "So this is CJ?"

CJ tugged and pulled every which way.

"Are you looking for the knife I keep hidden? It's not there," Ben said, and winked. "It's in my other one."

CJ stared at him with wide eyes, then handed Ben back the cane. "Do you wanna sit next to me at dinner?"

Ben nodded. "Of course. I'd be happy to."

Dad came in then. "Hi, Ben," he said. "It's good to have you over." And he took him into the dining room, where Mom was chatting with Miss Jenny.

Jude walked up to me. "I never, ever would have believed that I'd be having dinner with Ben Folger."

"Yeah, it's crazy, isn't it?"

"You're doing it, Sunday," he said. "You brought the hermit out of his house and he's making friends."

Just then Mom called everyone in and we squished around the table. Dinner began, and it was chaos as usual.

May and Emma were fighting over some shirt.

"Mom, tell her it's mine," May whined.

"Is it?" Mom asked.

"Yeah," Emma said. "But it doesn't fit her anymore."

"Does too."

"Yeah, right."

I took a bite of my hamburger and watched as Henry dumped forkfuls of his peas onto the napkin in his lap.

I knew that later he'd carry the napkin outside and throw each and every pea onto the roof.

CJ and Bo spent every spare minute they could asking Ben Folger questions like: "Have you ever eaten a cat?" "What's in your basement?" and "Do you like raw meat?" before Mom threatened to make them clean the toilets.

After that, Miss Jenny talked to Ben about the library, something that seemed to make his face light up.

"I'd really like it if you could help me with a few things," Miss Jenny said. "I have some ideas for programs I want to start, but I'm not sure where to begin."

I watched Ben fiddle with his napkin. "Well, I don't know if I'd really be any help—"

"But you would. And I'd really appreciate it."

The rest of the conversation was lost when Henry toppled over his glass of milk.

"Sunday, could you help clean this up?" Mom asked, steering Henry toward me.

After mopping up my brother, throwing away his pea-filled napkin, and helping him into a new shirt, I found CJ in the bathroom preparing to give Bo a haircut.

"It can't be hard," he said. "Besides, Mom said that if we got gum stuck in our hair one more time, she'd just shave it—"

I noticed a thick wad of gum mashed into Bo's hair. At least I'd come before CJ took the buzzer to his head.

"I didn't mean to get it stuck, Sunday," Bo whimpered, hugging my waist. "Don't tell Mommy."

I sighed and said, "Just wait here," and went downstairs, where I secreted away a jar of peanut butter. By the time I was done getting the gum out and rinsing his hair a few times so it didn't smell like an old sandwich, the table was empty and Ben Folger was starting off toward his house, his silhouette barely visible in the dusk.

"He's leaving already?" I asked.

Mom smiled and waved to Miss Jenny, who had just hopped onto her bike and was riding away. "It's getting late and Ben said he needed to get back home. But he's stopping by the library to help out, so you'll see him then."

I'd missed everything! "And what about Jude?"

"He just left. Wally came by and got him. But he said he'll see you tomorrow." Mom turned toward me. "Why do you smell like peanut butter?"

I started back inside. "Don't ask."

"So where did you go last night?" Jude asked the next morning. The reopening party was in a little over a week and there were still a ton of books that needed to be logged into the computer and then shelved.

"Well, I cleaned up Henry, and then Bo had gum stuck in his hair. It was a mess. What did I miss?"

Jude shrugged and swallowed down a piece of chocolate chip muffin. "Not much. They just talked about the library a bunch. And Ben is coming over to help today."

"Yeah, that's what my mom said."

Ben Folger was already bent over a box of books when Jude and I walked into the library. Mom was helping Dad move some of the newly finished desks around, and Miss Jenny was sitting at the computer.

"Hi, Ben," I said, walking over to him.

"Hi, Sunday. Jude." He turned. "I think you'll like this one, too, CJ."

CJ? My brother who couldn't stand to read? My brother who had helped at the library only when he was forced to?

CJ strutted over to Ben with Bo and Henry. He took the book from Ben's hand and read the cover. "*Captain Underpants?*" He grinned and fanned out the pages.

"Yep, it's funny," Ben said.

"You read *Captain Underpants?*" I asked.

Ben nodded and winked at me. "I like to know what kids are reading these days."

"You know, Ben"—Miss Jenny looked up from her computer—"I'm going to need help with the kids' program. Would you be interested?"

He shrugged. "I don't know. I'm awful old and grouchy these days."

Miss Jenny laughed and then turned to Jude and me.

"Those stacks over there are all logged into the computer. Do you two want to help shelve them?"

When lunchtime came around, Jude and I went over to Ben's house and sat out on the porch and talked while we ate peanut butter and jelly sandwiches. And that night, he had all of us over to his house for dinner.

The lasagna he made was kind of burnt in places. But me, Jude, and my brothers got to look down in Ben's basement, which was a big disappointment for CJ.

"Not even one single bone or instrument of torture," he whined on the way home.

The next two days went the same way, working in the morning, talking in the afternoon. The mysterious manuscript and the letters still bounced around in my head, but I hardly had time to think about them with the work at the library and afternoons with Ben and Jude. But on the third day, when Muzzy came over to the library carrying a blueberry pie, I realized I needed to get back to my investigation.

She pushed through the library door. "Yoo-hoo!"

"Hi, Muzzy," I said, and waved.

She just about dropped the pie all over the polished floors when she saw Ben Folger. "Land sakes! What's he doing here?"

She left a little while later, promising Ben Folger and Miss Jenny their own pies.

By that afternoon, half the town had "dropped by" and I watched as Ben Folger gave his shy smile as he separated and shelved books.

"Your brothers and sisters and your mom and dad, Sunday," Ms. Bodnar said, "why you all seem to have performed quite a miracle. And that brother of yours, CJ, seems completely taken with him. Who would've thought–?"

But the rest of her words were lost to me.

My brothers and sisters.

My mom and dad.

CJ.

I was lost in the shuffle again. Sure, I was happy that Ben Folger was smiling and talking and sort of making friends. But knowing how hard I'd worked–the cookies, the spying, the gardening, inviting him over for dinner– and my family getting the credit, I felt like I was back on the orange bench at the gas station, blending into the background.

If only I was someone that really *was* special. Like Harry Potter finding out he was a wizard or Matilda finding out she had a secret power. It would be so much easier to stand out.

But I was just Sunday.

Jude tugged on my arm, and I blinked back to reality. "Are you okay?"

I had to do something. "Bye, Ms. Bodnar. Come on, Jude, we have stuff we have to do."

I pulled him toward the house.

"Where are we going?"

"To my room."

"Sunday!" Great. Bo had spotted me. I ignored him and sped up.

"Wait up, Sunday!"

What was the use? "What do you want, Bo?"

He shrank back a little bit, but I couldn't find it in me to feel sorry. "I . . . what are you doing?"

"Nothing. Jude and I have some things we need to do. Alone." I started up the porch stairs.

Bo's footsteps slapped after me. "I won't get in the way. Promise."

"No, Bo!" I yelled. I stopped. I never yelled at Bo.

His eyebrows scrunched together. "You don't have to be mean. Maybe CJ's right. Maybe you are getting old and boring like May and Emma."

I felt horrible. "Bo. I'm sorry I yelled. Jude and I just need to do something for a second." I went to Bo, kneeling down and wrapping him in a hug. "We'll be down in a little bit. And . . . tonight you can sleep up in my room again and I'll tell you a story."

"The story about Lilly and Mark?"

I smiled. "Yeah, that one. Okay?"

Bo shrugged and said, "All right," as he started off toward the woods, where I could hear the banging of CJ's hammer.

Jude and I raced up to my room.

"So what's this about?" Jude asked.

I pulled out the manuscript from beneath my mattress, "This. I need to find out who wrote it. It's the only way that I'm going to make my mark."

"But you got Ben to come out like you wanted to."

"You heard Ms. Bodnar. It's just like how I told you it would be. My brothers and sisters got as much credit as I did. Nobody knows, or cares, what part I had in it."

Jude plopped onto the bed and flipped through some of the manuscript. "Tell them, then."

I paced the room and shook my head. "You don't understand. It doesn't work like that." I reached for the story and held it up. "This is what's going to help me stand out. Finding out who the author is."

"Okay," Jude said. "So what do we do now?"

I handed him the Librarian letters and then started reading the manuscript where I had left off.

Though she pretended to be fearless, there were times when Lilly found it hard to keep herself from shaking. Shaking and trembling like one of the last leaves of fall clinging to a branch.

She was not afraid of spiders or heights, not of swimming or performing, or even dying.

Thunderstorms—great gray clouds hanging in the sky, the rumbles and clapping of thunder and the sudden brightness of lightning—that truly terrified her. And no amount of wishing or thinking of other things could overcome her fear.

On a stormy afternoon when she was twelve years old Lilly finally smiled at the thunder and lightning. Well, perhaps not smiled. It was a grim determination that made her stand tall with fists clenched to face that storm.

Mark had tapped on her windowpane. She had been clutching a pillow when she looked over and saw him. He smiled and waved. What was he doing?

Mark fascinated Lilly. He seemed to fear only crowds of people. Even then, he walked through with a grace that always fooled everyone.

He tapped again, and Lilly rushed to the window. The smell of rain already saturated the air.

"Come on in, quick," she said, and slammed the window shut just as he pulled himself the rest of the way inside.

Mark's glasses fogged over and he took them off, rubbing them with his shirt. "My mom says it's going to be a big storm."

Lilly didn't answer. She turned her back on the dark afternoon and clutched the pillow tighter. "What do you want?" she asked, knowing she sounded harsh the moment the words left her lips.

Mark didn't notice. "I know you don't like storms, so I came over to keep you company."

Lilly hated when Mark knew things about her that she had never told him. "I never said that. I don't mind them . . . but they aren't my favorite."

He was silent for a moment, his blue eyes never leaving her face. "It's okay to be afraid."

"I'm not afraid!" she said.

A flash cut across the sky followed by a rumble of thunder. Lilly jumped, her knuckles whitening around the pillow.

Mark stood up and held out his hand.

"What are you doing?"

"We're going to go outside and dance in the rain."

"It's not just raining. It's like a tornado out there." A loud clap echoed from the outside.

"Then we'll sit on the porch and watch it come in. And then we'll dance in the rain."

I stopped reading. "Dancing in the rain."

Jude looked up at me. "Huh?"

"Isn't dancing in the rain in one of the letters?"

"Yeah. I just read that one. Here." He pulled out one of the yellowed letters and read aloud. "'Dear Librarian, today I took a walk in the park. To tell you the truth, I had not been to the park in a long while. I've hardly stepped outside, it has been so wet. I know you would remind me of how you made me dance in the rain with you when we were kids. Yes, though I blame you for the cold I got afterward.' Blah, blah, blah, 'Daisies and hearts, Me.'"

I was inching toward a discovery. "Listen to this." I read him the scene in the story.

"That could be something."

I grinned and clutched the manuscript to my chest. "I think it's definitely something."

19

JUDE and I headed toward town and passed a yard with those same crazy zigzags as the library grass.

"I guess it's the same guy that mows the lawn at the library."

Jude laughed. "You know it's Papa Gil who drives the mower, right?"

"No way!" I tried to imagine Papa Gil switching gears and zooming across the thick, green grass.

"Yeah. He used to work in a pit crew for some famous car racer a long time ago. Now he just races around the library and the cemetery."

"The cemetery?"

Jude nodded. "Yeah, it's right over there." He pointed to a wrought-iron archway leading to rows of gravestones dotted with flowers. "It sounds like he's there right now."

"Maybe we should ask him if he knows of anyone in town who writes," I suggested. "And I bet he would know if Muzzy had anything to do with the manuscript."

"Really, Sunday? Even after you read her article, you still think she could've written the story?"

I sighed. "I know it's not very likely, but we still need to find out definitely."

He shook his head and shrugged. "Okay."

The only cemetery I had ever been to had been my grandpa's. I remembered visiting his grave with my family. We had all placed something by the stone and then stood in awkward, sad silence. I'd left his favorite, a peanut butter cookie, wrapped in cellophane despite the fact that May told me I shouldn't because a bird would eat it. I remember thinking that it shouldn't matter since Grandpa wasn't going to eat it, either, but it made me upset to think that I didn't put something better down.

"It's very sweet, Sunday," Dad had said when he saw me reach down for the cookie. "It's the remembering that counts, and that comes in more ways than one."

As we walked through the gates, Jude pulled out two small pieces of wrapped chocolate from his pocket and held one worn piece out to me. I shook my head. *Gross.* He popped one into his mouth and looked to where the lawn mower flew across the ground. "There he is."

I shuddered as we crunched down the gravel path toward him, walking by the first row of names. Papa Gil spied us, turned off the mower, and stepped down.

"Hello, you two!" he said, hitching up his pants. "What brings you to the cemetery today?"

I decided to ask him about Muzzy first. "We read Muzzy's article in the newspaper the other day."

He rubbed his hand over his thinning gray hair. "She didn't put in anything about your family that you didn't like, did she?"

"No, not at all," I said. "Jude and I were just surprised when we saw that she wrote for the paper."

"Yes, the editor lets my Muzzy write an article each week. I admit she isn't the best writer out there, but she does love it, and her eyes shine and sparkle every Friday when the paper gets tossed on our doorstep."

"That's great," I said, then knocked Jude with my elbow. "Isn't it, Jude?"

"Yeah, great."

"So did she just start writing, then?"

"Well, let's see." He looked off in the distance, shielding his eyes from the sun, which was now peeking out through little holes in the clouds. "She's probably been writing for the paper for the past six months or so."

"Has she ever written anything longer?"

"Not that I know of. Why?"

I shrugged. "Oh, just asking."

"The only person in Alma that I know of who wrote

anything longer than an article was Lee Wren. *The Life and Death of Birds.* Now, that was a brilliant book."

Papa Gil was the second person to describe Lee Wren as brilliant. "I'm actually reading it right now."

He grinned. "Is that so? Do you want to know where her grave is?" He started off down one of the gravel paths before we could answer.

I hadn't even considered that she might be buried in Alma. Weaving in and out among the tombstones, I glanced briefly at the bouquets of flowers, their ribbons droopy from the morning dew. A few flags hung limply, sad but no less proud looking.

Papa Gil stopped and pointed at a simple gray gravestone. "That's it, right there."

The first thing I noticed was the daisy lying right in front of the stone, the bright white and yellow stark against the deep green of the grass. "The daisy is pretty," I said. I'd always thought of daisies as sort of plain flowers. But delicate against the grass, it looked perfect.

"One of her fans probably left it for her," Jude said.

Papa Gil shook his head and rubbed his chin. "Truth is, for as long as I've been helping take care of the grounds, every time I come, and I usually come pretty early, there's a single daisy lying in front of the stone. Even in the winter. Of course, sometimes it's a different flower."

"Really? Every morning?"

Papa Gil nodded. "Well, I'm not here every morning. But I come a few times a week and there's always a daisy. Curious thing, but I figure that if someone wants privacy, well then, I should give it to him." Papa Gil smiled, bent down, and wiped the misty dew from one of the petals. "And I like seeing the flowers."

"Thanks for showing us, Papa Gil," I said.

He nodded and smiled. "You're welcome. Now, I better finish the rest of my mowing before Joanne comes looking for me. Make sure you two stop by and see us soon. We restocked all our treats last night."

"More candy?" Jude asked as if maybe Papa Gil had a cupcake wrapped in cellophane stuffed in his pocket.

"Yep, all kinds."

"Thanks, we'll stop by soon," I said. We both watched Papa Gil walk back to his mower, start it up, and zoom off down the grassy straightaway. I turned back to the grave.

"'Lee Amelia Wren,'" I read aloud.

Jude was busy unwrapping the other chocolate. I rolled my eyes and continued.

"'Born 1944–Died 1995. Beloved author to the world and treasured friend to one.'" The next words stopped my heart in my chest. "'Daisies and hearts.'"

Jude's head snapped up as I read the words aloud. "Where have I heard that?"

"'Daisies and hearts,'" I repeated, unable to keep myself

from jumping up and down on my toes. "From the letters, remember? To the Librarian. They always ended with the words *daisies and hearts*. Do you—"

Jude stared at the gravestone, the chocolate square a lump in his cheek. "You don't think? I mean . . . letters . . . written by Lee Wren. *The* Lee Wren? Sunday, that would be . . . that would be huge."

"I know, I know."

A new vision filled my head. It wasn't just a headline in the *Alma Gazette*. It was me, sitting on the comfy red couch on the *Morning Show*, telling the hostess, Janey Price, about what I'd found and how I'd found it. My parents and brothers and sisters would be waiting backstage in the dressing room while the world memorized my face. SUNDAY ANNIKA FOWLER, THE GIRL WHO FOUND PRIVATE LETTERS FROM THE FAMOUS AUTHOR LEE WREN. With these letters I didn't even need the manuscript.

"Of course, we have to find more proof that the letters are hers," I said. "Maybe the person who leaves a daisy by the grave every day knows for sure."

Jude gave a small laugh and looked around. "So what are we supposed to do to catch this person? You heard Papa Gil, he's never even seen who does it, and he's been working here since forever."

I bent down and felt the soft grass beneath me.

"What are you doing?"

"It won't be like a mattress, but it'll do."

Jude bent down next to me. "Do for what, Sunday?"

"I think that'll work. The person won't be able to get around us without being seen. We'll bring flashlights and drink lots of soda so we can stay up—"

"No, you don't mean we're going to . . ." Jude stopped.

I looked at him and smiled. "It's perfect, Jude."

"But we'll be sleeping in a cemetery!" he yelled.

I started walking away from the grave. "Come on, we have a lot to get ready."

20

TO KEEP CJ from following us to the cemetery that night, I had to bribe him with ice cream.

"I'll try a different flavor every day," he said, pacing back and forth across my bedroom floor. "Double scoop, sugar cone. Sprinkles. The double scoop is nonnegotiable."

"Okay, okay."

He eyed me warily, then stuck out his hand. "First ice cream cone tomorrow. Shake on it."

I took his hand and shook hard. It would cost all my money. But getting credit for discovering Lee Wren's letters would be worth it.

The cemetery was blacker than black when we walked through the archway that night. The moon was covered by a thick layer of clouds, and I said a quick prayer that we wouldn't get rained on. Persuading Jude had been hard. If it rained, there was no way he'd stay.

Jude walked beside me in a rain jacket, hat, gloves, rain boots, and a backpack with seams pulled taut by all the stuff he'd packed. I had a flashlight, a disposable camera (for taking pictures of the secret person), a sleeping bag, a notebook and pen, *The Life and Death of Birds*, snacks, and a rain jacket. I had almost brought the letters, but I needed them in pristine condition if I was going to show them to newspapers and TV crews.

We moved as silently as we could across the gravel paths, to the grave.

"This is so creepy," Jude whispered. The orange-yellow beam of his flashlight bounced off the headstones and gave an eerie glow to the foggy night around us.

"Turn it off and then we won't think about the graves."

He gave a snort. "How could we not think about the graves when we're sleeping in a graveyard?"

"You know what I mean. Just turn it off."

He clicked the flashlight off, and the night thickened. I tried to ignore the creepiness and unzipped my backpack, pulling out my sleeping bag and laying it behind the stone so we couldn't be seen. Jude did the same.

"Now what?" he asked.

"We wait."

The trees rustled. A car drove by on the road below. A bird cawed loudly from somewhere in the black. I shivered and hugged my knees to my chest. I tried to remember why I had thought this was a good idea.

Jude broke the silence. "We have to do something, Sunday, or we'll go crazy."

"You're right. But I don't know—"

"I have snacks," he said. "I packed a bunch." I heard him unzip his backpack and then the loud crinkle of a bag. He threw something into my lap. "Here's some chips."

"Does your mom know about these?"

He crunched down on one. "She usually buys veggie chips. I bought these with my leftover birthday money."

"Ah, I see." I opened the crinkly bag and crunched down on a single salty chip.

We sat and talked. Jude told me about how long it had been since he'd heard from his dad.

"It was my fifth birthday." Jude's voice trembled and I was glad I couldn't see his face. "Dad sent me a card and told me that he was going to take me to California to see the surfers, and then we were going to go to Legoland. He said that we'd stay up late every night and swim in the ocean as much as I wanted." There was the rustle of his chip bag and a hearty *crunch-crunch-crunch-crunch.*

"Then what?"

"It never happened. No California, or Legoland, or

surfers. He never even wrote back after that. No calls. No visits. Nothing." He sighed and faked a yawn. "But I don't care. Whatever."

"How long has Wally been around?" I asked.

"About three years, I guess."

"And you still haven't given him a chance?"

"Why should I?"

I chose not to answer that one. "Has he asked your mom to marry him?"

"Nope. And he won't unless I say it's okay. That's what he told me."

"And he's still around? Jude, Wally adores you and your mom. Think about it. If he didn't, he would've been long gone by now."

There was silence, and I hoped that I hadn't made him mad. I didn't want him to leave me alone out here. "Jude?"

"You really think he might?" His voice was small, and the words were delicate as a spiderweb, like he was afraid the possibility of it being true could blow away at any moment.

"Yeah, I do."

He sniffled, but I ignored it and made a bunch of noise with my now-empty bag.

"So, what about you, Sunday? To me, it doesn't seem like you're invisible to your family."

I laughed. "Are you kidding me? Sure, sometimes my

parents get my name right the first time. But you've heard them. And then there's the whole gas station thing."

"Gas station thing? What's that?"

So I told him what had happened at the gas station when we were coming to Alma. "They never even realized I was gone. They still don't know."

"Oh," he said. "That's a bummer."

"Yeah, just a little." Sarcasm dripped off my words.

"And you haven't told them?"

"No, why should I? They should've realized and apologized." I sighed. I wanted to tell my parents, but then again . . . I didn't. "I don't want them to pay attention to me just because they feel bad, or just to try and make it all better. That's why I need to do something that will make sure getting left behind never happens again."

"Don't you think it was just a mistake? A bad one, sure, but still just a mistake."

I crinkled up the chip bag and stuffed it into my backpack. "Of course it was a mistake. I know that. It's just that it wouldn't've happened with CJ, or Bo, or Henry, or my sisters. CJ is always so funny and loud that he'd never be forgotten. Bo's the sweetest of all of us, Henry is the youngest and cutest, and Emma and May are both pretty and talented. Me? I'm just easy to look over and forget."

"Oh, come on, Sunday. I get what you're saying about

the boys because they're still pretty little. But I bet it could've happened to one of your sisters."

I shook my head hard. "No way. Never. But forget about it. It doesn't matter. I'm the one that got left behind and now I've got to make myself be recognized."

"But—"

"It doesn't matter what I do, okay?" I yelled. "No one ever sees me."

"I see you." His words were gentle and quiet.

My heart stuttered. I didn't know what to say.

"And I'm sure your parents do, too," he continued. "They just don't show it enough." He sighed. "But either way, we're here and we'll stay awake and find out who is leaving the flowers for Lee Wren and we'll get all the other evidence you need to prove that the letters are hers."

I felt my cheeks flush despite the cool air. "You know, Jude, you didn't have to start helping me . . . but thanks. Really, I—"

"Of course," he cut in. "Do you want a Twizzler?"

I clicked on my flashlight and took one from the bag he held out. "Thanks."

As we kept talking—about movies, school, and friends— I felt like something was different with us now.

We were officially friends, and I found myself liking that very much.

~~~~~

After a while, we both felt like we were going to have to prop open our eyeballs to stay awake. I yawned. "Maybe we should take turns sleeping."

Jude yawned back. "Yeah, that sounds good. It's only one o'clock. I don't think I could make it until the morning right now."

We agreed to take two-hour shifts, and because I drew the short Twizzler, I got stuck with the first watch. Jude settled into his sleeping bag next to me, mumbled a good night, and was out like a light a few minutes later.

I leaned back against the gravestone, then shivered and sat back up. That was too weird. I pulled out *The Life and Death of Birds* from my backpack and clicked on my flashlight. Reading would take my mind off the cemetery.

A twig snapped.

I jumped, my heart leaping and the book falling into the grass. I picked it up.

No, Sunday, stop. You're fine.

Leaves rustled.

You're sleeping in a cemetery.

A dog barked.

There are dead people beneath you, right now. You know that, right?

I took a deep breath in, tried to steady my racing heart, and wrapped my sleeping bag tight around my shoulders. I wanted to get inside it, but I was counting on the chilly air to keep me awake. I tried to focus on Jude's breathing and not on the sounds of the dark around me. I swept my flashlight across the blackness.

Nothing but foggy shadows and headstones.

Click.

I rested my head on my knees again.

Dead people sleeping beneath you.

Sleeping beneath you.

Sleeping beneath.

Sleeping.

I awoke to a beam of light shining directly into my eyes. "Cut it out, Jude," I moaned. The light seemed to brighten. Blinking, I sat up and looked around me. The sun was warm on my cheek, dew covered my sleeping bag, and Jude was still snoring beside me.

The sun!

I shook Jude awake. "Hey, Jude! Jude! Wake up! Did you see anyone?"

He rubbed his eyes, yawned, then sat up next to me, glancing around with a confused look on his face.

"Did you see anything?" I asked again.

"What?" his voice was gravelly with sleep. "No. I don't think I ever woke up."

"Drat! I must've fallen asleep." Looking at the gravestone, I groaned at the single daisy lying serenely on the grass, the old one gone. "Drat, drat, drat!"

Jude looked at the daisy and winced. "Oh, no."

How could I have fallen asleep? How? This was important and still I'd completely slept through the mysterious person walking right up and placing the daisy by the gravestone. I stuffed my sleeping bag back into my backpack, furious with myself.

Jude cleaned up all of his things in silence, knowing enough to keep his mouth shut. I was thankful for that, because I was afraid that I might bite his head clean off if he tried to utter a single word.

It wasn't until we reached his road that Jude broke the quiet. "Luckily, it's still pretty early," he said. "My mom won't be up for another hour or so. You think you'll make it back into your house without getting seen?"

"Yeah," I said. "It'll be easy. I'm invisible, remember?"

And with the reopening party getting even closer, if I didn't have another breakthrough soon, invisible was all I was ever going to be.

21

CAREFUL to keep from stepping on the creaky parts of the stairs, I snuck up to my room and flopped onto my bed, immediately falling into a restless sleep.

I dreamt that I had climbed Mount Everest, but when I finally reached the top, out of breath, tired, and hungry, I saw that CJ, Henry, and Bo were already standing by the flag, which Emma had sewn by hand.

"I can't believe we're the first ones to reach the top!" CJ said. "And now we have time to build a fort."

"I wanna build a fort with you, CJ," Bo said.

Then our van appeared. May honked the horn, screeched to a stop, and held up her license. "Excuse me," she called, sticking her head out the window. "I'm the first one to *drive* to the top of Mount Everest." Then Jude and Emma got out of the backseat and smiled.

"We're getting married," Emma announced, showing off the ugliest ring I had ever seen in my entire life.

A crowd of people appeared, cheering, and pressing

forward toward my family, microphones outstretched
and cameras ready.

"Wait!" I yelled. But in the bustle of everyone talking
at once and trying to take pictures, someone accidentally
pushed me off the side of the mountain.

I was falling, falling, falling.

"Sunday."

My eyes flew open and I jerked upright.

"Sorry," Mom said. "I didn't mean to startle you." She
sat down on the edge of my bed and smoothed my hair
off my forehead. Pressing her palm against my skin she
asked, "Are you feeling all right?"

I nodded and rubbed my eyes. Clouds had moved in,
covering the sun that had woken me earlier at the cemetery. Happy screams echoed outside followed by the
familiar sound of an engine starting and restarting.

"Yeah, I think so." The feeling of falling still clung to
me, and I pressed my hands into the mattress to ground
myself. "I'm just tired."

"Why don't you come have a little breakfast? You can
give Jude a break. Henry has become his shadow."

I yawned and stood. "I'll be down in a minute."

When the door closed, I slipped into a pair of shorts
and a clean T-shirt, and brushed my teeth. I thought of
my dream. Of course I knew that I'd never be pushed off
the top of Mount Everest.

But I couldn't let myself be forgotten again.

A screech came from outside and I glanced out. Jude was swinging Henry in the hammock while CJ stood over a big hole he'd dug. It was only one of a dozen others. Mom and Dad were going to love that.

My gaze rested on Ben Folger's house. Ben knew more about Lee Wren than he was letting on. I just needed to find a way to get him to spill his information.

I was almost positive that I had her letters.

That meant I was one step closer to the front page of the newspaper. One step closer to making my mark. One step closer to never being invisible again.

Downstairs, I made toast, set the pieces on a paper towel, and walked outside.

"Sunday!" Bo squealed, dashing over to me. "You slept forever and ever this morning." He collided with my toast, shoving the buttery pieces onto my reading-award T-shirt.

"Bo!" I yelled. Peeling him off me, I let the toast fall to the ground. "Look what you did! My shirt is probably ruined."

"I'm sorry, Sunday," he said.

Why couldn't he be more careful? "This was my favorite shirt."

Bo stepped back. "But you used to like it when I hugged you."

"Bo—"

The screen door opened and Mom stepped outside. "What's going on?"

I held out my shirt so she could see the greasy streaks. "Bo just completely ruined it."

"I didn't mean to."

"Now, now, it's probably not ruined, Sunday. Go upstairs and change. I'll take care of your shirt."

I scowled once more at Bo and then dashed back up to my room and tugged a different T-shirt over my head—one that I didn't really like—and slumped back outside.

I scanned the scene for Bo and found him, shovel in hand, helping CJ with one of the holes. Feeling guilty, I walked over to him. "Hey, Bo. Sorry for getting mad. But you need to be more careful next time."

He shrugged but didn't look at me. "Okay."

"Hi, Sunday." Jude pushed the hammock forward.

"Hey." I kept my eyes on Bo, who was attempting to stick his shovel in the ground. It barely sliced into the dirt. "Here, Bo. I'll help." I took the shovel and drove it deep into the dirt with my foot, then lifted up a thick clod and flung it off to the side.

"SUNDAY FOWLER!" Mom yelled from the porch. "What on earth are you doing?"

"I was—" I started.

"You know better. Now, fill that back in right now."

"But—"

"Now!"

What was the use in even trying to explain myself? I sighed, tossed the dirt clod back in the small hole, and patted it down with the back of the shovel. Of course, she didn't see the dozens of holes that CJ had already dug.

"Thanks, Sunday," Bo said, flashing me his usual grin.

"Glad I could help." I handed the shovel back to him and walked over to Jude. The day wasn't starting off very well, and I just wanted to get going.

"So guess what I'm going to do this afternoon?" Jude said, heaving the hammock forward as Henry squealed.

"What?"

"Wally is going to take me into the city to meet one of his friends, who's an architect."

"Really?"

I could tell from the huge grin on Jude's face that he was more than just a little excited. "He'd mentioned it to me before, but I just thought, *Yeah, right.* Then this morning at breakfast he called his friend and now we're going to his office sometime after lunch. Cool, huh?"

I smiled. "Yeah, that is really cool. So before we go over to Ben's, do you think we could stop by your house and look up something on your computer?"

"Sure." Jude slowed down the hammock and let Henry jump off. Henry gave Jude a quick hug and then followed after CJ, who was most likely going to the backyard to dig holes where he wouldn't be seen.

I hoped he got caught.

Jude sat down at his computer and clicked on the Internet. "Are we looking up something on Lee Wren?"

"Yeah."

His fingers flew across the keyboard and he clicked on one of the sites that had appeared.

"'Author Lee Wren (1944–1995) was born in Alma, Pennsylvania, the only child of Elizabeth and Edward Wren,'" he read aloud. "'Her first and only published work, *The Life and Death of Birds*, won the National Book Prize in 1969, among numerous other awards. The book was named a modern-day classic by the National Library Guild. Despite the great fame and success of her book, Lee Wren remained very private, rarely making appearances and declining interviews. Though it was said that she continued to write, another novel has never been found, much to the regret of her fans. She died in 1995 at the age of fifty-one and was buried in Alma.'"

Jude stopped reading and turned to me. "It doesn't say anything about letters."

"Of course it doesn't. Those were private letters." I paced the room. "It says that she never published another book. That doesn't mean that she didn't write one. Maybe the—"

"You don't think that the manuscript could be hers, too, do you?"

I shrugged. "I don't know. Maybe. I mean, there was the mention of Orion's Belt in the letters and in the story, and the dancing in the rain, and remember how both of them were locked away in the library together?"

Jude clicked off the Internet and swiveled around to look at me. "I don't want to be negative or anything, but the author of the manuscript could still be anyone."

"I know. I know. Still, wouldn't that be amazing? I'd have her private letters and a secret manuscript." There would be no chance that anyone would forget me after that. "I think that if we can find out who the Librarian is, that person will be able to tell us for sure about the manuscript."

"I think you're right," Jude said, standing. "Now what?"

"Well, maybe Muzzy and Papa Gil knew Lee Wren a little bit," I said. "We could go ask them."

"Good idea. And Papa Gil said yesterday that they just restocked their candy, so that's a bonus."

We walked into the thrift store, the gentle clanging bell above the door welcoming us inside.

Muzzy waved from the back, and Mr. Castor barreled toward us, his tail wagging, slobber dripping from his mouth, and tufts of hair flying through the air.

"Down, Mr. Castor," Muzzy said in a voice that sounded like she was trying to be stern even though it wasn't really stern at all. Mr. Castor ignored her, grabbing a shoe from off the nearest rack, and dashed to the back of the store. "Mr. Castor! You bring that back."

Jude and I could hear Mr. Castor's nails clicking and sliding on the wood floor and see Muzzy's curly white head barely skimming the top of the racks of clothing.

"I give up." She sighed, appearing down one of the aisles. "Come on back, you two," she beckoned, reaching for the bowl piled high with candy. The shoe still hung from Mr. Castor's mouth. After he was sure Muzzy wasn't going to chase him again, he settled down on the floor and started gnawing on it. "What can I help you two with?"

"Well," I said, pulling out a strawberry lollipop. "Jude and I were wondering if you ever knew Lee Wren. You know, the famous author."

"Oh, Lee, yes. At least, a very little bit. I think Ben Folger knew her fairly well. People said he moved away so that he could be closer to her. But I never believed it."

Jude and I looked at each other. Ben Folger and Lee

Wren? I had seen the picture of them in the yearbook, but Ben Folger was no Prince Charming.

"She visited town every so often—doing small appearances at the library, things like that. She kept to herself mostly, but was always pleasant when you did see her. Sad when she died. She's buried here, you know. The town did a big to-do, and there were all sorts of folks that came from all over to attend the service. You know, she had the prettiest little necklace. It was a small heart on a gold chain. I asked her where she got it once, when I met her in the grocery store. She was buying up all the cartons of blueberries, so I knew that her book must be doing well since blueberries are always ridiculously expensive. My sister, she lives in Washington State, she said that blueberries are—" Muzzy stopped and smiled. "Sorry, I get a little carried away sometimes. I asked Lee, 'Where did you get your necklace?' And she said, 'I got it from a friend who went to India.' It was so pretty."

India.

The photograph of Ben Folger standing in front of the Taj Mahal snapped inside my head. He'd been to India.

I glanced over at Jude, but he was still too busy pawing through the candy to know what was going on. "Did she say who this friend was?"

Muzzy squinted her eyes, her brows crinkling in

concentration. "No, I don't think so. But I liked to think it was from a secret love."

"Anything else? Did she write more?"

Muzzy shook her head. "I wouldn't know that." She stopped suddenly like she'd remembered something. "And fresh flowers. She seemed to love fresh flowers."

"Do you know what kind?"

Muzzy shrugged. "If she's anything like me, then she probably liked just about any kind of flower."

I smiled and nodded. "Thanks, Muzzy."

"Is there anything else you two need?"

I nudged Jude's arm. "No, that's all, I think," he said, deciding on a small Snickers bar. "Thanks."

"Anytime."

Just then Mr. Castor bounded forward, the now-torn shoe dangling from his mouth.

"Oh, Mr. Castor!" Muzzy cried, trying to pry the wet leather away from him. "That was very naughty of you. Very, very naughty. What will Gil say?"

"I think he likes to be chased." I said. "I know my dog does—she thinks it's a game. So I don't think you should chase him. And if he does grab something he isn't supposed to, try a command like 'leave it' and offer him a treat, like a small bone, instead. Then he'll know that if he does drop it, he'll get a treat. It might take him a little while to learn, but he'll get it eventually. Butters did."

Muzzy ruffled Mr. Castor's furry head. "I'm willing to try anything. Thank you, Sunday."

I shrugged. "Sure." After saying good-bye, Jude and I stepped out onto the sidewalk.

"I think we know where to go now," I said.

"Where?"

"Were you really not paying attention to anything except the candy?"

"Just not as much as you were."

"We need to go to Ben Folger's house."

"Oh, yeah."

"We need to ask him more about Lee Wren. I think Ben Folger is the key."

22

BEN was sitting out on his porch swing, the metal chain creaking with each backward motion.

"Hello, you two!"

He walked down the porch stairs and pointed to two trays of flowers. "How would you like to help me plant these this morning?"

We both shrugged. "Sure."

He handed us each a shovel, then showed us how deep to dig before placing a plant in the soil and covering it loosely—but not too loosely.

"Is your mother dating the mechanic Wally Treewell?" Ben asked Jude.

Jude reached for a bright purple flower. "Yeah. They've been dating for a while."

"He's a good man," Ben said. "And I can't say that about many people. That Wally has his head screwed on right, and he's always done a good job on my car. Fair and honest."

Jude smiled and shrugged. "He's taking me to the city after lunch today to visit his friend who's an architect."

"Well, that's nice of him." He turned to me. "And you're probably getting ready to go back to Pittsburgh soon, is that right, Sunday?" he asked.

"Yeah."

"Have you liked Alma?"

"A lot."

"Your father's done a really good job at the library. I was thinking, I have some work around the house that needs doing. Maybe he could take a look?"

"He'd like that a lot, Ben," I said. "Thanks."

He nodded, then bent down again. "I've enjoyed getting to know you and your brothers and sisters."

"Yeah, most people do."

"I always wished that I had siblings. I had a friend growing up who had a big family. I used to like all the chaos. But I suppose that might get old after a while."

"A little."

"It seems like you all get along well, though."

Until recently, I'd never really gotten upset with Bo. And just the other night Emma and I had had so much fun together, and we usually fought the most. It was all so confusing. I shrugged. "For the most part, I guess."

He nodded and patted down the soil around one of the flowers.

It was funny. Most people asked me questions like Ben Folger's. Do you fight? Do you like your siblings?

They never asked if I felt lost in the crowd, or if I felt invisible. They never asked if I wished that for just one moment I could have my parents' attention all to myself.

We were finished in an hour or so. Ben brought out a pitcher of lemonade, I carried a plate piled high with marshmallow crispy treats, and Jude carried the glasses filled with ice.

"You should become a baker," Jude said, taking a gooey square. "Every day you make something delicious."

"Actually, before two kids ruined one of my flower beds, I don't think I ever baked much of anything." He winked. Jude and I looked at each other and smiled.

"So how long were you a librarian?" Jude asked.

Ben gazed off across the field at the library. "Fifteen years there. Then I . . . I moved for a little while. I came back about twenty years ago."

I took a sip of lemonade. "Where did you move to?"

"New York City," he said. "A far cry from quiet little Alma, but nice in its own way."

I nodded solemnly, though my insides were screaming. He had to be the Librarian in the letters and the person that left a daisy by Lee Wren's grave every day. If anyone knew about another manuscript that she had written, it would be him.

Still, it was obvious that he didn't want to talk about Lee Wren. I decided to try a different angle.

"I'm still reading Lee Wren's book," I said. I hadn't picked it up in a few days, but if the manuscript tucked under my bed was Lee Wren's, then it wasn't really a lie.

"That's good," Ben said.

"Yeah, I really wish she had written another one." I knocked Jude gently with my foot.

He caught on and nodded. "Yeah, I wish she had, too."

Ben Folger eyed me over the lip of his glass. "Yes, it's a shame that she didn't."

"How do you know that she never wrote anything else?"

Ben Folger gulped down the rest of his lemonade. "Have you found something?"

"No," I said, hoping that my expression wasn't screaming YES! It's under my mattress at home! "I was just . . . wondering . . . since you two were friends."

"You know," he said, "the sun is getting a little too hot now. I think I might go in and rest. How about you two come back tomorrow for lunch?" Then he turned and walked inside the house, leaving us with the pitcher of lemonade and the plate of crispy treats.

"He definitely doesn't want to talk about her at all," Jude whispered, taking one last sip of his lemonade.

"I know. But don't you think that makes it even more likely that there was something between them? If there wasn't, then he wouldn't care about talking about her."

"Maybe. But since he's not going to help, we need to think of somewhere else we can get proof."

I wiped my forehead, squinting back across the field. It was getting hot. "Yeah, and the only place I can think of is the library."

23

JUDE and I parted ways when we crossed the field. "I'll see you tomorrow, right?" he called after me.

"Of course. Have fun with Wally."

I expected to walk in the house and find my siblings shuffling and scuffling around the table for lunch, but instead it was only Mom stirring a bowl of chicken salad at the kitchen counter.

"Where is everyone?" I asked.

She smiled. "They're all over at the library helping your dad. I told them I'd give them a ten-minute warning. Could you run over and help May carry up all the boxes on the table in the basement? I sorted through them yesterday and made piles for trash and recycling."

That's where I was going to look. "You didn't throw anything away yet, did you?"

She shook the saltshaker over the bowl and then opened a family-sized bag of chips. "Nope, that's what you're going to do."

I rushed out the door and down the stairs.

Flying across the grass to the library, I dashed up the stairs, pushed through the doors, then ran down to the basement. May was hefting a cardboard box.

"Oh good," she said, letting it drop on the table. "You can carry up the last one. It feels like Mom filled these boxes with bricks."

Standing on tiptoe, I saw the shiny metal box still sitting on the top shelf of the bookcase and sighed with relief. "So this is the last one?"

She rolled her eyes. "Didn't I just say that?"

I tried to hide my curiosity. "Sorry. Did you find anything interesting in the boxes?"

May examined her fingernails. "Not that I saw. Mostly just old papers and a few ancient cassette tapes."

"Cassette tapes?" I remembered seeing old tapes when I found the manuscript. They were in the cardboard box where I had tossed the letters the first time.

"Yeah," May said. "Somewhere in that box. If not, they're probably in a trash bag."

"Thanks." I shuffled toward the stairs, then turned. "Mom said it's almost lunchtime."

"Finally. She's had us working all morning."

When I reached the Dumpsters in the back of the library, I set the box down next to the others and sifted through a mess of old papers and broken pencils before finding two unlabeled cassette tapes. I dusted them off and carried them with me back to the house just as Mom rang the bell signaling that lunch was ready.

"Do you know where I can find a tape recorder, Mom?" I tried to make my voice rise above the din of the table, but I could tell she hadn't heard me. "Do you?" I asked louder.

"What? Henry, if you flush your sandwich down the toilet again, I will ground you until Christmas. Emma, I can help you with the costumes tonight, but only for a bit. Miss Jenny and I are going to finish shelving the last of the books. Yes, May, you and I can drive Emma tomorrow. Emma, don't make that face, she's getting much better. Bo, really, just eat the chicken salad, I promise there aren't any bones in it, and CJ, stop saying that the mayonnaise is liver juice, you're making me lose my appetite. Adam, can you pass the water pitcher?" She stopped to take a breath.

I took the pause to yell, "I said, Do you know where I can find a tape recorder?'"

Dad slathered a baby carrot with ranch dressing. "What do you need a tape recorder for?"

"I found some old tapes in the library and wanted to listen to them."

Mom was about to answer but stopped when she glanced over at CJ. "If you give one more bite to Butters under the table, you'll have chicken salad for breakfast, lunch, and dinner tomorrow. And you'll be cleaning up the dog's diarrhea when she gets an upset stomach."

CJ giggled. "Diarrhea. Diarrhea."

"CJ, I mean it!"

Dad swallowed some milk. "You didn't find one in the library?"

"No." I'd found old catalogues and stamps but I hadn't seen a tape recorder.

"How about the thrift store? They might have one."

Of course!

CJ looked at me. "I might want ice cream tomorrow, so maybe I'll come along with you, Sunday. I'm thinking a double scoop of cotton candy with sprinkles."

Ugh. That's right. Any money I had was now in CJ's ice cream fund. Still, maybe the tape player was super cheap and I could find change somewhere.

"I want ice cream!" Henry cried.

Bo tugged on my arm. "Me too."

"I can drive you down to the thrift store tomorrow when I take Emma," May said.

CJ poked at his chicken salad. "Maybe if she wants to crash."

May let her fork and knife clank onto her plate.

I shrugged and nodded, hoping to prevent World War III. "Yeah, okay, I'll go."

May grinned and turned up her nose at CJ. "See, some people in this family have faith in my abilities."

CJ silently ran a finger across his throat.

As the afternoon dragged on, I realized that I'd just have to wait until tomorrow to go to the thrift store.

So that night after dinner I snuck up to my bedroom, locked the door, and pulled out the manuscript. I flipped through the pages, my gaze landing on the beginning of one of the last chapters.

When Lilly received what was to be Mark's last post-card, something in her froze. He was coming home.

Finally, after two years away, he was coming back to Price.

Price.

Price.

The name—the town—hit heavy in Lilly's stomach. It reminded her of all the dreams she'd had.

Mark had traveled as she had longed to. He had left Price behind and seen the world. Her world.

The thoughts sat with Lilly, frightening her, embarrassing her. What if he came back to Price only to see that she had done nothing? That she was unchanged, walking her four blocks to town and her four blocks back, writing a story that would probably die a silent death, while he had flown over oceans, woven through busy streets in taxis, felt hot Indian sun on his face, tasted mangoes and passion fruit.

Lilly tucked the postcard inside her notebook. She couldn't let him see her like this. She wouldn't.

Packing up her books and clothes, Lilly left her small apartment in Price and drove up to New York City. New York City, the center of excitement, the center of publishing, the center of the world. Any fear disappeared as she dove into her new life. She began as a waitress at a small diner, barely making the rent for her dingy apartment. She wrote every spare moment she had. It was not the glamour Lilly had first dreamt of, but she had created it, and that was something.

Mark did not write her and she found, at first, that she did not mind. She wrote to him after she sent her first story, "The Day We Met, and After" to a publisher she had met one morning at work.

The man had sat by a window, spreading out a manuscript. The white pages reminded Lilly of her own story, which had sat on her table for the past two months.

"Coffee. The strongest you have," he said, not looking up.

Lilly nodded and returned, careful not to let the coffee spill onto the manuscript. She watched the man over the next couple of hours, refilling his cup every so often.

"You're a writer, then?" the man asked, his eyes never leaving the pages.

At first, Lilly didn't realize the man was speaking to her and kept her focus on the stream of coffee that dribbled into the cup.

The man looked up and Lilly could tell he was used to getting quick answers. "Well, am I right?"

Lilly wiped down the already clean table. "Yes."

"And what do you write?"

"Fiction." Was that right? Her nerves jostled her thoughts around so that nothing was clear.

"Are you any good?"

Humility told her to shrug off his question with a loose answer, but she knew she wasn't a bad writer. Besides, she might never get another chance. So Lilly turned up her nose and said, "Yes, actually I am. I'll send you my manuscript if you'd like," then blushed at her brazenness.

The man nodded, then pulled out his business card. "I guess we'll see."

Lilly tucked it into her pocket with trembling hands and finished her shift. When she arrived home, she took the pages straight from their place on the coffee table to the post office. At the counter she also purchased a postcard, filled in Mark's address, and scrawled across the bottom, "I've sent in my story. Love, Lilly."

Then she went home and cried.

This had to be Lee Wren's manuscript.

After sliding the pages back under the mattress, I flipped the fan on to high. The library reopening was just days away. My hands trembled just as Lilly's had when she placed the business card in her pocket. I finally found something to make me stand out, but what if I couldn't prove it to the world?

I hoped that the tapes held another clue. In my heart I knew this was Lee Wren's manuscript.

I just needed to find a way to prove it.

24

THE NEXT morning after breakfast, May, Emma, and I walked over to the library to let Mom and Dad know that we were going into town.

"Mom, can I just drive Emma and Sunday into town by myself? It's not far—three blocks. Please?" May asked.

Mom shook her head. "Sorry, May, but someone with a license has to be with you. I'll come along."

We walked back to the van and took our seats.

"Is everyone ready to go?" May asked from her place behind the wheel.

I gulped and stole a glance at Emma.

May turned the key and the van rumbled to life. "See, it's going to be a smooth ride."

But smooth wouldn't be the word I'd use as we jerked our way out of the driveway and down the street, the van stalling twice as May tried to switch gears.

"It-it-it just takes me a minute to-to-to get it."

"That's okay," I said, the van hiccuping one last time before she shifted and we smoothed out.

"See?"

Mom clutched the armrest with white knuckles. "A rough start, May, but you got it."

Emma whispered something under her breath, and May shot her a look of death in the mirror.

The rest of the drive to town went relatively well. A renegade rabbit crossing the street gave us all a little whiplash, but we arrived intact and alive.

May idled the van, not pulling into the space. "I think I'm going to practice my parallel parking."

"That's a good idea," Mom said, yanking the handle and stepping onto the sidewalk. "I'll make sure you don't hit anything."

"Not with me in the van," Emma said. She unlocked her door and slid it open. "You three have fun. I'll walk the rest of the way to the high school."

I was about to get out, too, but was interrupted by a heavy sigh.

"At least I know you'll always stick with me, Sunday."

I settled back against the seat. "Yeah, of course I will."

For the next five minutes, May heaved us forward, the car jerking almost constantly, and then slid the stick into reverse, whipped the steering wheel every which way, and hiccuped us backward. I could see her frustration as she clutched the steering wheel with a death grip, and her cheeks reddened. Unfortunately she never made it close enough to the curb to actually consider it "parking," and the van was anything but parallel.

May slid the stick into PARK, turned the key, and then slumped her forehead against the steering wheel.

"What are you doing, May?"

"I'm the worst driver on the entire planet. I will never get my stupid license and then I'll always have to get a stupid ride whenever I want to go somewhere and everyone will know that I'm a stupid driving failure."

"Oh, don't worry," I said. "You'll get it."

"No I won't!" she said, looking up at me with a line of snot pouring out of her nose.

"Sure you will. I've heard that automatic cars are super easy. You need to try and convince Mom and Dad to let you drive one of those."

Taking a napkin from the cup holder, she blew her nose.

"And there are lots of people who can't drive that well."

Sob.

"No, I'm serious. And some people don't even need or want to drive. In this book I read there was a girl whose family lived in a big city. Her mom didn't have a license. The family didn't even own a car because they always took the bus and the subway and taxis and stuff."

I knew mentioning taxis and subways would convince

her. May had been to New York City on a class trip last summer and spent two months trying to talk our parents into moving. Her room was covered in posters of Broadway shows and the New York City skyline.

"Yeah, I guess that's true," she said, stuffing the soaked tissue back into the cup holder.

"Of course it's true. And not driving is also good because . . . because of the environment. It's very 'green conscious' to not have a car."

She looked up at me, her eyes puffy and red. "I learned about that last year in science class."

I nodded. "You'll get the hang of it, I'm sure. Besides, even if you don't, it's not that big of a deal."

She turned and looked at me. Her smile was small but hopeful. "You really think I'll get it?"

I unlocked the door, hopped out, and then peered in at her. "Definitely."

She took a deep breath and slid the key in the ignition. "Thanks, Sunday," she said.

I waved as Mom got back inside. The van jerked to a start and May whipped back out onto the street, the tires squealing on the pavement.

Ms. Bodnar hailed me from down the street. "Hi, Sunday!" she called.

"Hi, Ms. Bodnar."

"I've missed you and Jude at the café. When are you two going to come by and visit? Crepes are on me."

"We've been busy at the library. But I'll tell Jude."

"Well, I better get back to the café. Enjoy your day."

"You, too. See you later."

I watched her as she crossed the street, stopping momentarily to wave at a woman who barreled past her without a smile or a hello. The woman's mouth was set in a deep frown, and her white knuckles clutched the collar of none other than Mr. Castor.

Mr. Castor trotted along oblivious to his dirt-covered muzzle and the partially eaten stem that hung out of his mouth. I pulled open the thrift store door just as she barged through. Maybe I'd wait out on the sidewalk until she left.

The door was flung open a few minutes later, the bell above dropping to the cement with a hollow clang. "This is ten times too many, Joanne!" the lady yelled.

Muzzy stood in the doorway, casting worried glances at Papa Gil, who seemed to be trying to calm the lady down.

But she wasn't about to give him a chance. "If I catch that beast in my yard again I'm calling the police, the pound, and anybody else who might be able to keep him under control." Then she turned on her heels and stomped out onto the sidewalk.

"Oh dear. What are we going to do, Gil? We can't have the police take away our sweet Mr. Castor."

Just then sweet Mr. Castor lunged at the front window, leaving drool dripping down the glass.

Papa Gil shook his head. "I don't know, Joanne."

Muzzy buried her head in his chest and began to cry.

"It'll be all right, Muzzy. Maybe you could take him to obedience school."

"We tried that already," Papa Gil said. "He did well for a while. He knows how to sit and give you his paw, but then he takes off running the moment he gets loose and tears up anything he can get his mouth around."

I remembered when Butters had run off a few times, her ears flapping and her little meatball legs carrying her faster than I ever thought possible. We had to pick her up at the pound twice. It was only when I started—

I thought about how I'd started taking her on two long walks a day after that. She came home and conked out for the rest of the night, barely opening up an eyelid she was so tired. "Maybe all he needs is more exercise?"

Muzzy lifted her head, sniffed, and tried to smile. "We take him on walks, really we do. But Gil and I can't go as far or as fast anymore."

"You could take him with you when you mow the library lawn, Papa Gil," I said. "It's fenced in. That'll get him some exercise. Or ride your bike and hold on to his leash so he has to jog next to you. I've seen people do that."

Papa Gil looked down at Muzzy, who snuffled again and swiped at a tear. "You think that could work?"

"It's worth a try. I've heard that's one of the main reasons why dogs misbehave. They just need more exercise."

"Really?"

I nodded. "And I know how to teach him to leave something alone. I saw it on a show. It worked for Butters."

"We'll try just about anything."

For the next half hour, I ran my own obedience school in between a rack of ugly Christmas sweaters and stacks of old, scuffed-up shoes. Mr. Castor wasn't fully trained by the end, but he looked like he was getting the hang of it.

Muzzy and Papa Gil were thrilled.

"Oh, Sunday, thank you!" Muzzy said, kissing me on the cheek. "I'm just sure this'll work. I know it will."

"You're an angel, Sunday Fowler," Papa Gil said, and held out the basket of candy.

"No thanks. I should probably get going." I started toward the door.

"But wait," Papa Gil called. "Did you come in here looking for something?"

The tape recorder. I'd almost forgotten. I did an about-face. "Yes, actually. I'm looking for an old tape recorder. Do you have one?"

Muzzy went to a shelf against the back wall lined with video tapes, old cameras, phones, and cassettes identical to the two in my backpack. She scanned the shelves, then pulled a big silver box down. "Will this work?"

I looked at the big buttons and the large speakers. "It's perfect. I've never actually used one, though. Does the tape go in here?"

Muzzy took the tape recorder from my hands. "Here, let me show you." She taught me how to put the tape inside, then how to rewind, fast-forward, and stop.

"Thanks," I said. "It seems easy enough."

"Compared to the contraptions you young people use nowadays, I'd say it's about as simple as you could get."

I flipped over the recorder and noticed the white sticker on the bottom. Seven dollars. "Um . . . I don't really–"

"That's on us," Papa Gil said. He held up his hand as I started to protest. "I won't take no for an answer. You've saved us from having to bail our dog out of the pound. The least we can do is give you that old tape recorder."

I hugged both of them. "Thank you so much," I said.

They walked me to the door, Mr. Castor drooling on my heels. "Our pleasure, Sunday."

I WAS convinced that the letters and the manuscript were Lee Wren's, but I knew that it probably took a lot more than a few coincidences to prove it to reporters.

I didn't have anything else.

"I bet there's something on the tapes," Jude said when we met up at the gate leading to Ben's house."

I sighed. "Yeah, maybe."

We found another tray of flowers waiting for us by the porch steps along with Ben Folger, who was sitting out on his porch swing. He stood up and grabbed his gardening hat, meeting us on the walkway.

"Hi."

"How was your trip with Wally?"

"It was so cool. His friend has this huge table where he draws the plans. That's architect lingo for a drawing of a house. I got to see some of the plans and then a picture of what it looked like once the house was built. Then he let me draw something on my own with his rulers and protractors and tools, and he said that he thought I had natural talent and to call him when I got older."

"Cool," I said. "And you had fun with Wally?"

Jude nodded. "Yeah, he was awesome. He took me out to a burger place afterward, and they weren't organic burgers, either. We're going to play some more catch so that we're ready for the fair tomorrow."

"That sounds like a great time," Ben said. He turned his gaze toward me. "And how is the library coming along? The reopening party is in a few days, right?"

"Yeah, on Saturday," I said. "It looks really good."

Ben Folger nodded. "I spoke to your dad this morning about coming over once the library's finished to take a look at the work I'd like done. And at the grocery store yesterday, I mentioned your dad's name to Mr. Simmons, who is looking to add a deck onto his house." He shrugged. "I'm not sure if anything'll come of it. You might not even be able to stay in Alma longer, but maybe."

"Thanks, Ben."

He nodded, his cheeks flushing red.

A half hour later we stopped and went inside to make lemonade and bring out a plate of brownies. Then we took our glasses onto the porch.

After a few quiet moments, Ben got up and went inside. He returned, holding a deck of cards. "Why don't we quit for today and play some cards?"

Jude shrugged, and we each pulled up one of the porch chairs to the small table.

"Sure," Jude said. "I don't know too many games, though."

I held out my hands for the deck. On a trip to visit my cousins, I had spent the entire car ride perfecting my ability to shuffle.

"Crazy eights?"

Both Ben and Jude stared at me with open mouths.

"When did you learn how to shuffle like that?" Jude asked. He took the remainder of the deck and attempted to splay the cards together and then form a fluttering bridge. I laughed when they *thunked* lifelessly in his hand.

"Last summer," I said. "So do you want to play?"

Ben Folger picked up his eight cards. "I'm ready."

We played three rounds of crazy eights (I won two and Jude won the other), and then Ben and I taught Jude how to play spades (Ben won all four games).

I took the deck and started shuffling again.

"Do you have a chessboard?" Jude asked.

Ben's face lit up. "Sure do. I haven't played chess in years."

He went to get up, but I beat him to it, the empty brownie plate in my hand. "I can get it. Just tell me where it is."

Ben sank back into the chair. "I think it's in the right-hand drawer of the coffee table."

Chess was not one of my favorite games. It moved along slower than dripping honey, and I didn't have the patience for it. But maybe this was my chance to talk to Ben about Lee Wren.

I walked into the kitchen, set the plate in the sink, then pulled the wooden chess box out of the drawer and carried it out to the porch.

Ben and Jude were talking about their favorite foods, so I lifted the lid and pulled out the small pouch filled with pieces, then the board. A photograph fluttered out and landed on the ground.

I picked it up.

Immediately I recognized the smiling face of Lee Wren beneath a wide-brimmed gardening hat. She wore green gloves dusted with dirt and held the delicate roots of a flower in her hands—a daisy.

My heart thumped. I pressed the photo to my chest.

"All right," Ben said, emptying the contents of the pouch onto the board. He took a white pawn and set it in place. "You want to be black?"

My mouth went dry. "This is a picture of Lee Wren, isn't it?"

His eyes drank in the picture. He took it from my hands. "Yes." Ben set the picture down, glanced at it again, then continued setting up his pieces. "She was always beautiful."

"You knew Lee Wren really well, didn't you?" I whispered.

He dropped one of his pawns on the chessboard and reached again for the picture. "It's been a long time since I've seen this."

Afraid that if I made any noise everything would disappear, I held my breath.

"Lee was my best friend," he said. He smiled up at us. "And she was my wife."

I looked wide-eyed over at Jude, whose own eyes were the size of two York Peppermint Patties. Yes, I'd heard Ben right.

All the pieces started to fit together. The letters, the manuscript, maybe even the tapes.

"It sounds so strange to say that out loud, especially because we took such pains to keep it secret. But I know I can trust you two."

"Why was it a secret?" The question came out before I could stop myself.

"When her book was finally published it was an instant success. She found the publicity unbearable. We had been friends since we were little and I loved her from the moment I laid eyes on her. But after high school, I left, traveled around the world. She stayed here for a bit and then eventually moved up to New York City. We kept in touch and occasionally she would come for a visit. After her book won the award, she became even more private than me, so reporters knew they'd only be asking in vain. But she never wanted to get married." He smiled. "I guess I wore her out in the end. I moved up to New York, to show her that I'd do anything for her. We got married with just the two of us and the justice of the peace. We didn't tell anyone, though I know people suspected. When she got sick . . ." He stopped and coughed into his hand. "When she got sick . . . she wanted to come back here, to Alma. But obviously with her health she didn't want anyone to know she was back. 'There'll be visitors night and day, and our house will be filled with banana bread,' she said. 'And you know how much I hate banana bread.' So I brought her back here, and because everyone knew me as the nonsocial type, no one even bothered the doorstep. We lived here for a little while before she died." He swiped at his eyes and stared at his pieces on the board.

It was hard to believe what I was hearing.

"I think about her every moment of every day. But it's been a long time since I've talked about her." He cleared his throat. "I still miss her. She was almost like a fairy—a mythical little thing that you were afraid would vanish if you held on too tight. But she had a good right hook." He rubbed his jaw as if he had just been punched.

"She punched you?"

He smiled and nodded. "Oh, yes. Hated my guts when we first met. She didn't like being wrong. I didn't care too

much, not when it came to her, so most times I'd let her
be right. But when she got sick it was a different story.
'You'll live a lot longer,' I told her. She shook her head and
smiled sadly. When she passed away a few weeks later,
I was so mad at her for being right. Hated that she was
right." His voice had slipped to a barely-there whisper.

"And now you put a daisy by her grave?" Jude asked.

Ben Folger slipped the picture inside his shirt pocket
and patted it gently. "Every morning." He looked up at
both of us. "Please, don't speak a word of this to anyone.
I would rather it remain just like it always has ... unknown."

"Why don't you want anyone to know? I mean, you
were married to a famous author!"

"I was married to a woman named Lee, and our love
was big and real and that's all that matters. People knowing about it doesn't change a thing."

I looked into his face but didn't answer. Thankfully,
the dinner triangle ringing from across the field saved
me. I started down the steps, leaving Jude still sitting in
front of the chessboard.

My chance had finally come.

26

CJ called to me as I walked up the driveway. "You can try out your grave after dinner, Sunday. I worked on it all afternoon and I think it's deep enough now."

"Gee, thanks." I walked up the stairs, stored my backpack in my room, then went to the table. But knowing about Ben and Lee and the letters made it almost impossible to concentrate on anything anyone was saying. I did say *yes* to something that Dad had asked, and *stop* to CJ, who was flinging something across the table. But I didn't know what Dad said or what CJ was flinging.

Oh well.

After I put the dishes away and wiped off the table, I avoided Bo's calls for me and dashed up to my room. Carefully taking the tape recorder out of my backpack, I slipped one of the tapes inside and pressed PLAY.

"—and I was living with my aunt and uncle at the time."

I pressed STOP, then I pressed REWIND and listened to the whirring sound as the tape zipped backward.

As I waited, I pulled out the manuscript and flipped to where I had left off the night before:

Waiting to hear from the editor was like torture. Of course, Lilly knew that the editor had authors—real authors—who were all competing for his time, but Lilly still woke each morning hoping to hear from the man. She now found herself lurking in the lobby of her apartment building, checking and rechecking her small mailbox on the off chance that she had missed something.

One evening, after her shift at the diner had ended, Lilly returned to her building and checked her box for the third time that day. Once more there was nothing from the editor. It had been two months since she handed over the brown package to the mail clerk, and every day a different scenario played in her mind.

Someone had found it and stolen it, putting his or her name at the top.

It had gotten lost in the post office and was languishing on a shelf.

The editor had received the package, but was so disgusted having wasted his time reading its contents that he had thrown it into the trash.

Lilly was so busy imagning the death of her

manuscript and the pain of rejection that she did
not see or hear him at first.

"Lilly?"

She jumped, startled. When she turned, it took
her a moment to focus. It was Mark's tousled hair,
Mark's blue eyes, Mark's small smile, Mark's nervous shuffle. Mark, standing in front of her—so far
from home.

I jumped as the REWIND button popped up. Mark had
gone to the city to visit her! Just like Ben had done with Lee
Wren. Setting the manuscript down, I pressed PLAY and
held my breath. Maybe this is where I would find the proof
I needed. I turned up the volume and listened, straining to
hear words over the gentle rustle of papers, the scraping of
a chair, the clatter of the tape player being moved. A sigh.

"I can't remember exactly where I left off the last time.
Oh well. The manuscript is coming along. It's completely
terrible, but I hope I'll be able to clean it up enough to
give it to Ben. I just want this story to be perfect for him."

Ben. Ben Folger! The manuscript!

Get ready, *New York Times*, Sunday Fowler has a story
for you!

"All right," the voice said. "Well, let's see. He left after
graduation and I didn't see him for a while after that,
though I did get letters from him every now and then."

As I listened, I realized that the manuscript wasn't a story at all. At least not a made-up one.

It was her life.

I grinned, clutched the manuscript to my chest, and flipped over onto my back, staring at the ceiling. This was even better than I had hoped!

I kissed the first page. Glancing at the clock, I realized that I couldn't call the newspapers or TV stations until tomorrow. I pulled out the other cassette and slipped it into the player, too excited to wait till I had finished the first. I listened to Lee Wren as she described her time in New York, how Ben came to visit her more and more every year, how she decided to marry him, and how she felt when she knew she was returning to Alma for the last time.

It was somewhere around this point that, exhausted, I drifted off to sleep.

I WAS startled awake by Bo. "Wake up, Sunday," he said through a yawn. "Come on, wake up."

I blinked my eyes open, remembering my discovery the night before. "'Morning, Bo." I pushed myself up, only then realizing that I wasn't in my pajamas or under the covers, and that the lamp beside my bed was still on. I saw the tape recorder, tapes, and the manuscript spread around the bed. "What happened? What did you do, Bo?"

"Nothing. I came up last night and you were already sleeping with all this . . . stuff everywhere. I tried not to mess it up. I just got underneath the covers. You were snoring awful bad and I hardly had any room at all."

"Are both the tapes still here, all the pages to the manuscript?" I quickly gathered everything.

"I told you I didn't do anything," Bo said. "You made the mess, not me." He hopped down off the bed and stomped to the door. "You're grouchy."

I reached out for him. "No, Bo. I'm . . . I'm just tired, and well, I'm doing something really important."

"Important?" he said, walking back over and sitting on my lap. "What is it?"

"I can't tell you right now, but you'll find out soon. It's big, though. Something that'll finally get me recognized."

"What's 'recognized'?"

"Being noticed."

"I notice you."

I kissed him on his cheek, which smelled a little like toothpaste. "I know. Now, let me get dressed. I'll be down in a minute. We'll eat breakfast, then go find Jude. Okay?"

Bo hopped out of my room. I closed the door behind him and dressed quickly. What a night! Today Jude and I would call the newspapers and TV stations. I'd tell Ben Folger what I'd found, and then maybe we'd all go out and celebrate. Of course, I couldn't tell my family yet. They'd find out when the rest of the world did. This was one time that Sunday Fowler was not going to be forgotten.

An hour later, I took a seat on Jude's bed. "You won't believe what I found out." I told him about the tapes and the manuscript and how the story was really Lee Wren's. "Isn't that exciting? This is it! Finally." I fell back onto his bed.

"Yeah, cool."

I sat up and stared at him. "Yeah, cool?" Unzipping my bag, I pulled out a piece of notebook paper. "I made a list of newspapers and television stations that we're going to call to announce something huge and all you can say is 'yeah, cool'? Jude, we're going to be famous."

Jude's face sort of twisted up. He looked like he was forcing himself to be excited. "I don't know, Sunday. Ben didn't really want anyone to know anything. Remember?"

"Yeah. About him being married to Lee Wren. But I'm not going to tell anyone about him. I'm talking about Lee Wren's life. The life that no one knew about, written by her. And if they find out about him, it doesn't really mean that he'll be in the limelight or anything."

"I'm just not sure," Jude said. "He obviously knew about the letters and tapes and the manuscript." He shrugged. "He might've wanted to keep them private. Maybe Lee Wren did, too."

What was he saying? "You mean I shouldn't tell the newspapers about this? I shouldn't tell the world about Lee Wren's manuscript? This is my chance to not be meaningless anymore."

"You're not meaningless," he said softly. "You just think that because—"

"Whatever," I snapped. "Besides, I'm planning on

going over to let him know about everything. I could just let him find out all on his own!"

"Sunday, I'm not—"

"Forget it." Tears stung my eyes.

"I'm not saying you shouldn't do it. It's just that . . . maybe you should think about it a little more. Let's just go back to your house. You can decide what you should do—"

"What I should do? I've been trying to find a way to stand out since I got to Alma. I finally solve a huge mystery that the world is going to go crazy over, and you're saying I shouldn't tell anyone? Maybe you should go to my house and hang out with my family. They're the whole reason you're friends with me anyway. You liked Emma from the moment you saw her. Well, she would never like you, even if you were the last boy on earth."

I knew I had hurt Jude, but I couldn't stop the words. I didn't want to stop them. I plunged on. "So fine. Go ahead. You can just slip into my place in the family. No one would even notice anyway. I thought you wanted to help me. I thought you were going to stick by me."

I slammed his bedroom door and stomped out of his neat little house. What did he know? He was a stupid, fat, only child who had all the attention he could ever want, and could have whatever he wanted whenever he wanted it. How could I think he could ever understand?

Ms. Bodnar leaned out of the café as I passed. "Hi, Emma!" she shouted.

I didn't wave or smile. I kept right on moving.

If that wasn't reason enough to go to the newspapers, I didn't know what was.

"Yes, that's Sunday," I said into the phone. "Like in the first day of the week. Then Fowler. F-O-W-L-E-R."

"And where are you calling from, Miss Fowler?" The man on the line was asking all the wrong questions. Didn't he want to know why I was calling? Not where I was calling from? Besides I'd already answered these same questions for two other people in his office.

"I'm living in Alma, Pennsylvania." I needed to tell him what I'd found or he'd have me answering his silly questions all day. "You've heard of Lee Wren, right?"

"Of course. *The Life and Death of Birds*."

"Well, I'm calling because I've found a second manuscript written by her, along with other personal items."

The man laughed. "That's very funny, Miss Fowler. Now that you and your friends have had a good laugh, why don't you run along and play hopscotch."

He thought I was joking. "If you knew anything about Lee Wren, you would know that she grew up in Alma and is also buried here. I just so happen to have recorded tapes of her talking about the manuscript, letters that she wrote, and the manuscript, itself. But if you don't want to come see for yourself, then maybe I'll just call another newspaper."

There was a brief silence. "This isn't a prank?"

"No, it is not."

"How old are you?"

"I'm eleven, almost twelve, though I don't see why that should matter."

"Can I talk to your parents?"

I knew I'd get this question and I was prepared. "You can, but they don't know anything about this. I found the manuscript in the library when my parents were remodeling, and I've done all the research by myself." I thought of Jude and forced the words out, "With a friend."

There was a sigh from the man on the line. "Fine. I guess I can send someone down to Alma to see what this is all about. But if this is a joke, I'm warning you, my boss will take this to the police."

"I hope he does," I said. My heart was pumping wildly. He was sending someone down! "The library is holding a big reopening party in two days. If you'd like to come then, I'm planning on making the announcement. I'm also contacting other newspapers and TV stations about this, so I hope you'll be smart enough to take me very seriously."

He mumbled a quick "nice speaking with you," and we both hung up the phone. I turned to my right, thinking that Jude was sitting there beside me, but remembered our fight. Pushing aside the words I had yelled at him, I glanced at myself in the mirror and smiled. I had done it.

And there was no going back now.

Crossing off the first newspaper on the list, I took a deep breath and clicked the phone. "On to the next."

By the time I was done, two TV stations and five newspapers had agreed to send reporters down to Alma on Saturday to check out my story. It was really happening.

Jude's uncertain face flashed into my head again, and I tried to shake off the guilt. What was there to feel bad about? I found the manuscript and the letters and the tapes. Shouldn't I be able to tell the world?

I walked to the mirror and took a deep breath. "Now I'll go and tell Ben," I said to myself.

When I got to the house, Ben was bent over one of the flower beds, watering can in hand. He glanced up and welcomed me with a small smile.

"Hi, Sunday." He stood up, his eyes searching behind me. "Where's your partner in crime?"

"He decided not to come," I said, shrugging.

Ben grunted in reply and patted the soil around one of

the flowers. "Daisies," he said. "They were Lee's favorite. I forget when I first started leaving them for her on her windowsill." He looked up at me, his eyes squinting in the sun. "But you probably already know that."

Did Jude tell Ben what we found?

Ben turned back to the garden. "No. I can tell what you're thinking. Jude didn't tell me anything. But it wasn't hard to figure out what you had. Only someone who had found Lee's story and the letters would try and sneak around the house of the most feared man in town—the man who eats raw meat—and keep coming back."

I knew I should say something, but I didn't know what.

"I couldn't remember where I'd put Lee's papers until a few weeks ago. I went to the library basement when I was helping out. The silver box had been raided."

"Yeah, um—"

He waved off my embarrassment and continued down the flower bed with his watering can. "Don't worry about it, Sunday. I should've taken those things out of there a long time ago. Truth is, I thought I had. And you, being just as smart and curious as my Lee was, found the box and opened it. But tell me, is the manuscript all right? And the letters?"

I shook my head. "I've taken really good care of all of it." And I had. I sat down, the walkway warm on my bare legs. "I'm sure glad you know. Jude thought you'd mind that we found out and that I called the newspapers, and everything."

Ben Folger's head jerked up. "What do you mean 'newspapers'?"

I shrugged, my mouth instantly drying out again. He definitely didn't look excited. "You know . . . the newspapers and TV stations that'll be interested in the fact that I found a manuscript written by the famous Lee Wren."

He sighed and sat down beside me, bringing his legs up and leaning back on his hands. He didn't say anything. I half hoped that meant that even though he was a little disappointed, he was really fine with everything.

"And, of course, I won't mention your name," I said. "I don't think they'll figure out that you were the Mark that was in the manuscript."

He sighed. His shoulders slumped, and when he looked up at me again, his face was droopy with sadness.

I stood up and looked out over the neatly clipped grass, attempting to push away the guilt that was now rushing over me. "I better get back." I started away and then turned around. "I'll be making the big announcement on Saturday at the reopening of the library."

"Did you ever finish the story, Sunday?" he asked, his voice soft.

I shook my head. "Almost."

"*The Life and Death of Birds* was her masterpiece. It

was beautiful–as beautiful as the person who wrote it. When it was published, I'd never seen her so happy.

"But then the fame that she'd always wanted, well, it wore on her fast. Newspapers calling for interviews. People asking what she would write next. The pressure to write something equally brilliant. The possibility of failing. I encouraged her to write another story, convinced that it would be just as beautiful as her first. 'I can't,' she told me. 'I spent all I had and all that was inside me on that book. I don't think I have another one in me.'

"Oh, she'd write little things here and there. Articles, essays, her thoughts, but nothing more serious, and nothing she was willing to show to the world. Instead she read and tended the tiny garden we had at our apartment in New York City. Then, one day, about a year before she died, she woke up and told me, 'Ben, I have one more story to write. But this one isn't for anyone but us. You have to promise me. It's not for the world. I can bear them picking apart my words, but not my life. And not us.'" Ben stopped and looked up at me.

I hadn't moved a muscle.

"She gave it to me on our tenth anniversary. I read it a hundred times over, and each time I loved it more than the last. But I put it away when she died. Locked it up so that no one would find it. It's not what the experts and critics would call brilliant. Oh, it's good. She couldn't write anything that wasn't good. But she knew, and I know now, that it isn't what people would want. They'd find out that it was her story. They'd pry into her childhood and label her. They would criticize and pick apart every word, every moment. Maybe they'd praise her, or maybe they'd pity her, or maybe they'd be disappointed in her. But what they wouldn't know, what they wouldn't think about, is that she didn't write it for them. It was like her diary, never meant to be shared." He stopped and whispered, "She didn't want it to be shared."

"But someday," I started, "someone was bound to find the manuscript and figure out who wrote it. Like *The Diary of Anne Frank*. It's a classic."

He nodded. "I know. And there wouldn't be anything I could do about it then." He ran his hands through his white hair. "But now . . . well, I should've protected it for her. Like she asked me to."

I swallowed. "But . . ."

He looked up at me. "Please, Sunday. Please don't give it to the newspapers."

I turned away, starting down the pathway. "I'm sorry. I . . . I have to."

As soon as I had passed through the gate, I dashed off across the field toward my house.

Everything that had seemed to fall perfectly into place last night was now turning out all wrong.

28

THE YARD was empty. There were no saws buzzing, CJ wasn't ordering anyone around, Bo didn't rush out to greet me, and the horn wasn't honking. In fact, the van was gone. Had I missed hearing the triangle ringing? I checked my watch. 4:35. Mom didn't usually start dinner for another hour.

I flashed back to sitting on the orange bench in front of the gas station, staring into the wavy heat. Waiting for them to remember me.

"Mom!" I called out. "Dad?"

Nothing. Just the hammock swaying between the trees and the triangle gently clanging against the side of the house.

"This is why I need to tell the world what I found," I said aloud, making my way up the porch stairs and through the front door. "Mom?! Dad! Bo!" My voice rang through the silent house. Our house was never silent. Butters barked excitedly, her tail wagging and her ears dragging on the ground as she ran up to me on her little sausage-y legs.

"Where is everyone, Butters?" I said, bending down and scratching her long, velvety ears. "They forgot me again, huh?"

Something fell up above me, and then there was the sound of footsteps.

"Sunday? Is that you?" Mom.

I sighed. "Yeah, it's me."

She walked down the stairs, pulling her hair back into a ponytail. "Where on earth have you been? Everyone else left for the county fair an hour ago."

"What? What fair? No one told me that we were going to a fair."

"Your dad talked to everyone about it last night at dinner. Since we're pretty much done with the library, we wanted to take you guys all out to celebrate. I'll call your dad to come pick us up. Where were you?"

"At Ben's house."

"You okay? You look upset."

I pasted on a smile hoping that it looked sort of genuine. "I'm fine." I wasn't really in the mood to go to a fair, but I started up the stairs. "I'll be ready in a minute."

In my room, I flopped onto the bed, staring up at the ceiling. Like the story of the princess and the pea, I could practically feel the manuscript underneath the mattress. *Why did I ever tell Ben?* I could've just made my announcement and then he would've found out what I knew with everyone else. Now I felt guilty about something that wasn't even wrong.

And Jude probably hated me. I rolled over onto my side and stared out the window.

There was a knock on my door. "Sunday?"

I sat up, remembering that I was supposed to be getting ready for the fair. "Come in."

Mom opened the door. "Your dad'll be here in about twenty minutes with CJ and Henry. I guess they rode the Tilt-a-Cup five times in a row. Now both of them are feeling sick. I'll just stay back here with them."

"I can stay, Mom. I'm not in the mood for the fair."

She stepped toward me and tucked a loose strand of hair behind my ear. "Everything okay?"

I shrugged. "Yeah, I'm just tired. Really. You go ahead with Dad. I'll be fine here with the boys."

"Are you sure?"

"Yeah. I can handle CJ and Henry. Besides, if they're not feeling well, maybe they'll go straight to bed."

Mom went to the small mirror, let her hair down from the ponytail, and fluffed it up with her fingers. "I think that's wishful thinking. But I trust you. You can call us on our cell phones if you need anything at all. Lock the doors and . . ." She sighed. "You'll be fine."

I nodded and followed her down the stairs.

About fifteen minutes later a horn honked from out-side and Mom looked at me again, her eyes filled with the same concern I saw when May went out with her friends for the evening. I pushed away the urge to ask her to stay.

"You sure you're all right?"

I nodded, enjoying the bit of attention. "Yeah, like I said, I'm just tired. We'll be fine."

"All right. Well, we'll see you when we get back."

The door opened and in trudged all three of my brothers, shoulders slumped, faces pale, all moaning softly. There was definitely something wrong if CJ wasn't racing through the door followed by the other two.

"Ooo, *all* of you feel sick?" Mom asked.

CJ groaned and lay down on the steps. "I feel like I'm going to throw up everything all over again."

Henry grabbed onto Mom's foot and sank to the ground. Bo fell into my arms. "Sunday, I don't feel so good."

I walked him over to the steps where CJ still lay, and then went and disentangled Henry from Mom's ankle. He reached for her again.

"I think I should stay," she said, looking down at the boys piled on the steps. "I'll just go out and tell your dad."

I lifted Henry onto my hip, something that he hadn't let me do recently. He lay his head on my shoulder, and I could feel the rumbling of his stomach against my own.

"No, Mom, really. You go out with Dad. I'll call if something goes wrong. I think they'll just fall asleep." But for the first time ever, I hoped they wouldn't. I needed something to distract me from replaying the day over and over again in my head.

She thought about it, then kissed each of my brothers on the head. "We'll just go for an hour or so, okay?"

I nodded and the door closed. "So, boys," I said, turning and hitching Henry up higher on my hip. "Are you okay?"

"I will never eat again," CJ said. His face was stuffed in his elbow, muffling his voice.

"Yeah," Bo said. "Me neither."

"Sure you will. You just need to rest for a bit. Why don't we go upstairs and you guys can—"

"I can't move," CJ moaned again.

I nudged him with my foot. "Come on, CJ. You can't just sleep on the stairs."

He groaned.

"Why don't we all lie down in Mom and Dad's room and watch a movie? I think that couch pulls out." Besides family movie nights, Mom and Dad banned the TV every summer, unplugging it from the wall and slipping it into one of the closets, so what I was suggesting was a huge deal.

Henry lifted his head up. "Really?"

I shrugged. "Sure. I can make some popcorn."

CJ whined. "No. No popcorn."

"CJ barfed up popcorn," Bo said.

"Yeah, and cotton candy, and two hot dogs, and French fries with cheese all over them. My throw-up looked like mashed-up oatmeal, and mashed potatoes, and there were chunks of pink stuff floating inside it."

"Don't forget the green and yellow stuff, too."

I felt my own stomach heave. "Gross. Thanks for that description. We'll have ginger ale. I saw some in the pantry."

"But what if I throw it up?" Henry moaned.

"You won't. Ginger ale is what you're supposed to have when you don't feel good."

"Why?"

I shrugged. "Just because. Now, come on."

I opened the door to Mom and Dad's room, pushed the couch that was against the window in front of the TV, and set Henry down. CJ fell onto the cushions, resting his head on one of the arms. Bo slouched in the middle.

"I'll go and get the ginger ale and then we'll turn on something to watch, okay?"

I returned with four golden, fizzy drinks, saltine crackers, and the phone in case Mom or Dad called. The boys lay where I'd left them, talking about food.

"Eww," Henry whined. "Could you eat a hot dog with mustard and ketchup and sauerkraut on top?"

The other two moaned.

CJ said, "How about macaroni and cheese?"

"What about a big cinnamon roll with icing dripping off the sides?" Bo said. "Yuck!"

I handed him a glass. "But that's your favorite."

He took a sip. "I know. But now I can't even think about it or I'll throw up."

I handed the other two their glasses, the small bubbles rising to the top. "Then why are you guys talking about it?"

CJ sat up. "I don't know. Just 'cause."

I rolled my eyes, reached for the remote, and flipped on the TV.

"Will Mom get mad?" Henry asked.

I pressed the CHANNEL button until we came to a station that played cartoons all day. "She'll understand. And we won't watch too much."

The couch was cramped, but I grabbed a blanket for each of my brothers and then squeezed myself in between Bo and CJ. Henry, realizing that my lap was unoccupied, crawled up and leaned his head back against my shoulder.

The cartoon was silly, and we found ourselves laughing at all the same parts. But within the hour, when the door to the room opened and Mom walked in, all three of my brothers were fast asleep. CJ and Bo rested their heads on my shoulders, and Henry breathed rhythmically against me. Mom smiled and flicked off the TV.

"They look so sweet piled around you like that. You'd

never be able to tell what a mess they can get themselves into when they wake up."

I nodded.

My shoulders ached and my right arm and left leg had fallen asleep, but I felt strangely cold and alone when Dad carried them one by one to their beds.

"Thanks, Sunday," he said, bending down and kissing me on the forehead. "You know it's still early. I could drive you back to the fair if you'd like. Jude's there with his mom and Wally."

I shook my head, stood up, then helped him push the couch back underneath the window. Jude wouldn't want to see me. "No thanks. I'll just go upstairs and read."

As much as I didn't want to think about what Ben had told me, and the guilt that kept nagging at me, I needed to finish the manuscript and listen to the parts of the tape I had missed.

"If you're sure, sweetheart."

I nodded.

"We'll see you in the morning. Lots to do to get ready for the party."

Upstairs in my room, I slipped the manuscript out from underneath the mattress and set the tape recorder and tapes beside me on the bed. I started to read but couldn't concentrate. I kept thinking about the look on Jude's face when I had yelled at him.

I snuck downstairs, grabbing the phone and phone book. I'd never called Jude before, so I found his mom's name in the phone book and dialed the number.

I didn't know what I was going to say, but maybe if I called he'd say something first. Maybe he'd tell me that I was right to call the newspapers. A woman picked up the phone on the third ring. "The Trist residence."

"Um, hi, Ms. Trist," I managed to say. "Is Jude there?"

"Yes, may I ask who's calling?"

"It's Sunday. Sunday Fowler."

"Oh hi, Sunday. Just a minute."

I heard the phone being set down and then two voices talking, though I couldn't understand them. Then someone picked up the phone again.

"Sunday?" It wasn't Jude. My heart dropped.

"Yeah?"

"Jude can't come to the phone. We just got back from the fair and, well . . . maybe you could try back tomorrow."

"Oh, okay," I said. "Thanks. Good-bye."

"Good-bye."

The phone clicked and the line went dead. He didn't want to talk to me. Fine. Whatever. I needed to figure out what I was going to tell the TV stations and the newspapers anyway.

Whether Ben and Jude liked it or not, reporters were

coming all the way to Alma for a story, and I couldn't just not tell them.

Right?

I sighed, stuffing the guilt away, and then picked up the manuscript to finish reading.

And so Mark and Lilly tucked themselves away in the hometown Lilly swore she'd never return to. They created a life in a little corner that was just theirs. Away from the hounding reporters and the fame that had, at first, felt like a gentle rain but quickly became the painful pelting of hail.

Their story may not read as "happily ever after." But it is their ever after.

Each night they climb out onto the rooftop of their little home. They find Orion's Belt. And then, in the morning, when Lilly rolls over to greet the sun, a daisy rests on the windowsill.

Please don't show this to anyone. This is only for you and me.

Daisies and hearts,

Lee

I tried to ignore the last line. I had my proof, and I was going to tell the media about what I'd found.

Why wasn't I more excited?

Ben might be upset for a little bit, but he would get over everything eventually, and maybe he'd even find that he liked the fame. The town would get a lot more attention—that was good for business—and the library would get publicity, which was good for my dad, my family, and the entire town of Alma.

I yawned and set the tape recorder and manuscript on the floor, then flipped off the light. Actually I was doing everyone a huge favor and sooner or later they'd realize it, too.

Wouldn't they?

29

"**CJ**, please stop talking about your throw-up," Mom said the next morning. She flipped over a pancake dotted with chocolate chips.

All the boys had woken early that morning, their appetites and mischief returning as strong as ever. CJ slathered butter on the top of one of his pancakes. "Okay. But it was just so nasty. All those chunks, and the pink—"

"CJ!"

He plugged up his mouth with a large bite.

"Are you feeling okay, Sunday?" Mom asked when I brought my plate over.

My pancake consumption could usually rival CJ's, but that morning, my stomach anxiously fluttered over my announcement.

"I'm good. Just excited for the party tomorrow."

"Are you still up for helping me decorate and cook today?"

"Yep."

Mom looked around as if she were missing someone

or something. "Is Jude coming over?" She looked down at her watch. "He's usually here by now."

I shrugged. "I don't know." Honestly I had hoped that he would just show up and neither of us would need to say anything. Then everything would just go back to being the way it had been.

I turned away from his empty chair. He wasn't going to spoil the event that was going to change things for me.

"We have a busy day, so I need all of you to help. Emma's play is tonight at seven o'clock, and May is going for her driving test after lunch." Mom ran her fingers through her hair. "I can't believe this is all falling on the same day. Maybe we should move the party to next week."

"No!" I said a little too loudly. Mom glanced over at me. "It's just that we've already . . . we've told people that it's tomorrow. We'll get it all done. It's not that much when you really think about it. The decorating and cooking will take the longest, but I know that Ms. Bodnar is bringing food, and so are Muzzy and Papa Gil. And we can do some of the cooking tomorrow before the party."

Mom sighed and flipped over six more pancakes. "I guess you're right. And your dad will be done with cleaning the library this morning, so he should be able to help decorate before he has to take May for her test."

"Why doesn't she just try for her driver's license at home? We only have another week here."

"She thinks that maybe the test will be easier here."

CJ laughed, splattering orange juice across the table-cloth. "She just wants to fail here instead of back home."

"CJ, just eat, please," Mom said. "And Sunday, could you go over to Jude's house and see if he'd like to come and help? We can use all the hands we can get today."

"Really. Mom? I—" I stopped when she shot me a desperate look. "I'll be right back."

On my way through town, I checked with Ms. Bodnar to see if she was still bringing something. "Of course, sweetie! A friend is going to help me bring my whole setup to the library. Crepes for everyone!"

Muzzy and Papa Gil remembered, too. I saw Papa Gil out riding an old bicycle, Mr. Castor trotting along beside him. "Pies," Papa Gil said, coming to a halt. Mr. Castor was panting. "She's making every kind of pie you can imagine. And I thought that since the lawn needs mowing, I'd give rides to kids who want to jump on board."

"Great. How is Mr. Castor doing?"

"You're a genius, Sunday Fowler. He's like a brand-new dog. Hasn't had enough energy to run away, and he's getting better about not chewing on everything in sight."

"Good," I said, and then started toward Jude's house.

I had been hoping to find Jude on my way over, but he hadn't been at the café or anywhere else. I walked up to the door and knocked.

Nothing.

I knocked louder. He woke up just as early as my brothers, so I knew he wasn't still sleeping.

Out of the corner of my eye I saw a curtain flutter. I knocked again, louder and longer. "Come on, Jude," I said. "I know you're in there. My mom needs help."

Nothing.

I shoved my way through a bush and peered into the window. He was standing by his bedroom door like he was listening, just waiting for me to go away. I rapped on the glass, sending him about a foot into the air. "Come on!" I yelled.

He stared at me for a moment, walked over to the window, stuck out his tongue just like CJ would do, and closed the blinds.

Now I was just plain angry. "JUDE! You come out here. You're being a big old baby."

Nothing again. "Fine!" I yelled, and stomped through the grass and down the sidewalk toward home. I guess he wouldn't be helping us today.

Mom, Dad, Miss Jenny, my brothers, and I decorated the rest of the morning. We hung balloons on the outside of the refinished door, wound streamers around the cleaned stone banisters, and set up long tables on the grass.

Though I had been in the library on and off throughout the weeks that Dad worked on remodeling, it still took my breath away when I stepped inside. The floors and stairs shone glossy in the light that poured in through the cleaned, trimmed windows. I walked among the shelves, letting my fingers run along the colorful spines. I noticed that there was a new copy of *The Life and Death of Birds*. It was because of Lee Wren that I was finally going to mean something. I smiled and slid it back in place.

I walked to the circulation desk, where Mom was placing a large jar of jelly beans with a GUESS HOW MANY? sign, and Bo was taping balloons every which way. Above the desk hung the newly framed picture of Lee Wren. Now that I knew her story, her smile seemed mischievous, and in the sparkle of her eye I could picture the girl serving coffee and eggs and toast at a diner in New York City. But there was something I hadn't noticed until now. Her hands rested on her lap, her fingers wrapped around a bright and cheery daisy.

A daisy that Ben had given her.

Maybe he'd stood off to the side when they took the picture. Maybe the smile was not so mischievous after all, but meant for him. I tried to ignore the thorn of guilt that pricked me in the chest.

"Sunday, could you arrange the flowers?" Mom asked. "I brought over all the vases that I could find in the house.

It needs to look bright and cheery tomorrow, so put them everywhere."

She slid two large boxes of flowers over to me and pointed to a table in the corner that was filled with vases of every kind. As I began to arrange the flowers, I felt Lee Wren's gaze on my back.

Was her picture one of the ones that followed you wherever you were in the room? I turned and looked. Her eyes were definitely on me. The guilt I had tried to stuff away returned. Would she really mind? Did it matter that she minded? I shook my head and turned back to the flowers, placing a daisy in each vase. She would like that.

But the manuscript and the tapes and the letters and her husband. Would she like all that being brought into the open?

"Sunday," Mom said. "I know I keep asking, but are you okay? Did something happen with you and Jude?"

Jude. I had managed to forget about him for most of the morning. Now he and Lee Wren and Ben Folger were coming at me from all sides.

"Oh, I think he's mad at me. It'll be fine, though."

Mom pulled a few stray leaves from one of the arrangements. "Anything you want to talk about?"

I shrugged. It would be nice to talk to her about everything, but I . . .

"Mom!" Bo yelled. "Can I have a snack?"

"Yeah, me too, me too!"

I sighed and watched her walk over to the boys. I couldn't talk to her. Besides, everyone would know everything tomorrow. "It's fine," I said halfheartedly, knowing she couldn't hear me.

"Sunday," she called back to me, "once you're done with the flowers, why don't you fold these brochures in half and put them in this basket. They're just for people to see the 'before' pictures of the library so they know all that your dad, and everyone, did."

"Okay," I said, and then went back to arranging flowers.

The decorating was finished by lunchtime, and then it was on to the baking.

"We'll bake the cookies and brownies and cakes today, and then tomorrow I'll throw the appetizers in the oven and the Crock-Pot," Mom said. I slathered another celery stick with peanut butter and lined it with raisins.

"Can you put a few more raisins on that one, Sunday?" Henry asked. "I love raisins."

CJ picked his off and tossed them onto Henry's plate. "Have mine. I hate raisins. They look like rat poop."

Bo giggled and popped one in his mouth. "Look! I'm eating rat poop, I'm eating rat poop."

Mom sighed. "Really, CJ? Do you have to get them started?"

He crunched down on the celery, a look of satisfaction on his face.

Dad strolled into the kitchen, May behind him, looking pale and nervous. "Well, May and I are off to her driver's test. We'll be back in about an hour or two with a new driver in the family."

"Hopefully not," CJ whispered.

Mom knocked him on the shoulder, then went and kissed my sister on the cheek. "You'll do fine, sweetheart. Just relax and try your best."

May nodded, and I watched as her bottom lip trembled..

"Good luck," I said. She was going to need a whole lot of luck or maybe a driving instructor who was blind and didn't mind getting whiplash.

May glared at CJ, then turned to me and smiled. "Thanks, Sunday."

"We'll be back," Dad said, and they disappeared out the front door.

I thought I heard Mom mutter "She's going to need a miracle" as they backed out of the driveway, but I wasn't sure.

"Should we make a sign for May when she comes back?" Bo asked, licking the peanut butter out of his celery stick.

"That would be really nice, Bo," Mom said. "Go find some paper and you can make her one."

Bo hopped down from his chair, licked his fingers, and ran off. "I'll make her the bestest sign ever."

"Wash your hands!" Mom called after him.

Mom set to work baking, and the kitchen turned into a hurricane of flour, sugar, oil, eggs, and butter.

As she popped a tray of cookies into the oven, CJ, Bo, and Henry tumbled through the kitchen.

"I'm going to hang up the signs I made," Bo said. He clutched a stack of papers and proudly held up one with a large A written on it. "All the letters spell out 'Congratulations May on Getting Your Driver's License.' CJ helped me spell it out."

CJ rummaged in the kitchen drawer, pulling out a roll of clear tape, a box of nails, and a hammer. "Yep. Now we're going to hang them up." He held the hammer and the nails behind his back while Mom busied herself with stirring a humongous bowl of thick, black brownie batter.

"Looks great, Bo," I said. "Where are you going to put them?" I handed him and Henry oatmeal cookies from the cooling rack.

"On the porch."

They started out of the kitchen when Mom said, not

turning from the counter, "I know you are not about to take that hammer and those nails outside, CJ."

"But Mom, tape never works. And don't you want May to see what we made for her? You know, her brothers supporting her and stuff like that."

Nice. I was impressed with CJ's attempt, appealing to my mom's yearning for brotherly and sisterly affection. Still, I doubted that she had forgotten when CJ had built a fort around Henry, Bo, and himself. It took two hours to pry out enough nails to get them free.

"I think that May will see the signs just fine without the hammer and nails," Mom said. "You better hurry, though. They'll probably be back soon."

When the last batch of brownies sat steaming on the cooling rack, next to the dozens of cookies, two cakes, and a few loaves of apple bread, and I had washed the spatula for the last time, I filled up a glass with lemonade and walked out onto the front porch and down the stairs. The pages they had hung flapped in the breeze.

In multicolored marker and big, bold letters, the sign read: I HOPE YOU DIDN'T FLUNK, MAY!!

I smiled. That's what Bo got for trusting CJ to help him spell. Taking a sip of my lemonade, I turned my gaze to Ben's house across the field and then quickly away, hoping he'd understand what I was going to do.

I still needed to arrange the letters, cassette tapes, and

the manuscript for tomorrow. Then I needed to pick out an outfit, and I was thinking that I should practice a little speech. With my brothers off somewhere, Emma at the high school, and May and Dad still gone, I'd have time to get everything ready without being interrupted. I managed to slip by Mom, who was stacking cookies, covering brownies, and wrapping up the loaves of bread, and snuck up to my room, closing the door gently behind me. I immediately went on a search in my closet for something to wear for the big announcement. Unfortunately I had packed mainly shorts, T-shirts, and tank tops but was pleased to find a skirt and top still stuffed in my suitcase. Mom probably tucked them inside just in case. I didn't have any shoes other than the old sneakers on my feet, but newspapers and TV cameras usually only took pictures or filmed you from the waist up.

I set the outfit out on the old stool. Now to gather everything together. The letters still sat on my dresser from the night before, but when I lifted up the mattress, my heart dropped to my feet.

The story was gone.

I lifted the mattress up higher.

Nothing.

I swept my hand underneath, my fingertips searching for a corner of paper. "No, no, no, no, no."

And then I remembered how I had just set the

manuscript on the floor, next to my bed, last night. I flopped onto the mattress, peered down, and gasped.

The pages of the manuscript were flipped upside down, scattered among a rainbow of colored markers.

Bo!

I scrambled for the pages. How could he? What was I going to do now? Even after I had been so careful, my brother had managed to ruin the only thing that was going to help me stand out. He'd ruined everything!

I stacked the papers together, angry tears spilling down my cheeks.

"They're here! They're back!" Bo shouted. Bo. The person who destroyed my chance at being recognized. My anger flared up fiercer than ever.

I stomped out of my room, down the stairs, and out the front door.

"She passed," Dad said, his voice showing his surprise. "I don't know how she did it, but she did."

I ignored my sister's outstretched hand as she showed off her license, and ran up to my brother. "Bo!" I yelled. "How could you?"

He had May around the waist and was asking, "Do you like my sign?"

My sister gave a confused smile. "Um, I think?"

I grabbed Bo by the arm and pulled him off her. "I said, 'How could you do that?'"

"Ouch, Sunday. That hurts." He looked up at me, the smile slowly disappearing from his face.

"What is this about, Sunday?" Mom asked. Her eyebrows were knit together and her arms folded.

I pointed up at the porch, where some of the pages had blown away. Now the sign read: YOU FLUNK MAY! "Great," I said, running up to the porch and pulling down the remaining pages. "Where did the rest of them go?"

Bo shrugged and looked around. "I don't know."

"We should've used the nails," CJ said, shaking his head.

Henry tossed the keys into the air and tried to catch them. "I saw some blow away."

I ran my hands through my hair and turned on Bo again. "How could you, Bo? How could you take the one thing that mattered most to me and completely ruin it?"

"I-I-" he stuttered.

I held up the papers. "You don't understand how important these were. They were going to make me special, and now—" My cheeks burned. "Now they're ruined. You ruined them. Just like you always do. Just like everyone always does!" I stared hard at him. "I . . . I don't ever want to see you again!" Then I pushed past everyone and ran back into the house and up the stairs to my room. I slammed the door and locked it, flopping onto my bed and burying my face in the pillow.

All the dreams I had had for tomorrow were crumbling

around me. Sure, I could still give the reporters the rest of the manuscript and the tapes and the letters. But now it was incomplete and some of the pages were colored on.

There was a soft knock on my door. "Sunday?" Mom called.

"Go away!" I yelled. "Just leave me alone."

"I don't know what this is about, but Bo is crying hysterically, and you need to apologize to him."

I sat up, my eyes stinging. "Apologize to him? He's the one that took something of mine, something more important to me than . . ."

"Than what, Sunday?" Mom yelled. "Than your brother? There is nothing more important than your family."

"You don't understand! Now, just go away."

"Fine, I'll leave you alone for now. But when you come downstairs you will be apologizing to him. He's still young, and he didn't know what he was doing."

I waited until her footsteps disappeared before I got up off my bed and went to the window.

"Sunday?" Bo said from outside my door. He sniffled.

"Go away, Bo. I don't want to talk to you."

"But I didn't mean to draw on your papers."

"Go away. And! Leave! Me! Alone!"

IT WAS almost time for the play. After trying to get out of going altogether, I threw something on, stomped down the stairs, and plopped onto the couch.

"Sunday," Mom said. "I think you have something to say to Bo."

My brother peeked out from behind her, his nose and eyes red. He swiped a hand across his face, bringing a disgusting booger-slime across his cheek.

"Sorry," I said, the word oozing with insincerity. I wasn't sorry. He's the one that needed to be sorry.

But that seemed good enough for him because he sniffed and then plopped down next to me.

I got up, brushing off his hand when he tried to grab ahold of mine. "I think I forgot something upstairs. Let me know when we're leaving."

Bo followed behind me. I turned and glared at him.

"Can I come with you, Sunday? Maybe we can look for the missing pages?"

I glanced down the hall to make sure Mom wasn't nearby. Whispering, I pointed my finger in his face. "I told you, Bo, leave me alone." His bottom lip trembled, but I didn't care if he cried.

Bo tried to squeeze in next to me in the van on the way to the play and then again when we got to the high school, but I switched seats or got up and moved. I could tell that Mom could see what was happening, but she didn't say anything. And Emma didn't give her any time. The moment we arrived, she dragged Mom backstage to help with a few minor adjustments to costumes before the production started.

"Everything okay, Sunday?" Dad asked, taking a seat beside me. May was on the other side, texting a play-by-play of her driver's test to someone.

"It's fine. I don't really want to talk about it right now."

He put his arm around my shoulder and pulled me to him, kissing the top of my head. "Well, you know I'm here."

Despite the hurricane of emotions swirling around inside me, I was able to slip into the eye of the storm for the first act and loved every moment. The actors and actresses were wonderful, the sets were beautiful, and I couldn't help feeling proud of my sister, who had created the "simple but elegant" costumes fluttering across the stage. At intermission, Dad handed me five dollars. "Go and get yourself something to munch on until the second act starts."

I took the money and stole away to the concession stand, hoping that Bo wasn't trying to trail after me.

Jude, cheeks red, stood at the backstage door with a small bundle of flowers in his hand. Ben Folger stood by him, dressed in a shirt and tie, a single daisy in his lapel. Were they best friends now? My stomach sank, and I tried to focus on the fact that reporters were coming tomorrow. Jude glanced in my direction, but I turned away from him. The world needed to know what I'd found.

The man behind the concession stand smiled at me. "What can I get for you?"

I quickly looked beside me, thinking that Bo would be there to order something. He wasn't. I could order whatever I wanted and wouldn't have to share it with anyone. "I'll have a brownie and lemonade, please." I paid, took my treats, and started for the auditorium.

"Sorry," the usher said. "No drinks or snacks inside."

Probably for the best. If I went in I'd have to share my brownie, and CJ would have my lemonade sucked down in seconds. Out here I could enjoy it by myself.

I went over and stood by the window. Muzzy and Papa Gil were both outside with Mr. Castor, who was tied to a tree. Papa Gil pointed his finger at the dog, and Mr. Castor dropped what was in his mouth, his tail wagging.

I smiled.

"Have you talked to anyone yet?" a woman asked.

She was wearing a knee-length black skirt and a white silky-looking blouse, the fanciest outfit I had seen on anyone since we came. I could tell that this woman did not live here. The man she spoke to looked a little more like someone from Alma, but I doubted it.

"A few people, but no one seems to know much about her except that she was pretty reclusive. But we already knew that. Everyone knows that."

I stepped closer, set my lemonade on the ground, and retied my shoe. The man had a camera slung over his shoulder, and the woman was pulling out a small note-pad and pen. It was one of the reporters!

Should I say something? Introduce myself? I stood, cleared my throat, and wiped my hands on my pants.

"I don't want to just wait for tomorrow," the woman said. "We need to get information now. I'll talk to the old ladies and you talk to the old men."

"And the kid?"

The woman pulled a piece of gum from her purse, unwrapped it, and popped it into her mouth. I bent down and tied the other shoe so I could listen a little longer. "Yes, we'll meet the girl tomorrow at that library thing and see what she has. And if she really did find a secret manuscript, this is going to be huge."

I knew it!

The woman continued. "But if we don't find anything

out tonight or tomorrow morning, I want to get first read of the manuscript and the letters."

"What about that critic from New York? He's going to insist that he get to tear it apart before anyone else does."

My heart *thunked* like metal in my chest. Tear it apart?

"Who? Albert? Oh, I've already told him that I want to look at it first. He agreed, but I'm not sure what other papers and networks that girl called. In any case, I want a read. I'm sure there's a juicy story there. A secret child, a hidden husband, a wretched home life. Albert can adore or loathe the manuscript. I don't care. Whatever Wren Lee wanted kept hush-hush, that's what I'm going to find out." She swiped red lipstick over her lips. "Nothing stays hidden forever."

"Lee Wren," the man said.

The woman turned to him, annoyed. "What?"

"You said Wren Lee, but her name was Lee Wren."

She waved him off. "Her name could be Napoléon Bonaparte and I wouldn't care. We came here for a story and that's what we need to get."

I was still hunkered down over my shoe, unable to move, as they walked off. They wanted to tear apart Lee Wren's manuscript, expose everything that she wanted to keep secret, turn it into a juicy story.

Well, what else did you think, Sunday? a voice in the back of my head asked.

I didn't know.

My mind flashed to Ben Folger's house. It was bustling with cars, reporters knocking on his door, cameras flashing, relatives hounding him, townspeople bringing over loaves of bread hoping to get the scoop. The pictures of Lee Wren and Ben would be taken and spread everywhere.

Lee Wren's manuscript would be printed up, talked about, criticized. Her letters published, her life over-analyzed. The tapes would be played, maybe sold.

The lights dimmed and the ushers closed the doors to the auditorium. The second half was starting. I slipped inside and found an extra seat next to Henry.

The act started and ended, and I hadn't heard a single word. When the lights were turned up at the very end, I wished that they hadn't been. I still needed time to think. What juicy story would the press create out of Lee Wren's manuscript and letters? Could I do that to Ben?

But if I didn't give the newspapers what I'd promised, I'd still be a nobody. Plus I'd be called a liar for bringing the media all the way down here and then not delivering. I did not want to be remembered for that.

"Ready to go backstage and see your sister, Sunday?" Dad asked. I nodded and followed.

Emma grinned ear to ear, loving the attention, the compliments, the hugs, and the flowers. Everything I had been hoping to get tomorrow.

"Thanks!" she said, bringing a bouquet of roses to her nose. "You really think everything looked good?"

"Your costumes were gorgeous," Mom said. "I'm so proud of you."

My heart sank at the thought of not hearing those same words. I walked out of the auditorium and stood by the van to wait for everyone else.

There had to be a way I could be famous and still not betray Ben Folger and Lee Wren.

But as I looked into the darkness, I realized there was no way I could have both.

I had to choose.

At home up in my room, I read and reread and re-reread the letters over and over again.

I knew what I couldn't do, and I knew what I needed to do. It's just that both of them left me with the same just "one-of-the-six" label I'd always had.

I set down the manuscript and the letters on the night-stand next to the tapes and flicked off the light. I'd go see Ben first thing in the morning.

"SUNDAY!"

The light came on and I sat up and squinted, trying to focus on what was going on.

Mom opened my closet, then bent down and looked underneath my bed. "Is Bo in here?"

I rubbed my eyes and glanced at the clock. One o'clock in the morning. "No, why?"

Tears welled in her eyes. "I don't know where he is. Your dad picked Emma and me up from the auditorium and I went to check on the boys. He's not in his room or anywhere in the house. Your dad and I have checked everywhere. We can't find him."

I jumped out of bed. "But he has to be here." I pulled on a pair of shorts. "He's probably just hiding. Or maybe he fell asleep somewhere crazy and can't hear you."

Mom wiped her tears, smearing her mascara. "I don't know, Sunday. I've looked everywhere."

I grabbed my flashlight and headed down the stairs,

Mom following behind me, sniffling. "Bo!" I yelled in the empty entryway. After I searched in every nook and cranny in the house, I burst out the front door and saw three flashlights bobbing in the blackness. "Bo! Where are you?" I called out. "It's Sunday."

I found Dad, May, and Emma out in the field. "Dad?"

He turned and grabbed ahold of my shoulders, his hands trembling. "You found him?"

"No . . . I-I" I stuttered. I had never seen my dad, usually so put together and calm, look so terrified. "I wanted to know where you've looked already."

"In the house, the library, the yard, and the field." He turned to May. "Could you call the police, May?" She sniffed and then rushed off to the house. Dad turned back to me. "I don't know where he could be. I just don't know."

"I'm going to ask Ben and then go over to Jude's house. They'll help." I dashed across the field, bolted up the porch stairs, and pounded on the door. "Ben! Wake up! It's me, Sunday! Wake up!"

A light flicked on, I heard footsteps, and then the door opened and a bleary-eyed Ben Folger looked out at me. "Sunday? What's wrong?"

"It's Bo. He's gone. No one knows where he is."

"I'll get my flashlight." Ben disappeared inside and then came back to the door. "I'll start around here."

"Okay," I said, running down the walkway. "I'm going over to Jude's. Maybe he went there. And Ben—" I said.

He turned.

"I already decided not to tell anyone about anything. You know, with Lee."

"Thank you." He gave a quick nod and a half smile, then disappeared into the dark.

Jude's house filled with light when I pounded on the door and rang the bell over and over and over. His mom, with Jude behind her, opened the door a crack.

"Please, Ms. Trist. My brother Bo. Is he here?"

She opened the door wider when she realized it was me. "No, Sunday. He isn't."

Jude shook his head no, too. "I haven't seen him since the play tonight."

Tears stung my eyes, and I told them that everyone was out looking for him. Jude ran back into his bedroom, reappearing with a T-shirt and two flashlights. Jude's mom pulled her bathrobe tighter around her waist, grabbed her cell phone, and started out the door. "I'll call Wally. He'll help. You go down the street this way and I'll go the other way."

Jude and I called to Bo until our voices were hoarse. When we reached Main Street, I sank to the curb, dissolving into sobs. Jude sat down next to me and put his arm around my shoulder.

"Don't worry, Sunday," he said, his voice shaking. "We'll find him. I'm sure he's just hiding somewhere."

"But it's my fault," I said. "I know it is."

"That's stupid, Sunday. He just–"

"No, you don't understand. He drew on some of Lee Wren's manuscript and lost some of the pages–they blew away. I . . . I told him I never wanted to see him again." My chest ached as I let everything out. "I was so . . . so mean."

Jude stood up. "Okay. So do you think he's out trying to find the missing pages?"

I nodded, still unable to speak. My brother. My sweet, sweet brother. I looked down at my hand and imagined feeling his small one in mine. He hadn't meant to ruin anything. And who cared if he did? He could draw on every sheet of the manuscript if it meant he'd come back safe and sound. I'd color on every sheet myself.

"Please." I couldn't manage anything more than a whisper. "Please come back, Bo."

Jude pulled me to my feet. "Come on, Sunday. You need to go back to your house and wait for him there. I'll keep looking around here. I'll get Muzzy and Papa Gil and Mr. Castor, too. Go! And don't worry. We'll find him."

I stumbled back to the house and slumped onto the porch swing, where Mom sat, staring into space. She reached for my hand. "He has to come home. He has to."

I tried to swallow another lump that was forcing its

way up my throat, but the lump won and I collapsed into her arms. "It's all my fault," I wailed.

She wrapped her arms around me and pulled me to her, quietly shushing me and stroking my hair. "Don't say that, sweetie. It isn't your fault."

And then everything spilled out: the gas station, the locked box, Ben Folger, the cemetery, and finally what I'd said to Bo. I left nothing out. She needed to know how awful I was.

"I'm sorry," I said, my stomach aching. "I'm so sorry."

Mom was crying, too, her cheek resting on the top of my head. "*I'm* sorry," she said. "So sorry that we left you that day. That's inexcusable. And I'm sorry that you felt like you had to earn our love or do something to get us to pay attention. I know it's not easy being in such a big family, but I promise you that once we realized you were gone we would've searched the ends of the earth to find you. You are my heart, Sunday Fowler. And I can't live without that part of me. Neither can your dad, and neither can your brothers and sisters."

I nodded, unable to speak.

"You are special. Only you can handle CJ so that he doesn't kill himself. And May and Emma. Well, they may think you're too young in certain ways, but I see the way they go to you for advice and help, and just someone to listen to them. Henry adores you." She stopped, her voice catching. "And everyone knows that you've always been Bo's favorite." She tilted my chin up so that her eyes were looking into my own. "It's not your fault that he ran away.

"And I do recognize you. I do see you. I guess I just don't say it out loud enough, and I need to." She squeezed my hand. "I'm proud of your decision about Lee Wren's manuscript. I think you're doing what's right."

The darkness was slowly turning into the light of the early-early morning. "It was hard. I really wanted to be in the paper," I said. "And on TV."

"I know. And that's the reason I am *so* proud of you."

We sat in silence for a few moments.

"We'll find him, right?"

Mom reached over and squeezed my hand. "We won't stop looking until we do."

We continued to rock back and forth, staring out into the dark, my cheek pressed against her shoulder. I said the same silent prayer over and over again.

Please bring Bo home.

"I remember the day you were born," Mom whispered. "I woke up early in the morning, knowing that it was going to be the day we'd finally meet you. Your grandma and grandpa came over and picked up May and Emma, still groggy in their pajamas.

"Your dad and I held hands on the way to the hospital,

and I remember how the leaves were just starting to turn on the tree outside our house."

"The oak tree in the front yard?" I asked. That one had always been my favorite, with limbs low enough to grab ahold of and thick enough to climb.

"Yes, that one. It was still mostly green, but I remember a small patch of leaves on the lowest branch beginning to change to a beautiful orangeish-red color.

"The hospital was bustling. Nurses raced down the hallways, the television in the waiting room blared too loudly, and even inside our little room waiting for you to come, there were people walking in and out, asking questions, taking my pulse, getting everything ready.

"And then, there you were," Mom said. She held out her hands in front of her as if holding a small baby. "Not making a fuss. Never crying. Your eyes wide open, looking around. So peaceful and calm." She looked at me and smiled. "Just like you still are today in all the chaos."

I let my head sink heavier against her shoulder as we rocked back and forth, back and forth.

Shouting in the distance jerked me and Mom to our feet, and we both ran down the porch stairs. When the words "We found him!" rang out through the air, Mom collapsed in a heap on the ground and I sobbed beside her.

There, in Ben Folger's arms, was Bo, one hand wrapped

around Ben's neck and the other clutching a bunch of white pieces of paper.

Ben set him down and he rushed toward Mom, who was crying harder now that he was safe than she had when he was missing. After a minute, she let him go and I picked him up, squeezing him tight to me.

"I'm sorry, Sunday," he said. "But I found your papers."

My eyes stung with tears as I kissed his cheek. "I'm so glad you're safe. I don't care about the papers, Bo. I'm sorry for getting so mad at you. It wasn't right." Ben walked up to us, my dad's arm around his shoulder. "They aren't my papers anyway, and I wasn't really supposed to see them. No one was."

When I set Bo down on the ground, May and Emma smothered him with hugs and kisses. Taking the papers from his hand, I held them out to Ben. "These are yours. If you wait, I'll get the rest." I turned and ran up the stairs, grabbed the letters, the tapes, and the manuscript, then came back down and handed them to him.

"It's been a long time since I've seen these." Then he looked up and met my eyes. "And a long time since I've had a friend. Thank you, Sunday."

I nodded and smiled.

"All right, Bo," Mom said, taking him by the hand. "Let's get you inside so we can warm you up and feed you. I bet you're pooped."

The porch door opened and slammed. CJ stood there, rubbing his eyes and yawning. "Who pooped?"

There was a soft knock at my door.

I laid down the worn copy of *The Life and Death of Birds.* "Come in," I said.

The knob turned and Bo stood there. "Hi, Sunday. Mommy wanted me to sleep in her room for the rest of the night, but she and Daddy are snoring worse than CJ."

"Come on." I pulled back the covers.

He dashed for the bed and crawled in next to me.

"Could you tell me that story about the boy and the girl?"

I yawned. "I don't know. It's almost morning and—" His big brown eyes gazed at me and I smiled. "And . . . yes, I'll tell you the rest of the story."

He grinned.

"Mark loved Lilly, but she didn't want to get married."

"I don't, either. I want to live at home with you and Mommy and Daddy forever."

I nodded, remembering a time when I had felt the same way. "Well, Mark was sad that she didn't want to get married, so he left their town and traveled all over the world. He went to India and England and South America. All sorts of places. Lilly just stayed and worked on a book that she was writing."

"Did they miss each other?"

I nodded. "But they wrote each other letters. Then, after Lilly's book became really famous, Mark went to New York City and asked Lilly to marry him again."

"What did she say this time?"

I smiled. "She said yes. And they got married, and–"

"And they lived happily ever after?"

I imagined Ben across the field, sitting in his chair with Lee's letters and story in his hands and her voice playing over the tape recorder.

"Yeah, they sort of did," I said. "And even though Lilly's not alive anymore, every morning Mark walks to the cemetery with a daisy and he puts it on Lilly's grave."

"You should've stopped at 'happily ever after,'" Bo said, yawning. "That ending wasn't very good."

I turned off the light, the stars blinking out, one by one, as the dawn crept up in the morning sky.

32

MOM motioned for me to join her.

"And now I think it's time for what all our out-of-town guests have been waiting for. Sunday?"

I climbed up the stairs and stood by Mom, clutching the manila envelope that Ben had given me earlier.

"This'll make them happy, believe me," he said, winking.

When I looked out at the small crowd filled with reporters and TV cameras, I completely forgot the speech I had tried to memorize. Instead I winged it.

"If you don't know who Lee Wren was, she was the author of the book *The Life and Death of Birds*. She lived here in Alma, and even though her book is really famous, she never wrote anything else." I smiled. "At least that's what everyone thought." I held up the envelope. "But I've found three short stories and two essays that she wrote." I stopped and met Ben's gaze from his place next to Ms. Bodnar. He smiled and nodded. "They were in the basement of the library and, well, I'm excited that now we'll be able to enjoy more of Lee Wren's writing. After the originals are sent to her publisher, they're going to be kept here, at the library. So, um . . . yeah, that's all."

I started off the stairs but stopped. "Oh, and my family and I are going to be here for a couple more weeks. So if you have any other remodeling or home repairs, ask my dad. As you can see by the library, he's the best. Okay, that's all. Have a good time." I handed the envelope to Miss Jenny.

The reporters surrounded her, and I was surprised at how relieved I felt that it wasn't me. I was glad to scurry away to the snack station with Jude leading the way and Bo clinging to my hand.

Jude's mom spotted him looking hungrily at the spread of cookies, pies, cakes, breads, muffins, and cupcakes. "I packed organic peanut and cocoa-bean cookies for you, Jude," she said, handing him a plastic bag with a few round blobs.

Just then CJ, who had been busy chasing a girl with a disgusting bug, stopped dead when he spotted us. He caught his breath and then reached for the plastic bag. "Fake poop? That's perfect." And he sprinted off after her again.

Jude and I laughed.

While he loaded up a plate with desserts, I glanced around at the party. The cast from the high school had arrived in costume and were putting on scenes from the play. Emma and May stood huddled to the side, pointing and whispering about the boy who had played Puck and the boy who had played Oberon. Papa Gil had Henry in his lap, and they were cruising down a straightaway together. Dad was giving people tours of the library, and Mom and Muzzy were manning the refreshment table next to Ms. Bodnar's makeshift crepe stand.

Jude and I sat on the grass, Bo squeezing between us. I leaned back and smiled, gazing up at the blue-icing sky. Whipped-cream clouds floated by.

"I think the party is a success," I said.

Jude smiled. "Definitely. You should be proud."

As I scanned the crowd once more, I spied Ben Folger sitting by the library stairs, a picture book in his hand and a crowd of little kids sprawled out on the soft grass.

Ben Folger had come out of his house.

I smiled. I was still one-of-the-six. I had two older sisters and three younger brothers. I couldn't change that. And really, it wasn't such a bad thing.

Not at all.

I was Sunday Annika Fowler.

And though I never would have thought it before, that was enough.

ACKNOWLEDGMENTS

If you look in the dictionary under the word *happiness* you'd see a picture of the table on Grubbs Road where I first sat and listened to story after story after story. So, to all the Devlins and Pooles for giving me a history and a childhood filled with laughter, and love as filling as MomMom's famous mashed potatoes. And for the entire Eland family who have made me their very own.

To Rebecca. If only every writer were as lucky as me. Thank you.

To Alison, your brilliance and loveliness are overwhelming and your pen on every page. And also to the entire staff at Egmont USA for their support and kindness.

To my critique group. Lisa Amowitz, Cyndy Henzel, Cathy Giordiano, Kate Chell Milford, Dhonielle Clayton, Linda Acorn, Christine Johnson, and Heidi Ayarbe. What would

I do without you guys? I'm afraid to even think about it. Thank you, thank you, thank you.

To my dearest friend, Kim, and her wonderful family (Stephan, Isabelle, Henri, Ames, and Uncle). Super Secret Spot, beaks and claws, nails, Minturn, thrift stores, and good-ole-fashion laughter. A recent friend who feels like a history friend. Mwah!

Everyone at Breckenridge Elementary, my home away from home. Thank you for taking care of the most precious people in the world to me, and for always greeting me with a smile.

To all the authors that have come before me and have taught me everything I know through their brilliance. I don't think this book would be here if it weren't for Roald Dahl, Matilda, and The Trunchbull.

To Harper Lee. Thank you.

Thank you Gracie, Isaac, Ella, and Noah. Thank you for every hug, every smile, every day, and every moment. You make it all worthwhile.

And of course, John. Always and forever. Where you are is home.